Airhead

BOOKS BY MEG CABOT

FOR A COMPLETE LIST OF MEG CABOT'S BOOKS,

PLEASE VISIT WWW.MEGCABOT.COM

CABOT

ead

Point

Library of Congress Cataloging-in-Publication Data

Cabot, Meg.

Airhead / Meg Cabot. — 1st ed.

p. cm.

Summary: Sixteen-year-old Emerson Watts, an advanced placement student with a dis-
dain for fashion, is the recipient of a "whole body transplant" and finds herself transformed
into one of the world's most famous teen supermodels.

ISBN-13: 978-0-545-04052-5 (alk. paper)

ISBN-10: 0-545-04052-3 (alk. paper)

[1. Models (Persons) — Fiction.   2. Transplantation of organs, tissues, etc. —
Fiction.   3. Identity — Fiction.   4. New York (N.Y.) — Fiction.]   I. Title.

PZ7.C11165Ai 2008

[Fic] — dc22

2007038269

12 11 10 9 8 7 6 5 4 3 2 1   8 9 10 11 12 13/0

Printed in the U.S.A.

First edition, June 2008

The display type was set in Century Gothic.

The text type was set in Adobe Jenson Pro Regular.

Book design by Kristina Albertson

FOR BENJAMIN

MANY THANKS TO
BETH ADER, JENNIFER BROWN,
MICHELE JAFFE, SUSAN JUBY, LAURA LANGLIE,
ABIGAIL MCADEN, RACHEL VAIL,
AND ESPECIALLY BENJAMIN EGNATZ

Airhead

ONE

"EMERSON WATTS," CALLED MY FIRST-period Public Speaking teacher, Mr. Greer, startling me from the light doze into which I'd drifted.

Well, whatever. Do they really expect us to be alert at eight-fifteen in the morning? Come on.

"Here," I called, jerking my head from the top of my desk and surreptitiously feeling the side of my mouth, just in case I'd been drooling.

But I guess I didn't do it surreptitiously enough, since Whitney Robertson, seated with her long, tanned legs crossed beneath a desk a few feet away from mine, snickered and hissed, "Loser."

I threw her a dirty look and mouthed, *Bite me.*

To which she responded by narrowing her heavily made-up baby blue eyes at me and mouthing back smugly, *You wish.*

"Em," Mr. Greer said, with a yawn. I guess he'd been up pretty late last night, too. Only I'm guessing it wasn't because he'd been frantically finishing his homework for this class, like I had. "I wasn't calling roll. It's time for you to give the class your two-minute persuasive oral piece. We're going in reverse alphabetical order, remember?"

Great. Just great.

Chagrined, I slid out from behind my desk and made my way to the front of the room, while the rest of the class tittered. All except Whitney, I saw. That's because she had dug her compact mirror out of her bag and was gazing at her own reflection. Lindsey Jacobs, seated in the row beside hers, stared at Whitney admiringly and whispered, "That shade of gloss is so you."

"I know," Whitney murmured to her reflection.

I fought off a reflexive urge to gag — because I was about to speak in public, not because of their exchange . . . although I guess that could have had something to do with it — and turned around to face the room. Twenty-four sleepy faces blinked back at me.

And I realized I had completely forgotten the speech I'd been up half the night writing.

"All right, Emerson," Mr. Greer said. "You've got two minutes." He looked down at his watch. "And . . ."

Amazing. The second he said that, my mind went even *more* blank. All I could think was . . . how did she know? Lindsey, I mean. That that shade of lip gloss was so right on Whitney? I have been alive nearly seventeen years, and I still have no idea what shade of lip gloss looks good on me . . . or anybody else, for that matter.

I blame my dad. He's the one who gave me a boy's name to begin with, since he'd been so sure I was going to be one — despite what the ultrasound had shown — because I kicked my mom so much while I was in the womb. Dad insisted on naming me after his favorite poet, which is what you get when your father teaches university-level English literature. I guess my mom was still high off her epidural or something, because she totally let him, even after the ultrasound turned out to be right. So *Emerson Watts* is what it says on my birth certificate.

I know. I was a victim of sexual stereotyping in utero. How many girls can claim *that*?

". . . *go*," Mr. Greer said, turning on his oven timer.

And just like that, all the research I'd done on my assigned topic the night before came flooding back.

Phew.

"Females," I began, "make up thirty-nine percent of people who play interactive computer games, and yet only a small fraction of the games created by the estimated thirty-five-billion-dollar worldwide gaming industry is geared toward female players."

I paused . . . but it didn't matter.

I guess I couldn't really blame them. It *was* so early in the morning, after all.

Even Christopher, who lives in my building and is supposedly my best friend, wasn't paying attention. He was in his normal seat in the back row, and he was upright.

But his eyes were closed.

"A study," I went on, "by the Higher Education Research Institute at UCLA showed that the percentage of computer degrees granted to women has now dropped to an all-time low of less than thirty percent. Computer science is the only field in which women's participation is actually *decreasing* over time. . . ."

Oh, God. No one in first-period Public Speaking was awake now but me. Even Mr. Greer's eyes had drifted shut.

Terrific. Way to be part of the problem, Mr. Greer, and not the solution.

"Many researchers believe this is due to our educational system failing to engage girls in the sciences — particularly computer science — during the middle school years," I battled on, staring directly at Mr. Greer. Not that he noticed. He was now gently snoring.

Great. Just great. I mean, I'd been slightly psyched when I'd gotten my topic, because the truth is, I *like* computer games. Well, one computer game, anyway.

"So what can be done to keep girls interested in gaming," I went on, desperately, "which studies show increases problem-solving and strategic abilities, and also helps develop social interaction skills and cooperative play?"

There was no point, I realized. Really.

"Well," I said. "I could strip off my clothes and reveal to you that under my jeans and sweatshirt I'm actually wearing a tank top and short-shorts, much like Lara Croft from *Tomb Raider* . . . only mine are flame-retardant and covered in glow-in-the-dark dinosaur stickers."

No one stirred. Not even Christopher, who actually has a thing for Lara Croft.

"I know what you're thinking," I went on. "Glow-in-the-dark dinosaur stickers are *so* last year. But I think they add a certain je ne sais quoi to the whole ensemble. It's true, short-shorts are uncomfortable under jeans and hard to get off in the ladies' room, but they make the twin thigh-holsters in which I hold my high-caliber pistols so easy to get to. . . ."

The oven timer dinged.

"Thank you, Em," Mr. Greer said, yawning. "That was very persuasive."

"No, Mr. Greer," I said, with a big smile. "Thank *you.*"

It's a good thing my parents aren't paying for my tuition — I'm on full academic scholarship — at Tribeca Alternative.

Because I have true reservations about the quality of the education I am receiving here.

I went back to my seat as Mr. Greer asked — himself mostly, I guess — "Now, who do we have next? Oh, yes. Whitney Robertson?" Mr. Greer smiled. Because everyone smiles when they say Whitney's name. Except me. "You're up."

Whitney — who'd gone for a quick nose-powdering after the oven timer went off — closed her compact with a snap and uncrossed her legs. I knew I wasn't the only one in the room who got a flash of her leopard-print thong as she did so. Suddenly, everyone seemed to be wide awake.

"Here goes nothing," Whitney said, with a laugh, and she unfolded her long, lean frame out from beneath the desk and sauntered — no, really, even though she was wearing four-inch platform heels. How do girls do that? If I tried to saunter in four-inch heels (even in two-inch heels) I'd trip and fall flat on my face — down the aisle to the front of the classroom, her short, ruffled skirt swaying behind her. When she turned to face us, there wasn't an eye in the room that wasn't on Whitney.

Except Christopher's, I noticed, when I turned around to check. He was still soundly asleep.

"And . . . *go,*" said Mr. Greer, adjusting the oven timer.

"My topic is about why I," Whitney began, in a singsong sweet voice completely unlike the one she uses when she is advising me to bite her, "don't believe in the fallacy that Western civilization's standards for female beauty are too high. Lots of women complain that the fashion and film industries are attacking the self-esteem of young girls and older women alike. They want these industries to employ more, quote, average-size women, unquote. I say this is ridiculous!"

Whitney tossed some of her long blond — dyed, apparently. At least according to my little sister, Frida, who knows about things like that — hair and asked, her blue eyes glittering with indignation, "How is promoting a healthy weight — which scientists have determined as a body mass index of below twenty-four point nine — as beautiful an attack on any woman's self-esteem? If some women are too lazy to go to the gym because they sit around all day *playing video games*, well, that's their problem. But they can't then turn around and blame those of us who take proper care of our bodies for being sexist or holding them to impossible standards of beauty . . . especially when so many of us are living proof that those standards aren't impossible at all."

My jaw dropped. I looked around to see if anyone else was as stunned as I was. *This* was Whitney's interpretation of the topic Mr. Greer had assigned her for her two-minute persuasive piece? That normal-size women should stop blaming the media for hyping stick-thin models and actresses as the beauty ideal?

Apparently, I was the only one in the class who thought she'd gotten it wrong. At least if the rapt way everyone else (the male half of the class, anyway) was staring at Whitney's admittedly extremely perky boobs was any indication.

"If wanting to look as beautiful as someone like Nikki Howard, for instance," Whitney went on, naming the current It Girl in the beauty and fashion scene, "was really so wrong, would women be spending an estimated thirty-three billion dollars a year on weight loss, another seven billion on cosmetics, and three hundred million or more on cosmetic surgery? Of course not! People aren't stupid! They know that, with a little effort and maybe a little more money, they can be as attractive as — well, *me*."

Whitney flung her long hair behind one shoulder, then went on. "*Some* people" —*insert the name Emerson Watts here*, the look she sent in my direction implied — "might think it's stuck up of me to call myself attractive. But the truth is, beauty isn't just about being five ten and a size zero. The most important accessory a girl can have is confidence . . . and I guess I just have plenty of that!"

Whitney lifted her shoulders in an innocent shrug, and almost all the boys — and half the girls — in class sighed as they gazed longingly at her. I whipped around in my seat and was relieved to notice that Christopher's head had lolled forward in sleep. One guy — out of fourteen — was safe, anyway.

I turned back around in my seat just in time to hear Whitney say, "And the truth is, contrary to what critics tell us about the ideal being unachievable and women dying to be thin, the only thing killing women in this country is obesity, which is at epidemic proportions."

Everyone in class nodded in agreement, as if all of this made perfect sense. Which it so didn't. At least, not to me.

"Well," Whitney said. "That's about it. Was that two minutes?"

Right on cue, the oven timer on Mr. Greer's desk dinged. He beamed and said, "Exactly two minutes. Excellently done, Whitney."

She simpered again and started back to her seat. Since I saw that no one else was going to say anything — as usual — I stuck my hand in the air. "Mr. Greer."

He looked at me tiredly. "Yes, Miss Watts?"

"Seriously," I said, lowering my hand, "I thought the purpose of the two-minute persuasive oral piece was to *persuade* our audience of something, using facts and statistics."

"Which I totally did," Whitney said, as she slid into her seat.

"All you did," I shot back, "was make everyone in this class who isn't as skinny and perfect as Nikki Howard feel totally bad about themselves. How about mentioning the fact that most of us are never going to look like her, no matter how hard we try, or how much money we spend?"

The bell rang, loud and long. I guess I'd been asleep longer than I thought, because that period seemed to have flown by.

And as everyone sprang from their desks to get to their next class, Lindsey got up and said to me, "You're just jealous."

"Totally," Whitney said, running her hands over her slender thighs. "And you got one thing right, Em: No matter how hard you try, you're never going to look *this* good."

Cackling with laughter at her own witticism, Whitney hurried from the classroom with a giggling Lindsey in tow, leaving me alone with Mr. Greer. And Christopher.

"You can bring up those points next week if you want, Em," Mr. Greer volunteered, helpfully, "when we do rebuttal persuasive pieces."

I just glared at him. "Thanks, Mr. Greer," I said.

He shrugged and looked sheepish. I looked at Christopher, who was slowly waking up, and said, "Thanks to you, too. You were a big help back there."

Christopher, blinking groggily, rubbed his eyes. "Dude, I heard every word you said," he said.

"Oh, really?" I raised an eyebrow. "What was my assigned topic again?"

"Um . . . I'm not sure." Christopher's smile was slightly crooked. "But I know it had something to do with short-shorts. And glow-in-the-dark dinosaur stickers."

Slowly, I shook my head. Sometimes I think high school is just something society puts teenagers through as a sort of test to see if we've got the stamina to handle the real world.

It's a test I'm pretty sure I'm failing.

TWO

YOU WOULD THINK ON WEEKENDS I'D
get a respite. You know, from the Whitney Robertsons of the
world.

The problem is, my little sister is turning into one. A
Whitney, I mean.

Oh, she's not quite as bad as the Queen of Mean. Yet. But
she's slowly getting there. As I realized to my horror on Saturday
morning, when Mom said I had to go with her to the Stark
Megastore grand opening, because at fourteen Frida's still "too
young" to do stuff like that by herself.

Substitute the word *silly* for *young* in the sentence above, and
you'll get my mom's gist.

Not that Frida is actually mentally diminished in any way. Like me, she got into Tribeca Alternative High School on an academic scholarship.

She's just turned into a Whitney Robertson wannabe . . . or, more technically, a member of the Walking Dead. That's the term Christopher and I use to describe the majority of our classmates.

To most people, zombies are the undead. But to Christopher and me, zombies are the popular people at TAHS, who are very similar to the undead in that they have no soul or personality. But they are, technically, alive.

However, because they have no actual interests of their own (or if they do, they squelch them in order to fit in) and merely pursue those that they think will look best on their college apps, they're zombies.

Ergo, the Walking Dead are what make up the majority of the student population of Tribeca Alternative High School.

It is kind of frightening to watch your own sister turn into one of the Walking Dead. But, unfortunately, there really isn't anything you can do to stop it from happening. Except try to embarrass her as much as possible in public.

Which would be why Frida (it was Mom's turn to do the naming when my little sister was born, and so she got stuck being called Frida, after Frida Kahlo — Mom's a women's studies professor at NYU — a Mexican feminist painter best known for her self-portraits featuring her unibrow and mustache) was as thrilled to have me along to the Stark Megastore grand opening as I was to be going with her.

Um, not.

"Mo-om!" she whined. "Why does *Em* have to come with me? She's going to ruin *everything*."

"Em is not going to ruin everything," Mom said, rolling her eyes at Frida's dramatics. "She's just going to make sure you get home all right."

"It's TWO BLOCKS away," Frida pointed out.

But Mom wouldn't budge. There've been people protesting outside the new Stark Megastore since before it was even built, back when the neighborhood found out that's what would be replacing Mama's Fruit and Vegetable Stand (located in the middle of an abandoned lot) on the corner of Broadway and Houston. Situated just two streets over from our university-subsidized apartment on West Third and La Guardia Place, Mama's was where we bought all our lettuce and bananas, since you can't trust the produce at the local Gristedes, and the gourmet food store over on Broadway, Dean & Deluca, was way too expensive.

Mom and I weren't the only ones who were mad when we found out what was going up in that empty lot. The whole community banded together to save Mama's and demanded that Stark get out.

But despite all the picketing, letters to the editor, sabotage of the construction site by the E.L.F., the Environmental Liberation Front (I swear I had nothing to do with it, never mind what Mom and Dad seem to think), and promises of a community-wide boycott, Mama's got pushed out, and a Stark Megastore, featuring three stories of CDs, DVDs, video games, electronics, and books (in the smallest and most inaccessible part of the store), went up, guaranteed to put all the locally owned shops that already sold these things out of business with its steep discounts, endless supply . . .

. . . and publicity stunts, like the one today: a super-size grand opening, including free food and drinks (Stark Cola and Stark cookies and pretzels), with live performances on all three floors by some of the hottest young entertainers of the moment, followed by an opportunity to get a personally autographed CD from them.

Which was why Frida was so determined to go.

Because unlike the rest of our family — and residents of our community — Frida was *thrilled* about the new Stark Megastore opening up within spitting distance of her bedroom window (not that Frida would ever do something as déclassé as spit). She could not have cared less that Mama's had relocated to a windy, desolate corner way over in Alphabet City, nowhere close to walking distance of our apartment building, or that we were being forced to eat wilted lettuce and brown bananas from Gristedes.

"Nothing's going to happen," Frida kept insisting to Mom. "I'll look out for E.L.F. protesters. I'll wear my bike helmet if I have to."

Mom just rolled her eyes. "It's not E.L.F. I'm worried about, Frida," she said. "It's Gabriel Luna."

Frida's round cheeks (well, they are. What can I say? Round cheeks — like stick-straight brown hair, brown eyes, medium height and weight, and size nine feet — is our genetic destiny, the way high cheekbones and perfect everything else are Whitney's) instantly turned bright red.

"Mo-om!" she cried. "Whatever! He's, like, twenty. He's not going to be interested in a kid like me."

That's what her lips said. But anyone could tell by the glint in her eyes that Frida didn't actually believe this. She honestly thought Gabriel Luna was going to fall madly in love with her as he personally autographed her CD. I could tell. I used to be fourteen, after all, just two and a half short years ago.

So it was a good thing when Mom replied, "Then you won't mind bringing your sister along. Just in case."

"Just in case *what?*" Frida wanted to know.

"In case Gabriel Luna invites you to a party back at his penthouse."

You could tell this was *exactly* what Frida had been hoping would happen. Not that she'd ever admit it. Instead, she snarled, "Gabriel doesn't have a penthouse, Mom. He's not into the trappings of fame."

When I burst out laughing at *trappings of fame*, Frida glared at me and said, "Well, he's not. He lives in a studio apartment somewhere here in NoHo. He's not one of those music-company-fabricated pretty-boy-band types Em hates so much. He's a singer-songwriter. Even though he's already a sensation back in his native London, hardly anyone outside of England knows who he is."

"Except everyone who reads *CosmoGIRL!*, evidently," I pointed out. "Since you just quoted that verbatim from their article on him last month. Including the *trappings of fame* part."

"How would you even *know* that, Em?" Frida demanded snarkily. "I thought you never read teen magazines. I thought you only read your lame *Electric Gaming Monthly*, or whatever."

I sighed. "Yes, but when I've finished that and your *CosmoGIRL!* is the only thing that's lying around, what choice do I have?"

"Mo-om!" Frida cried. You could tell she was really upset that Stark had been so shortsighted as to schedule their grand opening on the last warm weekend in September, which all of her fellow Walking Dead members were being "forced" to spend at their families' vacation homes in the Hamptons. They'd invited Frida along, of course.

But she'd as soon eat glass as miss an opportunity to meet actual celebrities — even ones who don't live in a penthouse.

"Em's going to ruin everything. Can't you see that? She's a dork, you know, Mom. Not even a geek, which would be semi-respectable, but a *dork*. All she ever does is play her stupid computer games with Christopher, study, and watch disgusting surgery shows on the Discovery Channel. And she's going to say something mean to Gabriel and embarrass me."

"I will not!" I protested, with my mouth full of microwave waffle.

"Yes, you will," Frida said. "You're always mean to guys."

"That is completely false," I said. "Name one time I was mean to Christopher."

"Christopher Maloney is your boyfriend," Frida said, rolling her eyes. "And I mean a *cute* guy."

This was such a slanderous statement — since no way is Christopher Maloney my boyfriend — that I nearly choked on my waffle. Not that I haven't sometimes *wished* Christopher were my boyfriend, and not just my *boy* friend — my best friend, actually.

But Christopher has never once expressed any sort of similar desire. You know, that we should take our friendship to a more-than-platonic level. In fact, I'm not sure Christopher has ever even realized that I'm *not* a boy. I'm not actually the most feminine girl in the world. I honestly wouldn't mind trying to be, but the two or three times I've experimented by putting on eyeliner or whatever, Frida has just burst into hysterical laughter and told me to "Take it off! Just take it off right now!" before I've even gotten out of the apartment.

So I've taken it off.

I guess it's unusual that my best friend is a boy. But the truth is, I haven't had a *girl* friend since fifth grade. The few occasions girls ever actually invited me over in middle school, it was always so . . . *awkward*. Because we ended up having nothing in common. Like, I always wanted to play video games, and they always wanted to play Truth or Dare (with an emphasis on the Truth part . . . like, "Is it true that you have a crush on that Christopher guy, but that you just tell everyone you're really only friends, and that even he doesn't know you secretly love him? Do you want us to tell him how you really feel? Because we'll be happy to.")

Yeah. Like that.

It just didn't work for me. I told my mother I'd rather stay home and read.

Which is one of the good things about having parents who are academics. They know how you feel. Because the truth is, they'd always rather stay home and read, too.

Christopher was different, though. From the day almost eight years ago that I saw him hanging out with the moving van that was delivering all of his family's stuff to our building, I knew we were going to get along.

And okay, mostly because I peeked into the box marked CHRIS'S VIDEO GAMES as it sat next to the freight elevator and saw that we liked all the same role-playing games.

But whatever.

I guess because we hang out so much, people think we're dating, but nothing could be further from the truth (alas).

Still, even though we're not dating — however much I might wish that were true — I resented Frida's implication that Christopher isn't cute. He isn't, under the standard Walking Dead definition of hottie, of course. I mean, he's over six feet tall and does have the requisite blond hair and blue eyes the W.D. so favor. Except that Christopher has been trying to see how long he can grow his hair before he drives his father, the Commander (he teaches political science), completely insane. It's almost past his shoulders now.

And he doesn't spend four hours a day lifting weights, so he isn't a muscle-bound freak like Whitney's boyfriend, Jason Klein.

But just because Christopher isn't what the W.D.s consider hot doesn't mean he isn't cute.

"Thanks," I snarled at Frida. "A lot. See if Christopher ever comes over to defragment your hard drive again."

"Christopher's hair is longer than mine," Frida hissed. "And what about yesterday in the cafeteria, when you screamed at Jason Klein to shut up while you were both in line for ketchup for your burgers at the condiment bar?"

"Well," I said, with an uncomfortable shrug. "Yesterday was a bad day. And besides, he deserved it. And at least Christopher can cut his hair. What's *your* excuse?"

"All Jason said was that he preferred the cheerleaders' spring halter-top uniforms to their winter sweater ones!" Frida cried.

"Well, that *is* sexist, Frida," Mom said.

I flashed Frida a triumphant look over my waffles. Still, she wouldn't let it go.

"Cheerleaders are athletes, Mom," Frida insisted. "Their halter-top uniforms are less binding than their sweater ones, allowing them more freedom of movement."

"Oh, my God." I stared across the breakfast table at my little sister. "You're trying out for cheerleading this year, aren't you?"

Frida took a deep breath. "Forget it. Just forget it. I'll ask Dad. Dad'll let me go by myself."

"No, he won't," Mom said. "And you will not disturb him. You know he got in late last night."

Dad lives in New Haven during the week, where he teaches at Yale, and only comes home to Manhattan on weekends (it's tough on married academics when they can't get hired by the same college).

Because of the guilt he feels about this, Dad will generally let us do anything we want. If Frida had asked if it would be okay if she went to Atlantic City with the men's swim team for the weekend to gamble away her college education money, Dad would have been, like, "Sure, why not? Here's my bank card, have a blast."

Which is why Mom watches us like a hawk when Dad's home. She knows perfectly well that he's a pushover when it comes to his teenage daughters.

"And what's this about you trying out for cheerleading?" Mom wanted to know. "Frida, we need to talk. . . ."

While Mom went on about how women weren't allowed to play men's sports in school until the nineteen-seventies and so were relegated to cheer for the male athletes on the sidelines, thus giving birth to cheerleading, Frida sent me a withering look that said, *I'll get you for this, Em!*

I had no doubt she'd get her revenge later, at the Stark Megastore opening.

And it turned out I wasn't wrong.

It just didn't happen quite the way I'd been expecting it to.

✳ THREE

FRIDA TURNED OUT TO BE RIGHT ABOUT
one thing: Gabriel Luna is a *great* singer-songwriter.

And — truth be told — he was pretty cute, too. He wasn't
one of those music company–fabricated pretty boys, the ones
Frida and her friends are always freaking out over on *TRL* or
whatever.

Nor did he seem to be harboring any tattoos, or the latest
popular trend among male singers, eyeliner. Gabriel, as far as I
could tell (which wasn't easy, since there was quite a crowd
between us and the stage on which he was performing), appeared
to be tattoo and makeup free.

He was even dressed sort of normally, in a button-
down shirt and jeans. His hair was choppily cut and a little

too long (though not compared to Christopher's) and very dark in contrast to his somewhat piercing blue eyes (not, you know, that I noticed), but it still looked good. His hair, I mean.

But it was his voice — oh, God, and that English accent — that got to me. Deep and rich and soulful — but also playful when the song called for it — his voice filled the Broadway Tunes and Soundtracks section of SoHo Stark Megastore, where the mini stage had been set up for him to perform. People who were in the aisles looking for discount CDs couldn't help but pause with their Megastore shopping baskets to listen, because Gabriel's voice was so compelling and his presence so commanding.

He came out onstage with a fast dance number, the first single off his new album. And it was, I have to admit, pretty catchy. I found myself kind of bouncing along to it.

But, you know, secretly, so Christopher wouldn't notice, since I knew he'd make some cynical comment.

Then Gabriel traded in the electric guitar he'd been using to accompany himself for a regular one and went acoustic for his second number, which he performed sitting on a stool.

And, okay, I'll admit, Frida wasn't the only one who might have swooned a little. I had a hard time reminding myself that I'm not a teenybopper . . . even though I might have been attending an actual teenybopper fest.

At least until it came time to get in line to get Frida's CD signed. That's when reality came crashing back, as we found ourselves surrounded by a mob of thirteen- and fourteen-year-old girls, all wearing sparkly low-rise jeans exactly like Frida's and all clutching slips of paper on which they'd written the name to whom they wanted Gabriel to personalize their CD . . . along with their cell phone numbers. Just in case Gabriel happened to ask for them.

What had been a magical few moments turned tedious. And fast.

"He's not looking at you," I assured Frida, as we stood in the long (did I mention it was long?) line to get Gabriel's autograph.

"Yes, he is," Frida insisted as she waved. "He's looking right at me!"

"No," Christopher, standing beside us, said. Good friend that he is, Christopher had come along to lend me moral support . . . and also to check out Stark's electronics section, which was featuring a newly released, Stark-designed handheld gaming device with a screen wide enough that you could actually play tactic-style games on it without going blind. Even better, they were selling them for under a hundred bucks.

Christopher and I are ethically opposed to Stark Megastores . . . but we're not above taking advantage of their heavily slashed discount prices.

"He's looking at *her*." Christopher pointed toward a plasma screen that was hanging from the ceiling above our heads, showing Nikki Howard — looking coolly beautiful in a filmy evening gown and ridiculously high stilettos — against a hot pink background, gyrating in time to the thumping rock music that filled the store.

There were dozens — maybe hundreds — of similar plasma screens suspended by thick wires from the open ductwork along the ceiling all over the store, each featuring Nikki Howard in various states of undress, urging patrons to try Stark Enterprises' new line of clothing and beauty products, which would be available exclusively in Stark Megastores worldwide in the new year.

"He's probably trying to see if she's got anything on under there," Christopher joked.

"Gabriel doesn't think of women as sex objects," Frida sniffed, with the merest flick of a glance in the direction Christopher was pointing. "I know. I read it in his interview with *CosmoGIRL!* He respects women with brains."

I nearly choked on my free Stark Cola at the suggestion that Nikki Howard had a brain.

Frida got defensive right away. "She does!" she insisted. "What other seventeen-year-old do you know who's gotten as many modeling and product endorsement contracts as Nikki has? And she started with nothing — *nothing*. Seriously, how could you not *know* that? Don't you people do anything but play that stupid video game?"

Fortunately, it wasn't all that easy to hear Frida going on about how out of touch Christopher and I were with our own generation, considering the rock music that was blasting all around us (except that it was all right, since it was Gabriel's music) . . . not to mention the hordes of people crowding the store.

Not all of them were there to meet Gabriel Luna, like we were, though. A lot of them, in fact, were there for an entirely different reason: to make trouble. Every few minutes we saw a uniformed security officer dragging another protester from the store. The rabble-rousers were pretty easily distinguished from actual customers, like Frida, by their combat fatigues . . . and the paintball guns they all seemed to be carrying beneath their trench coats. Their primary targets were the plasma screens, many of which had already been hit (in strategic locations) by giant blobs of yellow paint.

In other words, the place was a zoo. Which meant that Frida was in her element. My little sister was taking in all the excitement like it was pure oxygen, frantically text messaging her friends, letting them know what they were missing, and taking snaps with her camera phone.

"Besides, you guys," Frida was saying, as she pointed her phone in Gabriel's direction — even though we were still so far away, he was only going to appear as a white-shirted blob to whomever she was sending the photo to. "Gabriel's deeply spiritual . . . and intellectual. Just like I am."

I choked on another free sample of Stark Cola.

"I *am*!" Frida insisted. "Just because I'm not a math and science dork like *some* people . . . Besides, Gabriel says what matters is the size of a woman's *heart*, not her bra."

"Right," I said sarcastically. "I'm sure Gabriel'd rather be with a total dog than Nikki Howard."

Christopher got a good laugh out of that one — even though, as I said it, I was sort of hoping it was true. But Frida didn't find it funny at all.

"I'm not a total dog," Frida said, shooting me an injured look.

"Frida." I stared at her with my mouth open. "I didn't mean *you*."

But it was too late. I'd hurt her feelings.

"Maybe you think of *yourself* that way," Frida said stiffly. "But don't drag me down to your level, Em. At least I make an effort."

"What's *that* supposed to mean?" I demanded.

"Well, *look* at you," she said.

I looked at myself.

And, okay, I'm not the fashion plate Nikki Howard might be, in her stilettos and bikini and spray-on tan, or Whitney Robertson, with her flirty skirts and sexy camis.

But what's wrong with jeans, a hoodie, and Converse?

Frida was only too eager to tell me.

"You look like a guy," she complained. "I mean, maybe you have a figure, but it's not like anybody could ever tell, thanks to how baggy you wear your clothes. And have you ever even tried to do anything with your hair except throw it back in a scrunchie, which by the way is completely two thousand two? At least I *try* to look nice."

I could feel myself turning bright red under the less-than-flattering Stark Megastore lighting. It's one thing to be dissed by your little sister.

But it's another thing entirely to be dissed by her in front of the guy you've been secretly crushing on since the seventh grade.

"Gosh, I'm sorry," I said, stung. Really, did I need this? I didn't even want to be in this stupid store, in this stupid line, to meet this guy who, okay, was cute, but whom I'd practically never heard of before this morning. I could have been having a perfectly nice time at home, trying to reach level sixty of *Journeyquest* with Christopher. The last thing I needed on one of my rare days off from that hellhole otherwise known as Tribeca Alternative was *this*. "I didn't know I was supposed to conform to some random standard of beauty dictated by some tween queen fashion model."

This caused Christopher to snort with laughter.

"Tween queen. Good one," he said. I felt my blush turn into a flush. Of pleasure. Because Christopher had appreciated something I'd said.

Yeah. I'm that far gone. It's sad, really.

"Anyway," Christopher went on. "I think Em looks fine . . ."

Fine! Christopher thought I looked fine! My heart soared. I mean, I know *fine* isn't exactly the world's greatest compliment, but coming from Christopher, it was like being called earth-shatteringly gorgeous. I was pretty sure I'd died and gone to heaven.

". . . and at least she's not some big plastic phony like *her*," he added, nodding at the screen above our heads.

"*Yeah*," I said, throwing Frida a triumphant look. *Fine!* Christopher said I looked *fine!*

But Frida was barely even paying attention.

"For your information," she snapped, "Nikki Howard has taken the beauty and fashion industry by storm. She's one of the youngest models ever to have done so. Nikki and her friends —"

"Oh, here we go." I rolled my eyes. "A lecture on the F.O.N.s."

"What's an F.O.N.?" Christopher wanted to know.

"Friend of Nikki's," I translated. "According to last month's *CosmoGIRL!* she runs with a whole posse of F.F.B.F.s."

"Wait . . . what's an F.F.B.F.?" Christopher looked even more confused. If it didn't have to do with a computer or computer game, Christopher often didn't know what it was. This was what set him so adorably apart from every other guy at TAHS.

"You know. People who are in the media all the time, but they're only Famous for Being Famous," I explained to him. "They've never done anything to get famous — they don't actually have any talent? They're usually rich people's kids, like Nikki's on-again, off-again boyfriend, Brandon Stark" —I was in a good mood on account of the *fine* remark, so I lowered my voice to sound like a television news announcer — "nineteen-year-old son of billionaire Stark Megastore owner, Robert Stark. Or celebutantes, like Tim Collins's seventeen-year-old daughter, Lulu. *The* Tim Collins," I went on. "Who directed the *Journeyquest* movie."

Christopher's jaw dropped. "And completely ruined it?"

"That'd be the one," I said. "Lulu's an F.O.N."

"Why do you guys have to be so mean?" Frida whined. "It's like, everything fun, you look down on."

"That's not true," Christopher said, crumpling an empty Stark cookie bag, the contents of which he'd scarfed earlier, and stuffing it into the pocket of his copious jeans. Christopher had zeroed in on the bags of cookies Stark was giving away for free and seized as many as his pockets could hold for us to snack on later. The Commander doesn't allow junk food in the house. "We don't look down on *Journeyquest*. Well, the game. The movie freaking sucked."

"*Besides* that stupid computer game," Frida said, scowling.

"Music," I said, noting that Gabriel's voice was still booming over the speakers above us. "I like music." Well . . . *this* music, to be exact.

"Oh, right," Frida said. "Name one popular musician you listen to. And don't name any of that horrible metal crap Christopher likes, either."

"One popular musician?" I raised an eyebrow. "Fine. How about . . . Tchaikovsky?"

"Nice one," Christopher said, with a burst of laughter and an approving nod. "Mahler. He's good, too."

"Too dour," I said. "*Beethoven.*"

"That dude is rad," Christopher said, raising his fists — thumbs and pinkies upright — in a rocker's salute to Beethoven. "Beethoven rules my world!"

"Oh, God," Frida moaned, dropping her head into her hands in mortification.

"Come on, Free," I said, elbowing her chummily. "We aren't *that* embarrassing, are we?"

"Yes," she murmured. "You are. You really are. Don't you realize that you guys look down on everything normal people like? Like Nikki Howard and her friends —"

It was kind of funny that as Frida said this, Nikki Howard herself actually appeared — along with some of her friends — in front of us.

Except that Frida didn't notice right away.

That's because Frida was too busy defending her idol to me.

"You're always going on about feminism, Em," Frida continued. "Well, do you really think Nikki would have gotten where she is today — the Face of Stark, currently one of the highest-earning models — if she weren't a feminist?"

"Uh," I said. Because I couldn't believe the person we were arguing about was so close to us.

"And I don't see how you can even call yourself a feminist, Em," Frida went on, oblivious, "when you are so totally mean about a member of your own sex. I mean, Nikki's just a girl, like you are."

Except that I could see with my own eyes that Nikki was very far from being just a girl — let alone a girl like I am. For one thing, she was about a foot taller (thanks to a pair of five-inch heels, but even without them, she had to have been about five foot ten) and about half as wide as me. Seriously. Two of her would have fit into my jeans.

And for another, her shiny blond hair flowed smoothly down past her elbows, not a strand out of place, even though she was practically running — despite her heels — across the store.

Strangely, her filmy dress seemed to cover everything it was supposed to, too . . . despite the fact that it was the lowest-cut thing I'd ever seen — aside from what Whitney Robertson wore to school last year on Picture Day. How did Nikki keep those thin straps of material over her nipples, anyway? Double-sided tape? I'd heard about that kind of thing, of course, but never had a chance to observe its use in real life.

And it was a good thing, too (that Nikki had thought to use tape to hold in her breasts, which weren't huge enough to need their own zip codes, or anything, but — unlike my own — definitely stood at attention when called to duty).

Because she was carrying a tiny ball of fluff that appeared at first glance to be a pom-pom and at second glance to be a small dog, trying frantically to burrow its head between her boobs and get away from all the crazy lights and sounds in the store. If it hadn't been for the tape keeping him out, well, that dog would have dived right inside Nikki's dress.

Frida was still going on about what a bad example of feminism I am (about which, can I just say, *Hello, Pot? This is Kettle. Yeah, you're black*), completely oblivious to what was going on behind her — even though everybody else in line was staring, slack-jawed, at the rapidly approaching supermodel and her entourage of dog, some kind of agent or publicist (red-haired lady with a briefcase, jabbering into a headset), hairdresser (man in a silk shirt and leather pants, carrying a can of hair spray), and the number one F.O.N. herself, Lulu Collins, an equally skinny, equally pretty seventeen-year-old girl in a faux snakeskin-print wrap dress, who couldn't seem to stop looking at her Sidekick, even to watch where she was going.

I swear, it was just like at school when Whitney and Lindsey and the rest of the Walking Dead start their morning promenade from the front of the building to their lockers. Every single person in the vicinity just stops talking and stares as if transfixed.

And not just the people all around us, either. I noticed that Nikki had caught Gabriel Luna's attention, as well. He was still smiling at the girls clustered in front of him, thrusting CDs (and their phone numbers) at him.

But he was also keeping a pretty close eye on Nikki . . .

. . . as, I might add, was Christopher.

It was at that moment that Frida finally turned around to see what Christopher — his mouth slightly agape — and I were staring at.

And completely lost it.

"Omigodomigodomigod," Frida cried, waving her free hand (the other was still clutching her cell) in front of her face as if she were fanning tears from her eyes. "Omigod, it's her. It's her. It's HER!"

"I don't know what you're talking about, Free," Christopher said. "That Gabriel guy may be sensitive and all of that. But he is *totally* staring at her chest."

"Um, he wouldn't be the only one doing that," I muttered, noting — with dissatisfaction — the direction of Christopher's gaze.

He realized what I meant and began to turn bright red. But I noticed he didn't look away.

Funny how, all of a sudden, I wasn't feeling so *fine* anymore.

"Omigod, you guys," Frida said, clutching my arm. "Lulu Collins is with her! I have to get their autographs. I have to!"

But at that very moment, the line in which we'd been standing for the past hour reached the very table that, mere minutes before, had seemed so very far away and out of reach. Gabriel Luna himself was within autographing distance. Heck, he was within TOUCHING distance.

Not that, you know, I was going to reach out and grab a big hunk of his shirt or anything. I'm just saying I could have. If I'd wanted to.

Up close, he looked even better than he had when he was onstage. Up close, I could tell he definitely didn't have any tattoos. Nor was he wearing eyeliner. His eyes really *were* that blue. And his gaze really *was* that piercing.

Except that it wasn't looking anywhere near mine. It was, in fact, still glued on Nikki.

"Frida." I found myself as unable to tear my gaze from Gabriel Luna as he was apparently unable to tear his own away from Nikki Howard. "Uh. Frida?"

Except that when my sister didn't reply, and when I finally forced myself to look in her direction, I saw that Frida had actually stepped from the line and was heading toward Nikki and her entourage — not like she meant to be doing it, but like she simply couldn't resist the pull of Nikki's celebrity . . . kind of like how Leander was drawn into the Dark Castle by the beam of the Ring of Ashanti in the *Journeyquest* movie (which sucked).

"Frida?" I called after her. Then, realizing that Gabriel Luna had finally stopped staring at Nikki and was instead looking curiously at me, I turned toward him slowly and heard myself murmur, "Um. Hi."

"Hi," Gabriel said back. And then he smiled.

And — I'm not kidding — it was like reaching another level in *Journeyquest*. No, it was even better than that . . . it was like waking up in the morning and hearing your mother go, "Guess what? They just canceled school. It's a snow day." Seriously, that's what his smile did to me — gave me a jolt of pleasure that was almost physical, it was so strong.

Which is weird because I'd felt something very similar just minutes before when Christopher had called me fine. Boys are confusing.

Of course I couldn't say anything. Of course I could only

stand there gazing at him with my mouth hanging open, wondering how anyone so beautiful could be real and not a product of airbrushing or computer animation.

"What's your name, then?" Gabriel asked, in his gorgeous English accent.

"Um." Oh, God. He was talking to me. He was talking to *me*. What should I say? Why was this happening? Where was Frida? Where the frack was FRIDA? "Em."

"Em?" Gabriel smiled some more. "Short for Emily?"

"Um," I said. Oh, God. What was wrong with me? Normally, I had no problem talking to cute boys. Because normally, all the cute boys I met — Christopher excepted, of course — were sexist creeps who needed to be taken down a peg or two. They weren't sweet British hotties with a voice like an angel and blue eyes that seemed to pierce my soul. "No . . ."

"Do you have a CD you'd like me to sign?" Gabriel wanted to know, looking questioningly at my empty hands.

Oh, no.

"Hold on," I said, my heart pounding. "My sister —"

I spun around to find Frida and ran smack into Christopher, who was still staring at Nikki. Only now he wore a look of concern. "Uh, Em," he said. "Look —"

What happened next seemed to unfold as if it were in a dream. Or more accurately, a nightmare. I saw my sister walking toward Nikki Howard and her posse.

At the same time, I saw a guy standing nearby suddenly throw open his trench coat to reveal an E.L.F. T-shirt . . . along with a paint gun. A Megastore security guy with an earpiece, seeing this at the same time I did, grabbed Nikki by the wrist and jerked her back. Meanwhile, Paint Gun Guy, grinning balefully, raised his rifle and fired at the plasma TV hanging directly over Nikki's head, leaving an enormous yellow splotch across the screen where Nikki's boobs had been. Actually, it looked like she'd been eating a hot dog with mustard that had slid out onto her chest . . . something that happens to me not infrequently.

Only this time, the plasma screen came loose from the wires suspending it from the ceiling. First one wire popped. Then a second one.

And standing directly beneath it stood my sister, Frida, still holding her pen toward Nikki for an autograph.

"Frida! Move!" I yelled, my heart giving a lurch.

I darted forward to push her out of the way just as the last wire holding the giant television in place broke with a pinging sound that was easily audible, even over the music blasting from the Stark Megastore's speakers.

And then the whole thing came crashing down.

On me.

And — just like in *Journeyquest*, when I make a mistake and my character loses a life — everything went black.

FOUR

IMAGES. THAT'S WHAT I BECAME AWARE of next.

Like the kind you see floating on the backs of your eyelids when you press the heels of your hands against them when you have a headache. Just shapes, really, floating in space.

I watched them, wondering what they were. They looked like amoebas . . . no, like Christopher's hair, underwater in the swimming pool, when they made us do laps in PE last time, and I was spying on him with my goggles . . .

Wait a minute. What was I doing in PE? Had I fallen underwater? But I wasn't wet. At least, I was pretty sure I wasn't . . . I didn't *feel* wet. Did I?

How could I be seeing Christopher's hair underwater if I wasn't even wet? Maybe my eyes weren't open. Were my eyes closed or open? Why couldn't I lift up my hand to feel my face and see? My hand felt so heavy . . . I couldn't even lift it. . . .

Why was I so tired?

So tired . . .

I heard voices. The voices were saying things. What were they saying? I couldn't tell. I couldn't understand them. I was too tired to understand them. Who kept talking? Why wouldn't they let me *sleep*?

Wait. That was Mom's voice. Mom was the one who was doing all that talking. Mom and . . . who else? Dad. That was Dad. Mom and Dad were talking. They were saying things. They wanted me to wake up. Why? Why couldn't I just go on sleeping?

I knew I should listen to them — whenever Mom tells us to do something, Frida and I always do it. Eventually, anyway.

But I felt like I couldn't move. Like I'd been turned to stone. I just wanted to go on sleeping forever.

Still, I could hear Mom, her voice charged with urgency.

"Em! Em, if you can hear me, open your eyes! Open your eyes, Em. Just open your eyes for a minute, Em."

I knew that old trick. The second she knew I was awake, Mom would make me get up and empty the dishwasher or go to school or something equally hideous. I wasn't falling for that one.

"Em! Please! Please, just open your eyes."

She sounded pretty upset, though. Maybe the apartment was on fire. Maybe I should do what she said. Just open my eyes for a second to see what she wanted.

"Please, Em . . ."

She sounded like she was crying, actually. I didn't want to make my mom cry. That's the last thing I wanted to do.

So I tried to open my eyes. I really did. I *wanted* to.

But they just . . . wouldn't open.

My eyes wouldn't open.

I heard my mother crying, and I heard my dad comforting her, murmuring, "It's all right, Karen."

"In cases like this," I heard another, unfamiliar, man's voice saying, "it's not unusual for —"

I didn't hear the rest of what the man was saying because I was too busy concentrating on trying to make my eyes open. Only I couldn't get my eyelids to lift. I really couldn't. It was like they were made of lead, and I was just too weak to raise them.

So then I tried to open my mouth to tell my mom not to cry, that I was fine, just so tired. Maybe if they let me rest a little more . . .

But I found I couldn't open my mouth, either.

That was a little scary. For a minute. But the truth was, I was really so tired . . . it was so much easier just to go back to sleep. I'd tell Mom later, I decided . . . about my being too tired to do what she asked. I'd explain it all later, when I wasn't so sleepy. I needed to get my energy back. I'd be fine with a few more hours of sleep.

Finally, I managed to open my eyes. Not because anyone was calling my name. Not because I was seeing amoebas behind my eyelids. My eyes just . . . opened.

All by themselves.

But when they did, and I looked around, I was surprised to find I wasn't in a swimming pool, or even at home, but in a bed in a hospital room.

I could tell that I was in a bed in a hospital room because even though it was pretty dark — it had to be nighttime — nothing looked familiar to me. The walls were beige, not the Navajo White I'd painted my walls back home in a fit one day, because I couldn't stand the bland eggshell the rest of the walls in our apartment were.

And all my posters — from the *Journeyquest* movie, which, I know, had sucked, but the posters were cool — were gone. So were all my postcards from that field trip we took to the Metropolitan Museum of Art. Instead, all I could see were wires. Wires that appeared to be coming out of me. They were hooked up to machines beside the bed I was in, which were whirring softly and occasionally making pinging noises.

Fortunately, I didn't get scared or anything, because sitting in a chair next to the machines was my dad. He was sleeping.

I tried to think why I would be in a hospital with wires coming out of me. I am actually a very healthy person and have only been to the hospital once, when I broke my arm falling off the teeter-totter in our apartment building's playground in the second grade. Had I fallen off something again? I couldn't remember climbing on anything. How had I ended up in the hospital? I didn't feel hurt.

Just super-duper tired.

But I felt better than my dad looked. He had a lot of gray stubble all over his face, like he hadn't shaved in a long, long time (which seemed kind of funny to me, since when I'd seen him just last night, at dinner, he hadn't had a beard. Or had he? Looking back, I couldn't seem to remember . . . hadn't I had dinner with my dad last night? It seemed so long ago. . . .). Also, his shirt was super wrinkly and there were some stains on it.

The truth was, my dad looked pretty awful. I wondered why my dad would look like that. I didn't want to wake him up to ask, though. That seemed like it would be a selfish thing to do.

On the other hand . . . I was so thirsty. Seriously. I thought I was going to die of thirst.

But there didn't appear to be anyone else around. And it looked as if, whatever was wrong with me, it was kind of serious, given all the tubes and wires.

If I could just get a sip of water, I'd go right back to sleep, no questions asked. . . .

I opened my mouth and tried to say Dad's name. At first nothing happened.

That's right. I tried to say the word *Dad*, and no sound at all came out of my mouth. I had to try a couple more times before I was able to make any kind of noise, and even then, it was more of a grunt than anything else.

"Dad?"

Only the word sounded really strange. I don't know why. Maybe my voice was rusty from lack of use or something. Or thirst.

But my dad's head jerked up anyway, and he stared at me all bug-eyed. "Er . . . Em?" he asked hesitantly.

"H-hey," I said. "S-sorry —"

Except that came out sounding weird, too. What was wrong with my voice?

Dad seemed to think my voice sounded weird, too, since, his eyes still wide, he jumped up from his chair, yelling, "Doctor! Doctor!" and then rushed off.

Which indicated to me that I must be more hurt than I'd originally thought.

But I was too tired to wait around to find out how hurt. Seriously, I felt even more tired than I usually feel in first-period Public Speaking. Which is pretty tired. Probably if I didn't stay up all night playing *Journeyquest* with Christopher — then have to stay up the rest of the night, finishing my homework — I'd be able to get up in the morning, but . . .

I wanted to stay awake. I really did. I wanted to find out what was wrong with me, and why I was in the hospital. I wanted to get some water. . . .

But I just couldn't keep my eyes open a minute longer. I closed them, thinking I'd just take a little nap until Dad got back.

But of course I went back to sleep. Mmmm, sleep. Delicious sleep.

I hoped I wouldn't start drooling after I dropped off. But I figured, in a hospital, they must be totally used to that.

When I opened my eyes again, it was daytime. And my mom was sitting in the chair my dad had jumped out of. She was calling my name.

"Mom," I said groggily. Because the truth was, I was still pretty tired. "I don't want to go to school today. Okay?"

At least that's what I tried to say. I'm not positive those are the words that my mother heard, because they didn't sound much like what came out of my mouth.

Instead of arguing with me, though, Mom flattened her hand across her mouth and started to cry. That's when I noticed she wasn't the only person in the room besides me. Behind her stood my dad, and a couple of people in white coats I'd never seen before.

I figured the reason she was crying was because my voice still sounded so weird. It was kind of . . . I don't know. High-pitched.

Also, I still wasn't sure the words I'd said made sense.

"Honey," Dad said. He had his hands on Mom's shoulders and was looking at me funny . . . like the time I slipped and hit my chin on the side of the pool at the hotel we were staying at in Disney World, and I didn't know it but a big chunk of my skin had come off and I was bleeding copiously but since it didn't hurt I wasn't crying or anything, nor did I notice I was covered in my own blood because I was wet anyway. "Do you, um, know who we are?"

Whoa. Whatever number I'd done to get myself into the hospital, it must have been serious.

"Um, yeah," I said. "You're Daniel Watts and she's Karen Rosenthal-Watts."

The words didn't really come out sounding that clear. There seemed to be something wrong with my enunciation.

Maybe that's why my mom burst into loud sobs. Which was really startling. I've never seen her cry that way before. Not even at the end of the movie *Love, Actually*, which always makes her weep like a baby.

I'm pretty sure Dad had never heard her cry like that before, either. He looked totally startled by her outburst and kept going, "Karen, it's okay."

Fortunately, one of the people wearing a white coat stepped around my parents while they were huddled in their weepy hug and said, in a kind voice, "I'm Doctor Holcombe, Emerson."

"Oh," I said. Then I tried to clear my throat. Only it didn't work, because there was nothing in my throat to clear, apparently. "Why does my voice sound so weird?" I asked.

Dr. Holcombe had taken out a penlight and was flashing it into my eyes. "Are you in any pain?" he wanted to know. I wasn't sure if he was ignoring my question, or if he just hadn't understood me. My voice sounded so weird, I couldn't quite understand myself.

Meanwhile, another person in a white coat, this one a lady with her dark hair in a bun, said, "I'm Doctor Higgins. Can you wiggle your toes for me, Emerson?"

It was hard — I was still so tired — but I wiggled my toes.

"What happened to me?" I wanted to know.

"Can you follow the end of my finger with your eyes, Emerson?" Dr. Holcombe wanted to know. "Don't move your head. Just follow it with your eyes."

So I followed his finger with my eyes. I could see everything just fine now. No more amoebas everywhere.

"I mean, I know I'm in the hospital," I went on. "But what's with all these wires? And why does my voice sound like that?"

"Just keep looking here," Dr. Holcombe said as he continued to shine the light in my eyes as I was following his finger with my gaze.

"Can you squeeze my hand, Emerson?" Dr. Higgins wanted to know.

I squeezed her hand.

"Seriously," I said. Since Mom was still crying, and Dad was still trying to help her pull herself together, I had no choice but to address my concerns to these doctors I had only just met. "How much school have I missed?" Because I was in all AP classes, and it was no joke if you fell behind. And then, because I still sounded so weird to myself, I asked, "What is wrong with my voice?"

"We'll get to all that," Dr. Holcombe said, finally flicking off his flashlight, "in time, Emerson."

"Em," I corrected him. "I go by Em."

"Of course." Dr. Holcombe smiled and put his penlight away. "Now, why don't you try to get some more rest? Your family, as you can see, is fine —" He glanced at them, realized they were both still sniffling, and looked uncomfortably away again. "— er, at least, they will be. They've been very worried about you, that's all. It's quite a relief to see that you're doing so well. You can go back to sleep now, if you want to."

I was still pretty sleepy. But I was worried about the school thing. His assurance that we'd get to all that in time didn't mean I wasn't going to have bucket loads of work to make up.

And how come no one would answer my question about my voice?

But the doctor with her hair in a bun was jiggling some of my wires, and suddenly I got sleepier than ever. So I closed my eyes for another little nap.

And when I opened them again, it was nighttime, and the handsomest guy I'd ever seen in my life was sitting in the chair beside my bed.

FIVE

"OH, YOU'RE AWAKE, THEN," THE GUY said, when he noticed that I was staring at him.

And then he smiled.

And I knew exactly what it must feel like to reach level sixty in *Journeyquest*. Suddenly, it was a little hard to breathe.

Also, it wasn't at ALL annoying that one of the machines next to my bed started pinging like MAD in time to my heartbeat.

"Oh, no," the guy said, the smile disappearing as he glanced at the machine in alarm. "Did I do something?"

"No," I assured him, in my still-weird voice. But who even cared?

Obviously, this guy was a hallucination.

But one that I was going to enjoy as long as I could.

I smiled back at him and asked, relieved the pinging had gone back to normal (how embarrassing!), "Are those for me?"

Because he was holding a big bouquet of red roses. Like his presence wasn't enough of a treat. He'd brought me flowers, as well.

"Oh," he said, looking down at the roses like he'd only just remembered they were there. He laid them down on the bed beside me. "Yes, they are. Do you remember me? Gabriel Luna? From the Stark Megastore grand opening last month?"

I had no idea what he was talking about. I guess I semi-remembered something about a Stark Megastore. I definitely remembered *him*, though. Or at least I thought I did. That dark hair and those piercing blue eyes — those I knew.

Just not the name that had been attached to them. Or how I knew them.

I couldn't believe such a totally hot guy was visiting me in the hospital. And I *really* couldn't believe he had brought me flowers.

"Of course I remember you," I lied.

"That's good to know," Gabriel said, smiling again. And this time, even though my heart didn't speed up (thank God), I felt it melt. Just a little. Because of course even though he was handsome, he wasn't Christopher. "I wasn't certain you would. Couldn't have been the best day of your life . . ."

What was he talking about? I had no idea.

"Ha-ha," I said, smiling back at him. I reached over to touch one of the roses' silky crimson petals.

Which is when I noticed my hand . . .

. . . wasn't my hand.

I mean, it was, obviously. It was attached to my arm. But it looked . . . different. Instead of my chewed-up, raggedy finger-nails (I'm a hard-core nail-biter), I saw that I had what appeared to be a grown-out, though perfect-except-where-the-cuticles-needed-to-be-pushed-back, French manicure . . . pink on the bottom with white tips.

Weird. Also, did my fingers look . . . *thinner* than before? Could you lose weight in your hand? I suppose so, if you were unconscious long enough.

But still. How long had I been sleeping, anyway?

Then I realized: long enough for Frida to glue on those Lee Press On nails she was always threatening to make me wear.

Then I realized Gabriel was talking to me. He was saying, "You look well. They're saying — well, all sorts of things about you. I didn't know what to expect. No one would tell me anything about you. They aren't allowing visitors . . . I had to sneak onto this floor —"

He snuck onto my floor to visit me? That was so sweet. . . .

"How are you feeling?" he asked, actually sounding con-cerned.

"Fine," I replied. "A little sleepy . . ."

"Then you rest," Gabriel said, looking slightly alarmed. "I didn't mean to wake you."

"No, it's okay," I said, fearful he was preparing to leave. My hot-guy hallucination! It couldn't end so soon!

But the truth was, I was having a hard time keeping my eyelids up. They kept kind of falling closed, no matter how hard I tried to keep them open, just like in Mr. Greer's class.

"Don't go," I said to him. It was just an inch or two from the rose petal I was stroking to where he was resting his hand. And before I could stop myself, I had laid my fingers over his. What was I doing? I mean, *me*, touch a boy's hand? Especially the hand of a boy as cute as Gabriel Luna. Not that any boy as cute as he was had ever come close enough to me before in order for me to reach his hand . . . I mean, obviously there was Christopher, whom *I* considered cute . . .

. . . but I knew the rest of the world — or at least Frida and the rest of the Walking Dead — didn't technically agree with me. At least, not unless he got a haircut.

Then again, Christopher had never brought me ROSES. Christopher hadn't come to visit me in the hospital (don't think I hadn't noticed). Christopher had never stroked the back of my hand with his thumb, as Gabriel had just done. The few times I'd ever touched Christopher's hand with mine, he'd moved his out of the way with lightning-fast speed, thinking it was an accident (it so wasn't).

But the thing was, none of this was really happening, anyway, since it was all a hallucination . . . so what did it matter? This was the perfect opportunity to practice holding a boy's hand so that, when the opportunity with Christopher actually arose — and it was going to have to someday, right? *Right?* — I'd know what to do.

The minute my fingers touched his, Gabriel stopped looking like he was getting ready to get up and leave. Instead, his face kind of softened a little, and he even turned his hand over to hold mine and, doing that amazing thumb-stroking thing, said, in that deep, soothing voice of his, "I'll stay until you go to sleep."

Wow. That sounded nice. Super nice.

And exactly what a hallucination should say. I could only hope Christopher, when the time came, would be as nice.

But there was still something vaguely wrong. Something was missing from my perfect boy hallucination scenario.

Then I realized what it was.

"Will you sing me that song?" I asked, my eyelids so heavy I was looking out of mere slits. "The one you sang . . ." Where? I didn't even know what I was talking about. All I knew was that I'd heard him sing a song . . . somewhere. I was pretty sure.

He smiled. "I didn't know you even heard that song," he said.

"I thought you didn't show up until after my performance was over. But I'll gladly sing it for you."

What was he talking about?

But then he started singing, super softly, and it didn't matter.

And the sweet notes of the song he was singing soon lulled me all the way to sleep . . . but not before I heard, way off in the farthest reaches of my mind, a voice that sounded a lot like that of the lady with the bun in her hair going, "You there! What are you doing in here?"

And the singing stopped.

But by that time I was asleep anyway, and so I didn't care.

A hot guy named Gabriel Luna had sung me to sleep.

A hot guy named Gabriel Luna had brought me roses.

A hot guy named Gabriel Luna had held my hand.

It had to all be a dream. The most perfect dream I had ever had. If it had been a different boy and not Gabriel Luna.

I never wanted to wake up.

Except that of course I did. Wake up, I mean.

The next time I opened my eyes, it was daylight again.

And sitting in the chair beside me was a girl who kept shaking my arm and going, "Nikki! Nikki, wake up. Wake UP!"

Then, when she saw that my eyes were open, she went, "Oh, thank God. What are they pumping into you, anyway, to make you sleep so hard? I thought you were in a coma or something."

I just blinked at her. She looked familiar, somehow, but I couldn't quite figure out how. Was she someone I knew from school? And if so, why was she talking to me? Because she was totally gorgeous — perfectly smooth café-au-lait-colored skin, a funky bleached-blond pageboy, collarbones so sharp they looked like they could cut thought tin cans, like those knives on TV.

And the gorgeous girls at Tribeca Alternative do not speak to me. Except to ask me to get out of their way.

"You have no idea how long I've been trying to track you down. Do you know they've got *rent-a-cops* at all the elevators to keep people from getting up here to see you? Getting in to see you is harder than getting a table at Pastis for Sunday brunch," the girl prattled on. "I had to sneak up the stairwell, then hide in the ladies' room until the coast was clear. Thank God I had a copy of the newest issue of *Us Weekly* to throw onto the head nurse's desk in order to distract them long enough for me to sneak by. It's a good thing Britney's on the cover again, or it never would have worked."

Slowly, I realized how I knew this girl. Not because I'd been asked by her to move out of the way in the hallways of my school, but because she'd been on the covers of some of Frida's magazines.

She was Lulu Collins, daughter of Tim Collins, the famous film director whose cinematic adaptation of *Journeyquest* had made so much money . . . and almost ruined the whole game for me forever after.

Why in God's name was Lulu Collins sitting beside my hospital bed?

"Anyway," she went on, "since no one would tell me anything about what was going on with you, I just took matters into my own hands. I had to. I know Kelly's going to be mad, but whatever, I'm your best friend, what, she's not going to tell me what's going on with my best friend? Also, to tell you the truth, I couldn't take the whining anymore. You wouldn't believe how much she's missed you. So I brought her to see you. I know it's against the rules, but whatever, some rules are just stupid."

And without another a word, Lulu Collins reached into her colossal tote bag and pulled out . . .

. . . Nikki Howard's fluffy white dog.

Which she promptly deposited on my chest.

And can I just say, that dog went mental for me? I have never really considered myself much of a dog person. I mean, I like them well enough, but my parents never thought it was a great idea for us to have pets, given their wacky living situation (Dad in New Haven, Mom in Manhattan).

But this dog. Holy moley, this dog loved me. It was jumping all over me, licking my face, dislodging wires —

"Oh!" Lulu cried as one of the machines next to my bed began to ping crazily. "What the — how do you reconnect this thing? Oh, here . . . stick it back on. STICK IT BACK ON!"

I didn't know what she was talking about. Apparently, the wire had been connected by a sticker . . . to my forehead. I put it back where it had been, and the pinging stopped. Lulu immediately relaxed.

"Phew," she said. "Oh, my God, seriously, they are guarding this place like it's the freaking front door to Cave. And for once, I am so not on the list. Which, whatever. Did you know Kelly won't say what's wrong with you? The press is having a field day. You should see what they're saying, Nik, it's unfreakingbelievable. I'm just saying no comment 'cause of what happened last time. But you look way better than you did then. Seriously. Even though you're doing the no-makeup thing. Cosy, stop licking her."

I finally managed to pry the dog away from my face.

But then I saw something that distracted me from both the dog licking me all over and the girl I had never met before who was acting like she knew me.

And that was that there was a vase of red roses sitting on the windowsill — along with about a million other bouquets.

But none of the others was red roses.

Wait a minute. Had my hallucination been real? Had Gabriel Luna really come to visit me and sung me to sleep while holding my hand?

No. No way.

"So when are they letting you out of here?" Lulu wanted to know. "Also, what do you want me to tell Brandon? Because he's been calling and stopping by the loft nonstop. He's the one who figured out where you were. And, oh, my God, you know that guy from the Stark grand opening? That British guy, the singer, what's his name . . . ?"

"Gabriel," I said. And my heart gave a thud at the mere mention of his name. Man, I was in trouble. Especially since I didn't even like him. I liked another boy entirely. I mean, didn't I?

"Right, Gabriel," Lulu said. "Anyway, he sent a whole BASKET of roses to the loft. Seriously. The whole place stinks of roses now. That guy's got it bad for you. Anyway, Brandon saw them — he stopped by the other night, thinking he'd catch you at home, which, you know, *as if* — and now I think he thinks there's something going on with the two of you. You and that British guy. Which is good, right? Brandon totally deserves it, I saw him dancing with Mischa again at Cave, don't be mad, but you've been kind of MIA, and — Cosy, stop it." She tried to pry the dog's tongue off my face again, but it didn't do any good. For such a small puffball of a creature, Nikki Howard's dog possessed a surprising amount of saliva. "God, I'm sorry, maybe I shouldn't have brought her."

"No," I said, reaching up to stroke the little dog's soft, curly hair. "It's okay. It's just that . . ."

Lulu had taken a can of energy drink from her enormous tote, and now she cracked it open and took a sip. "Sorry," she said, when she noticed I was looking at the bright pink can. "I'm so hungover. Oh, my God, I was soooo wasted last night, all I had was a PowerBar for lunch and then some popcorn and, like, twenty mojitos, and, ooooh, did you see this?" She waved an enormous ring in my face. "Justin got it for me. Pink sapphire. What do you think? I'm worried he's thinking — you know. And I am so not ready to go there. What am I, gonna squeeze out a couple of spawn like Britney? No, thanks. But I'm keeping it, anyway, because it's so pretty."

I blinked at her. Was any of this really happening? Was Lulu Collins really sitting in my hospital room, telling me that Gabriel Luna had sent a basketful of roses to me, care of the loft we supposedly shared, and showing off a ring given to her by someone named Justin (she had to mean Justin Bay, star of the movie version of *Journeyquest*. That's who she was rumored to be dating, right? At least according to Frida's latest copy of *Us Weekly*, which I'd just happened to pick up and read. Cover to cover)? What was going on?

Maybe this was a continuation of the dream I'd had about Gabriel Luna.

Except that hadn't been a dream, had it? Because the roses he'd given me were sitting right there on the windowsill.

And what about this dog? This dog wasn't a hallucination. I could feel its little heart pounding next to mine as it licked my face with its hot, wet tongue.

No, I'm awake. I'm definitely awake.

Which was why I said to Lulu, "I'm sorry. But I don't have the slightest idea what you're talking about. I don't . . . I mean, have we . . . met?"

Lulu's little rosebud mouth fell open. And when it did, I could see she had a wad of pink gum in there.

"Oh, my God," she said. "Is that what's going on? Do you have amnesia? Because you hit your head pretty hard when you passed out, Nik. Although Gabriel was all over you in a second, and so were the paramedics. Well, they were already there, working on that girl the TV fell on —"

"That's another thing," I said. "My name's not Nik. . . ."

Lulu's mouth closed with a snap. Her eyes narrowed. And suddenly, she was on her feet, her hands on my shoulders, shaking me, while Cosy barked with alarm.

"What have they done to you?" Lulu shrieked. "Who was it? Who did this? Was it the Scientologists? I told you to stay away from those people!"

Being shaken — even though it was by a tiny girl who looked like a walking toothpick — was causing all the machines at the side of my bed to start pinging. Also, I can't say it felt all that good.

"Oh, my God, Nik, it's me, Lulu," the girl, who was now kneeling beside me on my bed, was screaming at me. "Your best friend! Your roommate! Or loftmate, because, you know, we never could share a bathroom, let alone a bedroom, because with your acid reflux, ew, but —"

"What's going on in here?" demanded a shrill voice from the doorway.

And I turned my head to see a nurse staring at us in horror.

"Get away from her!" the nurse yelled. "Orderly! Orderly!"

And the next thing I knew, a shrieking Lulu was being yanked off me by a burly man in blue scrubs, while a nurse had grabbed the little white dog — who was snarling pretty ferociously for such a powder puff — and was carrying it out of my room while my mom and Dr. Holcombe came rushing in, both looking white-faced and concerned.

"Nikki," Lulu screamed, as they carried her off. "Don't worry, Nikki! I'll be back! I'll get to the bottom of this, if it's the last thing I do —"

Then a door slammed, and both she and the yapping dog were gone. The only sounds were the insane pings and pongs coming from the machines by the side of my bed.

"Are you all right, honey?" Mom asked me, her eyes wide with alarm.

"I'm fine," I said as Dr. Holcombe bent over me, checking his wires. "But what's going on? Why did she think she knew me?"

"We're very sorry about that, Emerson," Dr. Holcombe said. He'd succeeded in shutting off most of the alarms. Now there was just the steady ding of my heart monitor. "The nurses are supposed to keep out non-family members. . . ."

"But I don't know Lulu Collins," I said. "Why did she think she knows me? Why was she calling me Nikki? Mom — *what's going on?*"

"Doctor," Mom said worriedly. She was chewing on her lower lip, something she only did when she was seriously upset about something — like Dad not getting back to Manhattan in time for one of Frida's clarinet recitals or my science fair. "Shouldn't we —"

"Absolutely not," Dr. Holcombe said. He was messing around with a needle. "Emerson needs rest."

"But, Doctor —"

"The best thing for her is to —"

I didn't hear the rest of their conversation. That's because Dr. Holcombe did something with the needle he'd been holding — even though I didn't feel a thing — and the next thing I knew, I was dozing off again, way too sleepy to keep listening.

If I'd known that that sleep was the last truly restful one I was to have for a long, long time, I'd have tried to enjoy it more.

SIX

WHEN I OPENED MY EYES AGAIN, IT WAS nighttime, and Frida was peering down at me. I mean, really staring, like I was some homeless guy passed out in a subway car, covered in my own vomit.

When she saw I was awake, she jumped about a mile back and stared at me with wide, terrified eyes.

I mean it. She looked completely freaked.

"What's wrong?" I asked her. My voice still sounded weird — all high-pitched and sort of . . . I don't know. Girlie or something. But whatever. "Have I got something on my face?"

I lifted my hand to feel my face. But all I felt was smooth skin. Which was . . . well, unusual. I do the best I can, of course, but let's just say I couldn't imagine after however long I'd been in the hospital, my complexion was looking its best.

But I didn't feel a single bump. Which was a miracle in and of itself.

"What —" I broke off. Man, my voice sounded strange. It had been a while, I realized, since I'd had anything to drink. In fact, I was drying up with thirst. Maybe that was it. Maybe I just needed to drink something. "Is there water in here or anything?"

"W-water?" Frida stammered. "You want s-some water?"

"Um, yeah," I said. I actually felt awake enough to try to sit up.

Big mistake. The machines next to me started beeping like crazy. Also, all the wires connected to me pulled me back down against the pillows.

Not to mention, my head kind of throbbed when I tried to lift it.

"I don't think —" Frida looked horrified. "I don't think you're supposed to try to get up yet."

"I kind of got the message," I said. I reached up to touch one of the wires and found that it was only attached to my head by a sticker. Using my new, long, press-on nails, I peeled the sticker off, along with the wire. No pinging. Hmmm.

"I don't think you're supposed to be doing that," Frida said, her gaze owlish.

"It's fine," I said, pulling off more stickers. Of course I had no idea whether or not it was fine. I just didn't want to be attached to machines anymore. Why should I be, when I felt all right? I mean, except for the throbbing head. Oh, and the parched throat.

"Is there any water around here?" I asked Frida. "Does my voice sound weird to you?"

But Frida just stood there, looking like she was about to cry.

And for the first time, I noticed she hadn't bothered with her morning blow-out. Her hair was a mass of staticky tangles threatening to engulf her pale, tearstained face. She didn't have any makeup on, either, and instead of being dressed at the height of teen chic, she had on one of Mom's old sweaters and a pair of her most faded jeans.

This, more than anything else — including the roses from Gabriel Luna, which I saw were still on the windowsill, though they were a lot droopier than before, and that extremely odd visit from Lulu Collins — disturbed me. I mean, Frida has been scrupulous about her appearance since . . . well, her whole life. I can't remember a time when she wasn't freaking out over a blackhead, much less leaving the house without mascara. And here she was, cosmetic free and looking like death warmed over.

"Hey," I said. "What's the matter with you? You look like

somebody just told you *American Idol* is fixed. Which I'm pretty sure it is, by the way."

"I . . ." Frida blinked a few times. And an actual tear slid out from beneath one eyelid. "I just can't believe . . . it's you."

"Well, of course it's me," I said. Seriously, what was wrong with my little sister? I've always thought she spent way too much time obsessing about how she looks and not enough time reading books . . . even comic books. But still. This was ridiculous. She looked like . . . well, as Lulu would put it, crap. "Who else would it be?"

Something about that question made Frida's face crumple. And suddenly, she was crying. *Really* crying.

"Hey," I said, concerned. "What's wrong?"

"Well, well, well, look who's up," boomed a voice from the doorway, startling both of us. I turned my head and saw Dr. Holcombe coming into the room, followed by my parents. Both of them smiled when they saw I was awake.

"She . . . she wants some water," Frida squeaked, still looking wide-eyed as a rat caught in the headlight of a Number 6 train.

"I think we can safely accommodate that request," Dr. Holcombe said, in a cheerful tone. "Go and ask the nurses for a pitcher and a glass, will you, Frida?"

Frida, looking relieved to have an excuse to get out of my room, skittered away. Meanwhile, Dr. Holcombe found some of the stickers — the wires still attached — that I'd pulled off. He made a tsk-tsking noise.

"Now, now," he said, lifting one and placing it gently back on my forehead. "I'm glad you're feeling better, but let's not get ahead of ourselves. You're still a very sick girl."

"I don't feel sick," I said. "Except for my head. My head hurts. But just a little."

"That's to be expected," the doctor said, still messing with my wires. "You've got to rest."

I looked at my parents for some sign they disagreed with the doctor. Because he had to be exaggerating. Since I felt relatively okay. I mean, if I were sick, wouldn't I feel worse?

But Mom and Dad both looked pretty worried.

"You should do what Dr. Holcombe says, honey," Mom said, patting my hand. "He knows what he's doing."

That was probably true. But still.

"I don't understand," I said. "What's wrong with me? What happened?"

"They've got you on some pretty heavy-duty medications," Dad said, in this weirdly cheerful tone. Kind of like he didn't actually feel cheerful, but someone had told him to act that way. Around me, anyway. I don't know what made me think of that, but once the idea occurred to me, I couldn't shake it.

"That's right," Dr. Holcombe said, sounding pretty cheerful himself. "And with luck, we'll be weaning you off some of those medications soon. But not quite yet."

So I was on drugs. Well, that made sense. I'd been pretty sure I had to be, considering how much I'd been sleeping . . . not to mention the hallucinations.

But a glance at the windowsill told me not all of it had been in my head. Also, the droopy state of the roses told me something else.

"How long?" I asked.

"Until we can start cutting back on your medications?" Dr. Holcombe was checking the machines next to my bed. "Well, that's hard to say —"

"No," I said. "I mean how long have I been in the hospital? How much school have I missed?"

"You don't need to worry about that, Em," Dad said, in his fake cheerful voice. "We've talked to all your teachers, and —"

They'd talked to all my teachers? They'd been to my school? Oh, my God. Why couldn't this part be a hallucination and not the part where Lulu Collins thought she was my best friend?

"How long?" I repeated, my weird voice — what was up with that, anyway? — trembling a little.

"Not long at all," Dr. Holcombe replied. "Just a little over a month."

"A month!" I tried to sit up, but of course all that happened was that the machines on either side of my bed started going nuts — especially the heart monitor, because I was having a panic attack thinking about all the work I was going to have to make up. Plus, I felt dizzy. And not just at the prospect of all the homework awaiting me.

It was of course at this point that Frida decided to walk back into the room, holding a water pitcher and glass she'd snagged from somewhere. Hearing all the commotion, she froze in the doorway, apparently thinking I was having some kind of attack.

"Is she — is she —" Frida stood there, bug-eyed and stammering.

"She's fine," Mom said, emphatically pressing down on my shoulder to keep me from sitting up. "Em, stop it. You have many more important things to worry about than school right now."

Was she kidding? What could be more important than school?

"I'm gonna be held back!" I insisted. "I'm going to have to repeat eleventh grade!"

"No, you aren't," Mom said. "Please, Em. Calm down. Doctor, can you give her something —"

"Oh, no," I yelled. "You are not putting me to sleep again! I need my laptop! Somebody needs to go home and get my laptop so I can start catching up. Does this room have Wi-Fi?"

"Now, now," Dr. Holcombe said, chuckling a little. "Let's take it one step at a time, young lady. Frida, come here with that water."

Frida, still looking at me like I was some creature who'd crawled from the deep, came forward, holding the glass of water she'd poured with a trembling hand.

"H-here," she said.

I lifted my hand and took the glass from her — noticing again, as I did so, the glamorous long fingernails she'd glued over my bitten ones. "Thanks — and for the manicure, too," I added sarcastically.

"I . . . I didn't give you a manicure," Frida said, in a voice that shook.

"Right," I said. I took the glass. . . .

But because I wasn't allowed to sit up, it wasn't easy to drink from it. Also, somehow I missed my mouth, so the ice-cold water went pouring down my neck and into my hospital gown.

Which just made me madder than ever. "What the —"

"Now, now," Dr. Holcombe said, mopping up the worst of it with his own handkerchief. "See what I mean? Let's take things one day at a time, shall we? Homework can wait. Want to try that again?"

I really was parched. I nodded, and this time Mom helped me get the cup to my lips, and the water — the coolest, most delicious water I had ever tasted — made it into my mouth instead of all over my pillow.

"There, now," Dr. Holcombe said. "That's better. Do you think you'll be wanting to tackle some food soon?"

Just the word *food* made my stomach rumble. I nodded eagerly, and Dr. Holcombe looked pleased.

"Frida," he said to my sister. "Why don't you run down to the cafeteria and get something your sister might like. What do you feel like eating, Emerson?"

"I know what she'll feel like eating," Mom said, her nose wrinkling a little, the way it always does when she's about to say something she thinks is funny. "An ice-cream sundae. Right, Em?"

"With a chocolate chip cookie on the side," Dad said, looking a little more like his normal self and not Fake Cheerful Guy.

"Is that what you want . . . Em?" Frida asked.

Except, weirdly . . . it wasn't.

"Sure," I said. Because I couldn't remember a time when I hadn't wanted ice cream and a cookie. Until now.

Oddly, though, that "Sure" turned out to be the right thing to say. Because for the first time since I'd woken up and seen her, Frida smiled. Tentatively, but still. It was a smile. Then she said, "Be right back," and took off.

Which was pretty strange in and of itself. I mean, when was the last time my little sister had ever been eager to bring me food . . . in bed? The fact that Frida was so willing to fetch and carry for me told me way more about how hurt I must be than my dad's fake cheer or my mom's teariness.

"So what happened?" I asked when Frida was safely out of earshot. "Why am I here? Was there an accident? A subway accident?"

Mom frowned. "You don't remember? Going to Stark? *Anything?*"

Going to Stark? Gabriel had mentioned something about Stark, too. A grand opening. Something about those words seemed to tickle my memory, but when I tried to remember, it was like it was just out of my grasp. . . .

"We don't have to talk about that now," Dr. Holcombe said hastily. "Let's concentrate on getting you better."

"I know," I said. "But I mean . . . I've been out of school for a month? What, have I been in a coma or something?"

"The, er, accident didn't cause the coma," Mom said gently. "Dr. Holcombe placed you in a chemical coma, so that you could heal more comfortably. He's been bringing you slowly out of it over the past few days, to see how you are doing."

"Well," I said, "what part of me is hurt, exactly? Because I feel pretty good. Except for my head. And my voice. Do you hear how weird my voice sounds?"

My mom and dad looked at Dr. Holcombe, who said to me, "Well, Emerson, the truth is, your injuries were extremely severe. We used a special technique we've developed in order to save your life, since the type of injury you suffered is, in fact, fatal."

I blinked at him. "But I'm alive."

"Because the procedure worked," Dad explained.

"*Worked* isn't the word for it," Dr. Holcombe enthused, his eyes glittering excitedly behind his plastic-framed glasses. "Your recovery up until now has far, far surpassed our expectations. We certainly didn't expect you to be speaking, much less possess any sort of motor skills, until many days from now, if not weeks. But as with any risky medical procedure, no one can be one hundred percent certain of the outcome. And you're going to notice that some things — like your voice, for instance, which you already mentioned — might not seem the same as they did before your accident —"

"That's why it's very important that you do what the doctors and nurses here tell you," Dad said.

"Such as, don't take off your sensors," Dr. Holcombe said, picking up one he'd missed before and attaching it to my temple.

"And no homework," Mom said. She'd recovered herself and wiped the tears from her eyes. Now she attempted a smile . . . and didn't do a half-bad job at it. "Understand? You need to concentrate on getting better first. Then we'll worry about what's going to happen with school."

"Fine," I said, glancing from her face to Dad's, looking for some clue — any clue — to what was really going on. Why were they treating me like I was in the first grade? Concentrate on getting better? Who did they think they were kidding? Why wasn't anyone leveling with me? "But . . . I've really been in here a month? Can I at least call Christopher and find out what's happening in school? He must be wondering how I am. I'm his only friend, you know. . . ."

But no one exactly rushed to get me a phone. Everyone said I needed to rest, that Christopher was fine, and that they'd get me my laptop (my other request) soon. Dr. Holcombe did call a nurse over to unplug some of my more intrusive and bothersome wires (not all of them, it turned out, were attached to a sticker. Some of them were attached to needles that went *under* my skin. It was quite a relief to get rid of those, in addition to the ones that pinged so noisily every time I moved).

By the time Frida got back with my ice cream and cookie, everyone was treating me less like a hospital patient, though, and a little more like a normal person.

"Here," Frida said, putting the ice cream — which she'd slathered with hot fudge, whipped cream, and nuts — on the bed tray one of the nurses had set up in front of me. Next to the ice cream lay an enormous chocolate chip cookie — the kind I used to eat four or five of a day, if I had the money for them.

Now the thought of putting any of that sugary stuff into my mouth actually made me feel a little sick. Which was weird, because normally, dessert is my favorite meal of the day.

Still, everyone — Mom and Dad. Frida. Dr. Holcombe. Three nurses who had wandered into my room and the orderly in my hallucination (because it had definitely been a hallucination. No way had Lulu Collins been in my room . . . with Nikki Howard's dog, no less) — seemed to be holding their breath, waiting for me to take a bite from the sundae Frida had brought me.

So I did the only thing I could. I lifted the spoon and dipped it into the bowl. Then I brought it — carefully, remembering what had happened with the water — to my lips and took a big bite.

"Mmmm," I said.

Everyone in the room exhaled at the same time. And smiled. And laughed. The orderly high-fived one of the nurses.

While I took a really fast gulp of water, because all that sugar? It tasted totally gross to me.

What was happening to me? Since when did I hate ice cream?

What had this doctor done to me?

Fortunately, no one noticed. Everyone chattered away about how great it was that I was making so much progress so soon.

Which was flattering and all, but might have meant more to me if I'd known exactly what I was making progress from. I mean, what was I supposed to be recovering from? What had happened to me? Which part of me was hurt?

And what, exactly, was this "procedure" they'd used on me?

Dr. Holcombe had been right about one thing: I was beginning to notice that some things were different than they'd been before the accident.

And not just my not liking ice cream anymore. That was the least of it. The weirdest thing so far was how the people in my own family acted around me . . . as if they didn't know me.

Almost as if — and I knew it sounded crazy — but almost as if I were someone else.

SEVEN

"WHAT — WHAT'S GOING ON?"

That's what I asked the doctor and nurse — both wearing full surgery gowns, including masks — who showed up in what seemed to be the middle of the night to shake me awake, then transfer me from my bed to a hospital gurney.

"Shhh," said the nurse, pointing at my mom dozing in the chair next to my bed. "Don't wake her up. She's exhausted."

"But where are we going?" I asked, stiffly rolling from my bed to the gurney.

"Just to do some tests," the doctor whispered.

"In the middle of the night?" I asked groggily. "Can't they wait until morning?"

"These are very important tests," the nurse said. "They can't wait."

"Okay," I said, sinking down against the thin gurney mattress. As usual, I was so tired. I was dimly aware that they were wheeling me down a long, empty hospital corridor. But they could have been rolling me down the middle of Times Square, and I wouldn't have known the difference, that's how sleepy I was.

"How we doing?" the doctor asked when he stopped the gurney to push the button to an elevator, way down at the end of the hall, about a thousand miles, it seemed, from my room.

"Fine," I murmured, at the same time that the nurse pulled her mask down to say, "Looks good so far. There was no one even sitting at the nurse's station. The whole floor is empty. I think we're going to make it."

That's when I got my first good look at her.

And I realized she wasn't a nurse at all.

"Hey," I said, feeling suddenly wide awake. I leaned up on my elbows. Suddenly, my head didn't feel at all throbby anymore. "You're —"

The elevator doors chose that moment to slide open.

"Go!" Lulu Collins yelled at the guy in the surgical mask.

"What do you think you're doing?" I demanded, as the two of them rammed my hospital gurney into the elevator.

"We're kidnapping you," Lulu explained, stabbing the button

marked *B* for basement. "But it's all right. It's us, Nik. Me and Brandon. Show her, Brandon."

And the doctor — although I guess that's not who he was after all — peeled off his surgical mask and looked down at me.

"It's me, Nik," he said, smiling broadly. "Brandon. See? Everything's going to be all right. We came to rescue you."

"Rescue —" I blinked right back at him. He was young, blond, and impossibly handsome.

And clearly completely insane.

"I think there's been a really big mistake," I said. Was I hallucinating again? Except that I couldn't be. Because hallucinations were never this detailed, were they? I could hear each ping of the elevator as it went down. And I could smell Lulu's fruity perfume (or maybe that was her gum). And I could see that Brandon was sprouting a pretty serious case of five-o'clock — in this case, five o'clock in the morning — blond shadow along his jaw.

It wasn't until we emerged from the elevator into the hospital's underground garage and my captors wheeled me toward a limo — yes. A limo. Black stretch — that I realized just how dire the situation really was. Because there wasn't even anyone around to hear me if I screamed for help. The place was echoingly empty.

That's when Lulu turned to Brandon and said, "She's not going to get in willingly. She still has no idea who we are," and he gave a sigh, turned around, and swiftly yanked me off the gurney and over his shoulder.

Now, I may have just spent a month in a coma or whatever. But I wasn't about to let myself get kidnapped by a celebutante and her F.F.B.F. henchman. I sucked in my breath and let out a shriek that I swear had to have been heard halfway to New Jersey —

— if there'd been anybody around to hear it, that is.

There wasn't. Brandon stuffed me, kicking and biting any part of him with which I came into contact, into the rear seat of the limo, then settled into the seat opposite mine and sat there, looking hurt. And not just physically.

"Jesus, Nikki," he said, as Lulu jumped in beside him and yelled at the chauffeur to go . . . *go!* "It's me. *Brandon!* You know me. We're going out!"

And the thing of it was . . . I kind of did recognize him. Seriously. From some of Frida's magazines. It was Brandon Stark — as in Stark Megastores. Brandon Stark as in *the* Brandon Stark, Nikki Howard's on-again, off-again, album-producing boyfriend. Brandon Stark as in heir to the Stark family fortune . . . which one magazine of Frida's put at a net worth of, like, a billion dollars or something.

Which pretty much makes him the richest person I've ever met.

But that still didn't mean it was okay for him to grab me and then stuff me in a limo like that.

"What's wrong with you?" I demanded, of both him and Lulu. "Can't you see I'm sick?"

"I'm sorry," Lulu said, pulling off her surgical gown and mask. I could see that underneath it, her makeup and skintight black catsuit were still perfectly in place. "It's just that we couldn't think of any other way to get you out of there. I mean, seeing as how they're brainwashing you."

"No one is brainwashing me," I cried. "What are you talking about? I don't even *know* you!"

This was the wrong thing to say. Lulu and Brandon exchanged glances.

"See what I mean?" she asked him, under her breath.

Brandon, meanwhile — all six foot four or five of him — gaped down at me. He was so good-looking, in a frat-boy way — sort of like Jason Klein, Whitney's boyfriend. He had a big square jaw and blond hair that hung a little bit into his green eyes . . . but maybe that was just because he was still partially wearing the surgical mask on top of his head. "Nikki . . . what did they *do* to you?"

"Yeah," I complained. "That's the other thing. Why do you people keep calling me Nikki?"

"Oh, God." Lulu dropped her head into her hands, while

Brandon just stared at me as if I'd asked him why carbon-based life forms need to breathe oxygen.

The limo driver turned his head and asked calmly, "Back to Ms. Howard's loft, Mr. Stark?"

Lulu lifted her head to say, "Oh, God, yes." She looked over at Brandon, slumped beside her. "Maybe if she sees something familiar . . ."

"Yeah, to the loft, Tom," Brandon said, in a dejected voice.

"You guys can't do this," I said, trying to stay calm. Which wasn't easy, considering everything that was going on. I mean, that I had just been kidnapped. In a hospital gown, no less. I didn't even have any shoes on. So it wasn't like I could throw myself at the car door and bail.

"Nikki," Lulu said, in a patient voice. "We're doing this for you. Because we love you. Whatever they've told you . . . it's a lie. All right? We're your friends."

"I'm *more* than your friend," Brandon said, coming to sit beside me. A little *too* close to me, actually. Why was he . . . *looking* at me like that? The neon lights from the signs on the buildings we were driving past along Second Avenue flickered across his face, turning it from pink to blue to green and then back again. "I'm your *boyfriend*. How can you not remember me?"

I had to hand it to him . . . he sounded genuinely upset. He wasn't faking it. His deep voice broke on the word *boyfriend* and everything. It was almost moving.

Or at least, it would have been, if I hadn't been convinced the two of them were completely off their rockers.

"If you guys make this limo turn around," I said, trying to keep my voice from shaking (yeah. Good luck with that), "and take me back to the hospital, I promise I won't press kidnapping charges. No one will have to know. Just drop me off, and I'll never mention it again."

"Kidnapping!" Brandon looked stunned. "We aren't kidnapping you!"

"Yes, we are, actually," Lulu said to him. She'd dug an energy drink from the limo's mini fridge and was gulping from it. "I mean, that's what this is, really. Only I prefer the term *intervention*."

"How can she not know who we are?" Brandon asked her. "Who *she* is?"

Lulu shook her head. "I told her to stay away from those Scientologists. . . ."

I took a deep breath, still fighting for calm.

"I don't know what the two of you are talking about, but I think there's been some kind of misunderstanding. My name is Emerson Watts. My parents — who are going to be very upset when they find out I'm missing from my hospital room, by the way — are Daniel Watts and Karen Rosenthal-Watts. I don't know why you guys seem to think I'm Nikki — Howard, I presume. But I'm not."

The two of them blinked at me with a lack of comprehension that was, to say the least, absolute. Their gazes were as blank as Frida's always got when I was trying to explain the finer points of role-play gaming to her.

But I'd never let that stop me before, and I wasn't about to now, either.

"Up until very recently," I went on, "I was an eleventh-grader at Tribeca Alternative High School. Then about a month ago, I was . . . I don't know. In an accident of some kind. I'm not real clear about the details, actually. But when I woke up, I was in the hospital you just kidnapped me from. Which I would like to go back to. Now."

My voice rose a little hysterically on the word *now*. But overall, I managed to deliver that speech with a reasonable amount of composure. Certainly more than I actually felt, considering I was being held in a limo against my will by a couple of teenage socialites.

Also, I noticed no one had offered me an energy drink. And I was really thirsty.

"*My God,*" was all Brandon said about my speech. And he sort of let that slip out like he hadn't wanted it to.

"I know," Lulu said, not taking her completely blank gaze off me. "It'll be all right when we get her home. When she sees her stuff, she'll be fine. I mean, look at that dress. You know she'd never be caught dead in a dress like that if she were in her right mind."

That's when I realized she was referring to my hospital gown. As a *dress*.

"That's it," I said. I leaned forward in my seat and spoke directly to Tom, the limo driver. "Pull over and let me out, or you'll be joining these two in jail for unlawful imprisonment."

To my surprise, the limo stopped. But only, it turned out, because we'd reached our destination.

"Sorry, Ms. Howard," the limo driver said, sounding like he meant it. "Just following orders."

"*Why does everyone keep calling me that?*" I practically shrieked.

"Calling you what, ma'am?" Tom wanted to know.

"*Ms. Howard*," I hissed. "And *Nikki*."

"Well," Tom said, looking uncomfortable, "maybe because that's your name, ma'am?"

"I told you people," I said, still addressing the limo driver. "My name is Emerson Watts. I'm not Nikki Howard."

"Um, actually, ma'am," he said, turning the rearview mirror in my direction, "you *are*."

And I raised my gaze.

And screamed.

EIGHT

WELL, YOU'D PROBABLY HAVE SCREAMED, too, if the face you saw looking back at you from a mirror belonged to someone else.

Not just someone else, but someone whose face happened to be plastered on magazines and the sides of buses and phone booths all over town. Wearing nothing but a bra and a pair of panties.

Seriously. I looked into the limo's rearview mirror, and I saw Nikki Howard's face staring back at me.

Only, when I raised my hand to cover my mouth in horror — Nikki raised her hand, too.

And when I dropped my hand away — so did Nikki.

That's when I started to shake.

And I couldn't stop.

"How . . . ," I asked no one in particular. "How could this have happened?"

"That's what *we've* been trying to figure out," Lulu said. "Now do you see why we had to kidnap you? I mean, stage an intervention on you?"

I lifted trembling fingers to my hair . . . I mean, to Nikki Howard's hair. It cascaded from the top of my head (or Nikki's head) from a sloppy ponytail, which was how I hadn't noticed the long blond strands around my shoulders: because they'd been just out of my sight line. And there hadn't been any mirrors in my hospital room.

"I'm . . . I'm a *model*," I wailed, to my reflection.

And now, finally, the reason my voice sounded so strange made sense. Because the voice I was hearing wasn't my own. It was Nikki Howard's voice, breathy, high-pitched, and girlie . . . completely unlike my own.

"Right," Lulu said slowly. "Do you remember me now? Lu-lu. Lulu Collins. Your roommate? I mean, loftmate?"

I looked at her. She appeared to be genuinely concerned about me. I mean, despite the ridiculous *Mission: Impossible* black catsuit — obviously her idea of how a kidnapper would dress . . . if any kidnapper in her right mind would put on black suede thigh-highs with five-inch stiletto heels — she looked vulnerable and sort of sweet, with her kohl-rimmed eyes, birdlike bone structure, and sparkly lip gloss.

But then I remembered. It wasn't ME she was concerned about. It was Nikki Howard.

Whom I — despite what the mirror was telling me — most definitely was NOT.

"Come on," Brandon said, gently taking my arm. "Let's go up to the loft to talk about this. You probably want to change into your own clothes, right? Have a little something to eat?"

In spite of everything — the fact that I was wearing someone else's face; the fact that Brandon Stark — voted one of *People* magazine's most eligible bachelors — and Lulu Collins had just kidnapped me; the fact that my parents had no idea where I was and were probably worried to death about me; the fact that my entire family had apparently been lying to me this whole time, not to mention keeping me from seeing my reflection — I couldn't keep my stomach from giving a massive, angry gurgle at the word *eat*. The truth was, whoever I was . . . I was starving.

Everyone heard it. Brandon put a hand on my wrist — or should I say Nikki Howard's wrist, which, now that I was looking at it, looked nothing like my own wrist, being both bony and devoid of a yellow Livestrong band and the forever bracelet Frida had made for me last summer when we'd both been camp counselors — and said, gently, "Come on inside, and we'll get you some food."

"Yeah," Lulu said, suddenly seeming to perk up. "There's some leftover blackened sea bass from Nobu. Your favorite. I just have to pop it in the microwave."

The next thing I knew, we were crossing a colossal marble lobby — Lulu Collins and Nikki Howard, it turns out, share a loft in a converted nineteenth-century police station in SoHo, not five blocks from my own apartment building — and getting into a brass and mahogany elevator, with a uniformed lift operator who tipped his gold-braid-trimmed hat at me and said, "Miss Howard. Nice to see you. Been a while."

"Yeah," I said queasily. It was a really good thing Brandon Stark was holding on to my arm, because otherwise I was pretty sure I'd have fallen down. Not just from hunger, but because I was so completely freaked out by everything that was going on.

Not to mention the fact that I was walking around in someone else's body. Barefoot. In a hospital gown.

Which the elevator operator didn't seem to find at all unusual, if the way he threw open the door when we got to Lulu and Nikki's loft and went, "Have a good night, Ms. Howard, Ms. Collins, and Mr. Stark," in a totally nice way was any indication.

And then my bare feet sank into deep, impossibly soft white carpeting. And I found myself standing in a gargantuan loft space, with a huge marble fireplace (fire unlit) at one end and a high-tech kitchen — all black granite and stainless steel — at the other, with ceilings that towered ten feet over the top of my head and windows all along both sides, looking out over the rooftops of SoHo on one side and the Lower East Side on the other.

The overall decor theme seemed to be expensive. And modern. Above the fireplace was a massive flat panel TV that was showing a video of the inside of an aquarium, to make it look like the TV was really an aquarium and not a TV. Scattered throughout the place were long white couches that looked as if they'd swallow you whole if you sat on them. On the coffee tables in front of the couches were magazines. On the covers of all the magazines was Nikki Howard's face.

Or, should I say, *my* face.

Brandon steered me toward one of the couches and then gently pushed me down onto it. Immediately, I was engulfed in softness.

"Sit right there, Nik," he said with concern. "Lulu, you got something for her to eat?"

"Coming right up," Lulu said, pulling open the door to the Sub-Zero refrigerator.

"And maybe something hot to drink," Brandon added, looking down at me. "She's shivering."

Brandon looked around, then found a cream-colored blanket that had been tossed down at one end of the couch. He picked it up, then settled it around my shoulders, gently tucking it around me. It felt soft as dandelion down. I glanced at the tag attached to one end of it.

One hundred percent cashmere.

It figured.

As he arranged the blanket around me, I looked up and happened to meet Brandon's gaze. He really was extremely good-looking. I mean, if you happened to like the totally cut, perfect-looking type, which I myself do not. I prefer the loose-limbed, long-haired, computer-genius type. At least, I always thought I did. I had to admit, though, that Brandon Stark's eyes, in the light from the crazy modern chandelier overhead, looked very appealingly green.

"Hey," he said to me, softly, when our gazes met. "Hi."

I had no idea what was about to happen next. That's because no guy had ever been that close to me before . . . except Christopher.

But Christopher has never thought of me as a girl. And then there was Gabriel Luna, of course.

But that had been a hallucination. Hadn't it?

In any case, how was I supposed to know that when a guy leans in that close, he's planning on trying something? I just assumed I had something on my face that Brandon was going to brush off.

Except that I didn't. Unless he was planning on brushing it off with his lips. Which suddenly landed on mine. Since the next thing I knew, Brandon Stark was kissing me.

Kissing me? I'm sorry. Brandon Stark was performing mouth-to-mouth resuscitation on me.

Which I found, to my surprise, that I thoroughly enjoyed.

Or at least, Nikki Howard's body thoroughly enjoyed it. How else can I explain the fact that I was totally kissing him back? And I had never even kissed a guy before.

Still, I could totally see why everyone was so crazy about kissing. In the romance novels that Frida left lying around the apartment all the time (and which I occasionally picked up when I had nothing else to read), the heroines were always going on and on about what it felt like when the guy they were in love with kissed them. They talked about their mouths burning like "liquid fire," and their loins being all aflame.

My loins definitely didn't go up in flames when Brandon kissed me. And my lips didn't burn like liquid fire (whatever that was).

But they felt pleasantly toasty. *Really* pleasantly toasty.

And I wasn't even in love with Brandon. Imagine what it must feel like to be kissed by someone you actually like.

Imagine what it would have felt like if, say, *Christopher* had kissed me. . . .

Which was when I realized, however much my body — or Nikki's body — might have liked what was going on, I totally couldn't let it go on a second longer. Especially since it seemed like kissing could very, very easily turn into something else if I didn't put a stop to it, *tout de suite.*

"Mmph," I said, pushing Brandon away so hard our mouths disconnected with a sucking sound.

And Brandon ended up losing his balance and almost careened face-first into the sofa.

"What?" he asked, looking hurt, as he stumbled back to his feet. "I missed you! Is that so wrong?"

I guess for a lot of girls, getting kissed by Brandon Stark — who is, admittedly, a known heartthrob — would be a total thrill. Frida, for instance, undoubtedly would have freaked (in a good way) over Brandon kissing her. She'd even have enjoyed being kidnapped by him, too, I'm sure.

And I wasn't unappreciative of the fact that Brandon was super handsome and seemed really very interested in me.

But that was the problem. He wasn't. Interested in me, I mean.

He was interested in Nikki Howard.

And I wasn't interested in him.

"I . . . I'm sorry," I said to him confusedly. Because I *did* feel sorry, when I saw his hurt expression. And also when I felt the rush of cold air that swooped in between where our warm mouths had been attached. A part of me wished I had just let him go on kissing me. Because kissing? Totally not overrated. *At all.* "It's just that . . . I don't even *know* you."

"We've been going out for two years," Brandon cried, looking even more hurt. "I mean, on and off. How can you not remember?"

I pulled the blanket around me more tightly. I didn't know what else to do. Or say. My mouth felt all weird from where his lips had been pressed up against it. His stubble had felt all scratchy. It kind of hurt.

But like . . . in a good way. There was no denying that my lips felt super tingly where his had touched them. And I was sort of starting to detect some fire in my loinage area now.

Oh, my God! Nikki Howard is a total slut! Or maybe *I* am, and I had just never had an opportunity to discover it until now!

What is *wrong* with me? Why had Christopher never made a move on me before, the way Brandon just had? We could have been making out this whole time, instead of playing stupid *Journeyquest!*

Oh, wait . . . did I just think that? God! What's *happening* to me?

Fortunately, Lulu appeared just then, holding a pile of clothes.

"Here," she said, depositing what looked like jeans, a T-shirt, and some frilly underthings onto the couch beside me. "I thought you might want to put this stuff on. I mean, that dress isn't exactly doing anything for you, you know?"

"Um," I said. "It's a hospital gown, not a dress. But thanks." I picked up the pile of clothes, then hesitated, looking around the loft.

Lulu heaved a sigh. "I can't believe you don't remember. Your room's down there," she said, pointing toward a door off to one side of the kitchen. "The food'll probably be ready when you're done."

I thanked her and got up, a little unsteadily, still clutching the blanket around me. I didn't look at Brandon as I made my way down the length of the loft. For one thing, walking in my new body was . . . well, weird.

For another, I could feel his gaze boring into my back the whole time.

I couldn't exactly blame him. If his lips felt anything like mine did, it was really hard not to go running right back over there and smack them right back onto his.

How do couples not just go around kissing *all* the time? Kissing is *fantastic*.

Oh, my God. I've known I'm a model for five minutes, and

this is how my thought process erodes? I've got to get a hold of myself.

I opened the door to Nikki Howard's bedroom, relieved to be out of Brandon's sight line — and was hit in the face by the overwhelming fragrance of roses.

I soon saw why. The "basket" of red roses Lulu had told me had been delivered to the loft — the ones from Gabriel Luna — sat on top of Nikki Howard's vanity table. Only the "basket" was actually a wooden crate . . . a wooden crate filled to the brim with roses.

Geez. Gabriel didn't mess around, did he?

Nikki's bedroom, I saw, was a lot like her living room . . . all white, with a thick furry carpet and a vast, soft-looking bed. In fact, the only color in the room came from Gabriel's roses. The floor-to-ceiling windows were covered with white satin curtains. A huge mirror — half hidden by Gabriel's crate of roses — hung over the white vanity table in one corner. In the mirror, I could see my reflection — a pale, skinny blond girl in a hospital gown, wearing a terrified expression and clutching a pile of clothes to her chest, a cashmere blanket around her shoulders.

Right. A pale, skinny blond girl who, if Frida's *CosmoGIRL!* was right, earned something like twenty grand a *day*.

Unlike in my own room, back home, Nikki hadn't decorated her walls with postcards of paintings or posters of movies she liked. Nor were there piles of science-fiction and fantasy books and journals and manga lying around, threatening to topple over at any moment. In fact, there wasn't even so much as a photo on her nightstand. Although Nikki did own a computer — a Stark-brand laptop (in a hideous shade of pink) that sat on the vanity near her bed — she didn't appear to own much of anything else, really, except a Stark-brand flat screen television that was affixed to the wall across from her bed.

And makeup. At least, that's all I found in every drawer I pulled open, looking for . . . I don't even know what.

But all I found? Mascara. And lip gloss. A *lot* of lip gloss.

Which I supposed she needed, considering all the kissing she was apparently doing. She probably had to reapply a lot.

And, when I opened another door, I saw that while Nikki didn't appear to own any books, she did own a *lot* of clothes. There was a whole walk-in closet full of them — what looked like thousands of shirts, blouses, jackets, jeans, trousers, dresses, and skirts of every description and color, each item hanging neatly on a wooden hanger. Some of them were so new, they still had price tags on them. I found more than one pair of four-hundred-dollar jeans, and a pretty plain-looking dress with a tag that said three thousand dollars (which *had* to be a mistake). Beneath and above the hanging clothes were shelves containing literally hundreds of purses, bags, totes, and shoes of every type imaginable . . . boots, sneakers, flats, heels, sandals, pumps, even, for some reason, wooden clogs, like the Dutch Boy wears.

Frida, I knew, would have felt as if she'd died and gone to heaven if she'd walked into Nikki Howard's closet. All I felt, however, was confused. What kind of teenage girl could afford four-hundred-dollar jeans? Who even needed four-hundred-dollar jeans? And who kept her stuff so . . . neat? It was kind of freaky, in a way. I didn't like being in that closet. Not one bit.

I hurried out of it and tried the other door . . . and found myself in Nikki Howard's bathroom.

Unlike the rest of the loft, this room wasn't white. The walls were made of a taupe-colored marble — the ones that weren't mirrored, that is. There was a walk-in shower and a separate Jacuzzi tub. The mirror above the double sinks was surrounded by lights, dressing-room style. The reflection I saw blinking back at me in that mirror looked scared.

I put down the pile of clothes Lulu had given me and reached up to undo the ponytail someone had put my (or, more accurately, Nikki Howard's) hair into. It came tumbling down my shoulders, looking as unlike my own hair as any hair ever could. Instead of being stick straight and brown, Nikki Howard's hair was silky and golden and hung in perfectly curled waves . . . even though it clearly hadn't been brushed — or washed — in a while.

And when I reached behind me to undo the hospital gown

and it fell away to land in a puddle at my (I mean, Nikki Howard's) feet, I saw a body as unlike my own as the hair was. It was the same absolutely perfect — by the Walking Dead's standards — body I'd seen in countless Victoria's Secret ads featuring Nikki Howard. There were no surprises there. None at all.

Except the main one — that suddenly, that perfect body appeared to be my own.

I looked away from the mirror and hurried into the clothes Lulu had given me — a pair of frilly pink panties and an equally frilly bra first. Then jeans, which slid on to fit like a second skin, and the T-shirt — bearing the words BABY SOFT across the front, in pink curlicue writing — which did little to hide what the underwire bra was emphasizing. This was certainly unlike the shirts stocked in my own closet, back home, which I'd selected based on their ability to *hide* what Nikki Howard apparently preferred to flaunt.

Hurrying from the bathroom and into the closet to grab a pair of Skechers, the lowest-heeled shoes I could find, I threw them on.

Then, giving a last look at this room that supposedly belonged to me — but that, in a million years, I'd never have been able to keep that clean — I staggered back to the bedroom door, threw it open . . .

And was attacked all over again.

NINE

IT WAS OKAY, THOUGH. BECAUSE THIS
time, instead of a couple of F.F.B.F.s in surgical masks, my assail-
ant was nine inches high and only weighed a half-dozen pounds.
The minute she saw me come out of Nikki Howard's bedroom,
she careened straight at me, like a fuzzy white bullet with a pink
lolling tongue.

"Sorry," Lulu called from the kitchen, as she saw me scoop
up the excited little dog. "I had her locked up in my room, and
I forgot to let her out until just now. God, look how glad she is
to see you! Even if you can't remember *us*, you have to remember
Cosabella. I mean, you named her after your favorite line of
lingerie!"

Except, of course, that I don't have a favorite line of lingerie. Except maybe Hanes.

Still, even if I didn't know Cosabella, Cosabella knew me. As soon as I sat down again on the comfy white sofa I'd vacated a few minutes earlier, Cosabella leaped up and, tiny stump of a tail wagging, promptly stood on her hind legs to give my face a thorough licking.

And I didn't mind. I really didn't. Because after the shock I'd had, a face licking actually felt pretty good.

"Okay," Brandon said, lowering himself onto the couch opposite mine and studying me with a worried expression on his face. But not, I soon realized, because he was trying to figure out how to get me to kiss him again. Unfortunately. "It's time to stop messing around. Who did this to you, Nikki? And be honest. Was it Al Qaeda?"

"Brandon!" Lulu shrieked from the kitchen.

"Well." Brandon shook his head. "If they want to strike a blow against freedom, why not go after the Face of Stark, one of America's most beloved models?"

"Al Qaeda doesn't know how to give people AMNESIA," Lulu declared, from behind the black granite-topped island. "Only the Scientologists have the technology to do that."

Brandon looked at me gravely. "Was it the Scientologists, Nikki?" he asked.

"Okay," I said. I'd reached up to rub my temples — I mean, Nikki Howard's temples. But apparently, they were mine now. "We need to get one thing straight. I know I look like Nikki Howard. And I know I sound like Nikki Howard. I realize that, right now, I am in Nikki Howard's loft and wearing her clothes, while her dog is licking my face. But I am not Nikki Howard. Okay?"

"Okay," Brandon said. "Except . . . you are."

"I'm not," I insisted. "Look, I don't know what's going on any more than you two seem to. But seriously, I'm not Nikki."

"But how is that even possible?" Lulu wanted to know. She came around the kitchen island . . . and I noticed that she was carrying food. Lots of food.

And that the smell coming from the food was sublime.

Which didn't make any sense, because when I saw what the food was (after she'd put it down on the white marble-topped coffee table in front of me) I could see it wasn't anything I'd ever get excited over — in the past, anyway. Just the promised blackened sea bass — which, being fish, I shouldn't like. A bowl of soup — it looked like warmed-up leftover miso, judging by the bits of tofu and seaweed floating in it, and which, again, yuck. I completely hate tofu, let alone seaweed. All of this was accompanied by a cup of green tea.

I totally hate green tea.

But apparently Nikki Howard doesn't, because the next thing I knew, I was gulping that tea down. And a second after that, I'd started in on the sea bass and the miso soup.

And all of it was the most delicious food I could ever remember eating.

Don't think Lulu and Brandon didn't notice, either. They looked at how I was stuffing my face, and Lulu went, almost admiringly, "The blackened sea bass from Nobu always was your favorite."

That was enough to make me put my fork down. Although of course the truth was that, by then, the fish was all gone anyway. And I'd put a pretty good dent in the soup, too.

"You guys," I said. "Come on. Obviously, I'm not Nikki Howard. I mean, I didn't even know who you two were at first. I've seen you in magazines and all, but . . . I don't know anything about you."

Brandon looked sadly at Lulu. "She pushed me away when I kissed her."

Lulu threw me a shocked look. "Nikki! Way to be a bitch!"

I felt myself blushing to my hairline. If only they knew the truth, that pushing him away was the last thing I'd wanted to do. . . .

"But that's what I'm trying to tell you!" I cried. "I'm not Nikki Howard! I'm Emerson Watts — honest, I really am."

"I know, Nikki," Lulu said, laying a sympathetic hand on my arm. "That's why we're staging this intervention. To help you remember who you really are — which isn't this Emerson Watts person. Look." She bent over and pulled a black portfolio out from beneath the couch. "I have your book. I know this will spark some memories."

She turned it to the first page, where there was a tear sheet from a magazine ad featuring Nikki Howard in a poofy prom dress, jumping into the air from a trampoline. "This is from your first-ever shoot for Stark Enterprises, when you were just starting out. Remember? This was before we met, when Rebecca first brought you to New York. You remember Rebecca, right? Your agent?" When I looked at her blankly, she prodded, "You must remember getting signed by Ford. They said you were the most professional fifteen-year-old they'd ever represented. They said you were way more mature than most of their twenty-year-old models."

"Uh," I said, "I told you. I'm not Nikki. I'm Emerson Watts —"

"Emerson Watts." Brandon's eyebrows were knit. He was concentrating . . . which you could tell for him wasn't all that easy. "Emerson Watts. Why does that name sound so familiar to me?"

"Shhh," Lulu said to him. "Don't confuse her." She turned a page in the portfolio. "Look, Nikki. Look at this. This is from your first runway show with Chanel. Remember, I was sitting in the front row? And at the after-party I asked you if those lace-up gladiator stilettos hurt, and you said they hurt like a mo —"

"Emerson Watts," Brandon said again. Now his expression suggested that he was in pain. But only from concentrating so hard. "Seriously. I've heard that name before. . . ."

"Ignore him," Lulu said to me, and turned the page. "He's just tired. He was up all night last night dancing at Cave. Oh, look! Here's your first Victoria's Secret spread!"

I stared down at the pictures, holding Cosabella close (she didn't seem at all inclined to leave my lap. Ever. Which I didn't mind. I liked the way her fluttering little heartbeat felt against my thighs. Or, er, Nikki Howard's thighs. There was something comforting about this little creature that seemed to absolutely adore me. Who cared if who she really adored was Nikki Howard?).

Looking at the pictures, I recognized the body I'd just seen in the bathroom mirror a little while ago. In the airbrushed ad for lingerie, that body looked even more perfect than it had in the mirror.

It seemed weird to me that, if Lulu Collins was really trying to jog my memory, she'd show me Nikki Howard's portfolio and not a family album.

But of course, given the context — that I was apparently a normal eleventh-grader trapped in the body of one of the world's most famous supermodels — maybe it wasn't that weird, after all. Maybe, under the circumstances, hoping to make me remember who I really was by showing me pictures of myself in a diamond-encrusted bra wasn't the worst strategy.

"Oh," Lulu said, turning the page. "Here's your first print ad for your new clothing line! See how pretty you look there? Your eyes are the same color as those sapphires. . . . That's not even Photoshopped, you know. Your eyes really *are* that color —"

"I know!" Brandon cried suddenly, startling us both — and Cosabella, who lifted her little head from my knee and cocked it at him inquisitively. "Emerson Watts! That was the girl who got hit by the plasma screen at the grand opening of my dad's new store in SoHo."

I blinked. The words *plasma* and *screen* triggered something deep within the recesses of my mind. Dimly — like a dream I'd had long ago — the memory of the day Christopher and I had taken Frida to the grand opening of the Stark Megastore came back to me . . . just a trickle at first . . . then a flood.

"Yes!" I cried, clapping my hands and startling Cosabella a little. "Yes! That was me! I'm Emerson Watts! I was there that day!"

"So was I!" Lulu squeaked, her dark eyes widening. "Oh, my God! That was so horrible! Nikki, do you remember now? You fainted!"

"I'm not Nikki," I reminded her. "I'm Emerson Watts. *I'm* the one who got hit by the plasma screen."

"And, Nikki, you, like, totally passed out," Lulu said, ignoring me. "And that Gabriel Luna guy ran over, and he totally, like, cradled you in his arms, but he couldn't wake you up. No one could. And the paramedics came, and . . ." Lulu swung her head around to stare at me accusingly. "And that's the last time I saw you! Kelly said you'd been diagnosed with hypoglycemia and were taking some time off to try to get it under control. But I knew that wasn't true. I mean, for one thing, you'd never said anything to me about having hypoglycemia. Acid reflux, maybe. But not hypoglycemia. And also because no way would you take time off without telling me where you were going. And no way would you leave Cosy behind."

I looked down at the little dog on my lap. No. There was no way anyone would leave Cosy behind.

Not if she'd had a choice.

"And no way would you not call me," Brandon added. And when I glanced at him, I saw that he was looking at me in a way that . . . well, no guy had ever looked at me before.

Except possibly for Gabriel Luna, that night in the hospital.

Only — I realized with a sudden pang of disappointment — it hadn't been *me* Gabriel had been looking at like that at all.

It had been Nikki Howard. Nikki Howard, whom he'd supposedly cradled in his arms after she'd passed out at the Stark Megastore grand opening, then later visited in her hospital room.

Of course! How could I have been so stupid? How could I ever have thought Gabriel Luna would bring *me* flowers? Those flowers hadn't been for me.

They'd been for Nikki Howard.

God. How naive could a person be? What guy would ever look at a girl like *me* — a normal girl — when a girl like Nikki Howard was around? Even Christopher hadn't been able to take his eyes off her the whole time she'd been within sight range, back at the Stark Megastore. And Christopher isn't the type to fall for a pretty face. I mean, Christopher has always laughed at Whitney and the other Walking Dead at TAHS.

But I remembered now the way his gaze had been glued to Nikki Howard's chest that day.

That chest was mine now . . . at least for the foreseeable future.

What did *that* mean? I mean, so far as my relationship with Christopher went?

The thought made my new chest feel a little tight.

Then I remembered something: Christopher had said I looked fine at the Stark Megastore grand opening. But that was back when I'd still been me, Em Watts. Would he still think I looked fine as Nikki Howard?

Somehow, I sort of doubted it.

"So I started looking for you," Lulu went on. "First I checked all the usual places you might go to get away from it all . . . Bali, Mustique, Eleuthera . . . but there was no record of you there under any of the fake names you usually use to register —"

"And that's when she asked for my help," Brandon said. "And so I talked to my dad. Because, you know, if anyone was going to know where you were, it'd be my dad. But he was all freaky about it."

"Right," Lulu said, looking indignant. "He told Brandon you were all right, but that you were working through some things. Which, you know, I knew right away was total BS. Because no way you'd work through anything without asking for my help. I always help you work through things. Like that time Henry put the café-au-lait lowlights in your hair, remember? So then I thought maybe they'd stuck you in a Promises somewhere — just for a rest, you know, because I know you'd never mess up your body by doing *drugs*, and so that the press couldn't find you —"

"— but you weren't registered at any of them, and finally I snuck into my dad's office," Brandon said, "and I looked through his stuff and I found your file and I saw that you were right here in the city, at Manhattan General on Sixteenth Street —"

"You were literally just down the street!" Lulu cried. "The whole time! So I went to scout it out," Lulu explained. "Because Brandon —"

Brandon looked sheepish. "I thought you might not be so happy to see me. About the Mischa thing, I mean. But honest, Nik, I thought you were mad at me, and that's why you hadn't called. And the thing with Mischa, I mean, whatever, she just won't stop calling me, she wants to cut an album, and you know I'm producing now —"

"But then when you didn't remember me," Lulu went on, after flashing him a glance filled with annoyance, "that's when I knew. That they'd gotten to you."

It was hard to take in, this not-very-lucid explanation of what had gone on, from their point of view, from the last time I remembered being myself — the day of the Stark Megastore grand opening — until now.

But one thing was apparent. Something very, very weird had taken place that day.

"Wait!" Lulu cried. "I figured it out."

Both Brandon and I looked at her. "Figured out what?" I asked.

"How come you look like Nikki," Lulu explained, "but you think you're this Emerson Watts person? God, it's so obvious! You've had a spirit transfer!" she cried. "Like in that movie *Freaky Friday!*"

Now it was my turn to blink. "Uh, Lulu," I said. Seriously. It is a crime that girls like my sister worship people like Lulu. Yeah, she's good-looking, and she's rich. And maybe — just maybe — she means well.

But she's got the brains of a clam.

"There's no such thing as a spirit transfer," I informed her.

"Of course there is!" Lulu cried, excitedly. "Why have there been all those movies about it, if there isn't?"

"Lulu," I said. How was I going to sum up quantum physics — let alone biology — for this girl who so clearly had dropped out of school after approximately the eighth grade, if not earlier? "What you're describing . . . that doesn't happen. Okay?"

"But what other explanation is there?" Lulu asked me, her brown eyes wide and innocent. "Obviously, when that girl was hit by the plasma screen, and you — I mean, Nikki — fainted, you two swapped spirits. All we have to do now is find this Emerson Watts person — who has Nikki's spirit trapped inside her — and you two can swap back and be normal again."

Brandon was frowning. "Except . . ."

"No *except*," Lulu said stubbornly. "That's how it works. I mean, maybe, since you two both passed out at the same time, and that's how your spirits got swapped, we'll have to hit you both over the head to make it happen again. But we'll be careful not to do any permanent damage. Also not bruise you, because you have the spring shows in Milan coming up —"

"We can't," Brandon said, before I could interrupt.

"What do you mean, we can't?" Lulu demanded. "Of course we can. Why do you always have to be so negative, Brandon? It's because you spend too much time with Mischa, and she's still bummed out about her last pilot not getting picked up —"

"No," Brandon said. "I'm not being negative. I mean, you can't do the spirit transfer thing."

"Why?" Lulu snapped, looking angry. Only, because she was so tiny and pretty, it was kind of hard to take her anger seriously. It was like seeing a Chihuahua growling. "If we need a spirit guide, or whatever, I can totally ask Yoshi from my yoga class. He's way spiritual."

"It's not that," Brandon said. He looked super uncomfortable. "It's just that . . . when I was going through my dad's files, looking for information about Nikki, I saw something. Something about that Emerson Watts girl."

I leaned forward in my seat — even though it wasn't easy, since the couch was so soft, it kind of enveloped you.

"What about me?" I asked.

"Well," Brandon said hesitantly. "It's just that, according to this report my dad had — when that TV fell on Emerson Watts — she — I mean, you — died."

TEN

"NO," I SAID, HORRIFIED, SHAKING MY head. "That's not possible."

Brandon looked like he felt sorry for me.

"I'm just telling you what I read," he said. "Dad seemed pretty upset by the whole thing. I mean, even though those E.G.G. people did it —"

"Egg? You must mean E.L.F.," I corrected him.

"Whatever," Brandon said. "It was still his fault. Dad's, I mean. He should have had better security."

"He should have made sure those plasma screens were better secured to the ceiling," Lulu said gravely.

"Well," Brandon said, looking uncomfortable. "It was secured.

Secure enough that it wouldn't have fallen down if someone hadn't shot it with a paintball —"

"I don't believe you," I said, cutting him off.

He shook his head. "I'm sorry," he said. "But it's true. If anyone's to blame, it's those elf people —"

"Not about the plasma screen," I said, getting up from the couch . . . but still clutching Cosy to me. "About me. Being dead. I can't be dead."

"Oh, believe me," Brandon said. "Emerson Watts? She's dead. It was in the paper and on CNN and everything. I even saw the obituary. It was in the file in my dad's office with the rest of the stuff."

It felt as if something moved over me. Nothing too massive. Just a steamroller.

Lulu, who'd been biting her lower lip, released it and said, "I'm sorry, Nik. But I think Brandon's right. I saw the way that thing landed on that girl, and she . . . well, I don't see how anyone could have survived that. It squashed her. Like a bug."

"If I'm dead," I demanded, when the steamroller finally moved off me and I was able to speak and also pace the length of the loft, which I promptly began to do, "how can I be here? How can I be talking to you? How can I just have eaten that blackened sea bass?"

"Because," Lulu said patiently, "I already told you. You had a spirit transfer —"

"Oh, my God!" I yelled. "For the last time! There's no such thing as a spirit transfer!"

"God, okay," Lulu said, blinking rapidly. "You don't have to yell."

"There's got to be some other explanation," I said, still pacing. "I mean, if Emerson Watts is dead, and I'm Nikki Howard, why are Emerson Watts's parents the ones who've been at my bedside all along in the hospital? Why haven't Nikki's parents been there?"

"Well, because Nikki doesn't have any parents," Lulu said matter-of-factly. "I mean, she became an emancipated minor the minute she landed her first modeling contract."

I quit pacing and stared at her. "What are you talking about?"

"Nikki never got along with her parents," Lulu said. "You know you never — I mean, *she* never — talked about them much."

"Try *at all*," Brandon said drily.

"Right," Lulu said. "Nikki didn't have any family. I mean, none that she spoke to. Or about. I think —" Lulu dropped her voice to a whisper. "I think Nikki's parents were poor. Like trailer-park poor."

"Why are you whispering?" I asked her.

"Well." Lulu shrugged. "I don't know. I mean . . . I guess because . . . Well, it's not very classy to talk about money. And

Nikki never mentioned her family, or where she grew up, or anything that happened before she came to New York and made it big."

"Fine," I said, beginning to pace again. "That still doesn't explain what my parents were doing in Nikki Howard's hospital room."

"Because they know that's where your spirit is," Lulu explained patiently. "Maybe her body is dead, Brandon. But her spirit is still alive. Which, of course, leads us to the real question: Where is Nikki Howard's spirit? Is it just floating around out there? If so, we need to *capture* it!"

"What we need to do," Brandon said, completely ignoring Lulu, "is call Kelly and tell her we have Nikki here in the loft. But that Nikki doesn't know she's Nikki. Then we need to ask Kelly where the *real* Nikki is. Nikki's spirit, I mean."

I looked back and forth between the two of them. And wondered if I could possibly have been kidnapped by two stupider people.

"Do you think Kelly did this?" Lulu asked. "I've always thought there was something wrong with her. I mean, what kind of publicist is she, when she can't even get Nikki on the cover of the *Sports Illustrated* swimsuit issue, right? She keeps saying there's plenty of time and that Nikki shouldn't worry. But what kind of lame answer is that? I'll bet you anything Kelly is behind this whole spirit transfer thing. . . ."

Only I didn't hear how Brandon replied. Because I had reached up to scratch my head and felt something.

Something that wasn't just hair and smooth scalp.

I stopped pacing and stood there in front of one of Nikki Howard's floor-to-ceiling windows, staring unseeingly at my own reflection — or Nikki Howard's reflection — and the bright lights of downtown Manhattan beyond it as I felt along my head. Something wasn't right. Something . . .

And there it was. All along the base of my — or Nikki's — skull. A puckered line of skin, hidden by long blond hair. It didn't hurt, but it was still tender. Something horrible had happened there. Something that had left a hideous raised scar, about a half-inch wide and five or six inches long.

The thing is, I knew what it was. I knew exactly what it was, from all the plastic surgery shows Christopher and I liked to watch on the Discovery Channel. Someone had made an incision at the back of Nikki's neck, then peeled her skin back, hair and all, until the gleaming white bone of her skull had been revealed.

Only why? *Why* would someone have done something like that? Unless . . .

And then I remembered something that made my blood — Nikki's blood — run cold. A rainy Sunday afternoon at the apartment Christopher shared with the Commander, a bag of Doritos we'd smuggled in from Gristedes, and a surgery show: "Brain Transplants: The Surgery of the Future Is Here Now."

No. No *way*.

What had they said in that documentary? It was all coming back — brain transplants, sounding like the stuff of science fiction.

But scientists in Europe had proved it was possible to transplant the brain as a separate organ into an intact animal and maintain it in a viable, or living, situation for many days.

"*Sweet,*" Christopher had said. "I want one."

The documentary had gone on to assert that it was only ethical considerations that were keeping the technology from moving forward. Bioethicists argued that it was immoral to harvest a brain-dead body for the use of a living brain.

"Immoral, my ass," Christopher had said. "They can transplant my brain into the Hulk's body anytime they want."

Christopher had been disappointed to learn that the technology for whole-body transplants — the correct term for brain transplants — in humans was far off.

But, as he pointed out, a generation ago, human cloning seemed an impossibility, as well. So how long would it be until whole-body transplants were as routine as heart transplants?

Was that it? Was I the first-ever recipient of a whole-body transplant? Had that plasma screen crushed my body but spared my brain? Had Dr. Holcombe then removed my brain and transplanted it into the nearest convenient brain-dead body on hand . . . the body of Nikki Howard, who'd apparently suffered from some kind of collapse at or around the same time as my accident?

No. No, that was ridiculous. First of all, it wasn't even possible. Hadn't the documentary said scientists were still years from being able to perform this type of surgery in humans?

And second of all . . . why would anyone use that kind of technology — if, indeed, it did exist — to save *me*?

Suddenly, some things that had only confused me before now were beginning to make sense, though. Frida's weird reaction to me — asking me if I was really me. Of *course* she wasn't sure if I was me . . . because I was Nikki Howard on the outside, not the sister she knew and (allegedly) loved.

And what about Dr. Holcombe's insistence that I not move or sit up? This would make sense in a postoperative brain surgery patient.

And his assertion that I'd made more progress than they could have hoped for? They'd transplanted my brain into someone else's body, and I was already speaking lucidly and in control (somewhat) of my motor functions (although, of course, my surgery had been over a month ago).

And what about the fact that I was the only patient I had seen on the entire floor as Lulu and Brandon had been wheeling me out? Obviously, they wanted to keep the whole thing top secret. Why? Because of what the documentary had mentioned, about the ethical controversy over such a procedure?

And what about the fact that, suddenly, I liked fish?

Or the fact that I, Emerson Watts, was looking out of Nikki Howard's sapphire-blue eyes, instead of my own muddy brown ones?

My God. It all made sense. I hadn't had a spirit transfer, as Lulu Collins kept insisting. Dr. Holcombe had sawed open Nikki Howard's cranium, removed her brain, and slid mine in where hers had been, carefully attaching all of the appropriate nerves and arteries and veins before fusing her skull back and finally stitching her skin and hair back into place.

The realization caused my knees to buckle. Next thing I knew, I was sprawled out on the white carpet, looking up at Lulu's and Brandon's anxious faces . . . and being licked on the cheek by Nikki Howard's dog.

"Nikki?" Lulu was crying. "Nikki, can you hear me? Oh, Brandon, this is all our fault. Maybe we shouldn't have taken her from the hospital. Maybe she really is sick!"

"Nikki?" Brandon was giving my face little smacks. "Nikki!"

"Ow," I said irritably. "Stop hitting me."

"Oh." Brandon lowered his hand. "You scared us. Are you all right?"

"I'm fine," I said. "Help me over to the couch."

Brandon pulled me up, and then, chivalrously, carried me over to the couch. Once I was settled onto it, Cosabella came running over to jump in my lap and gave me a few more restorative kisses.

"What happened to you?" Lulu wanted to know. "Was it hypoglycemia? Do you have low blood sugar? Do you want some Tab Energy drink or something? Brandon, go pour her a Tab."

"No," I said weakly, refraining from pointing out to her that Tab is sugar free, not really useful for hypoglycemics. "I'm fine. Really."

Lulu shook her head. "Do it anyway, Brandon. Nikki — Em — whatever your name is. I'm sorry. I'm so, so sorry. We never should have . . . we were only trying to help. What can we do? What can we do to make it up to you?"

"Nothing," I said tiredly. Because that's all I felt. Not outrage over what had been done to me. Not anger. Not even wonder.

They'd done it. They had done it.

I was the world's first brain transplant. . . .

"Oh, here," Lulu said. She took the can of Tab that Brandon had brought over and waved it under my nose. "I think you should drink this."

The drink actually smelled great. Which made no sense, because it was diet. And I hate diet. I reached up and took hold of the can, then took a sip. It was cold and sweet and delicious.

"Look, Nikki," Lulu said. "Or Em. Or whatever your name is. Do you want us to call someone? Your agent, Rebecca? Or your publicist, Kelly? Should we call Kelly and see if she can tell us what's going on?"

"Don't call anyone yet," I said. I wasn't ready to go back to the hospital. Not now. Not knowing what I suddenly knew. Or was fairly certain I knew.

Why hadn't they told me? *What had they been waiting for?*

"I'm really tired," I said, handing Lulu the empty can, which I'd drained. "Can I just hang out here and maybe rest a little, before I decide what to do next?"

"Of course you can," Lulu exclaimed. "I mean, this is your loft. I'm the one who pays *you* rent."

"Nikki Howard," I corrected her. "You pay Nikki Howard rent."

I was the world's first brain transplant . . .

. . . and the body they'd chosen to transplant my brain into was one of the planet's most famous supermodels.

Seriously. The Hulk would have been better.

ELEVEN

I WOKE TO THE SOUND OF A BUZZER.

At first I couldn't figure out where the sound was coming from. That's because for a minute or so, I thought I was in my own room. I reached out, fumbling for my alarm clock. But instead of my fingers coming into contact with hard plastic, all I felt was warm skin.

This was unusual, to say the least.

What was even more unusual was that when I opened my eyes, I saw I wasn't in my room at all. Or even in the last place I remembered waking up, the hospital. No, I was in Nikki Howard's downtown loft, where I'd apparently fallen asleep on the living room couch — with my head on Brandon Stark's chest, no less.

When I jerked myself to an upright position — completely startled by the intimate way in which I'd curled myself up to a complete and utter stranger — I got a head rush. Not just a head rush, but a head*ache*.

It only took a second or two to remember why.

And when I did, I groaned and dropped my face to my knees, Nikki Howard's long blond hair falling all around me, like a tent. Cosy — Nikki Howard's dog — didn't seem to like that very much. She wiggled her way past my hair and onto my lap so she could give me a good-morning lick.

Then the buzzer went off again.

"Oh, God," I groaned, and, lifting Cosabella, I staggered across the living room, looking for the source of the sound so I could make it stop.

It was morning. The sky outside the floor-to-ceiling windows was already a bright autumnal blue.

But that didn't seem to trouble the two F.O.N.s who'd fallen asleep beside me and who continued to doze undisturbed. Lulu Collins looked like a little angel, with her pageboy all messed up and her mascara smudged.

And Brandon Stark, all six and a half feet of him, lay half on and half off the couch, snoring lightly, the television remote in his hand. On the screen over the fireplace flickered soundless images of famous faces. It was MTV, on mute.

The buzzer sounded again, and Lulu, over on the couch, groaned and pulled the cashmere blanket we'd all been sharing over her head. I realized the sound was coming from some sort of intercom located to one side of the door to the elevator. Not knowing what else to do — but desperate to make the sound stop — I lifted the handset that was connected to the wall where the buzzing seemed to be coming from.

"Hello?" I croaked, into the handset.

"Sorry to wake you, Miss Howard," said a man's voice I didn't recognize (of course). "But Mr. Justin Bay is here, and he's asking to see you."

Justin Bay? The star of the *Journeyquest* movie (which sucked)? Justin Bay wanted to see *me*?

Then I remembered. He wasn't here to see me at all. He was here to see Nikki Howard.

But wait. Why? Wasn't he Lulu Collins's boyfriend? I remembered the pink sapphire she'd shown me that time she'd visited me in the hospital, when I'd been so sure she'd been a hallucination. Hadn't she said that "Justin" had given it to her?

Yes. Yes, that's exactly what she'd said.

"He must mean Lulu," I said. "But she's asleep —"

"No, Miss Howard," the doorman — because that's who it had to be, right? — said. "Mr. Bay says to tell you he's here specifically to see you, and that he'd appreciate it if you wouldn't tell Miss Collins, and if you'd come down to meet him. He says it's important."

I stood there staring at the intercom in confusion. Justin Bay wanted to see Nikki Howard, but he didn't want her to tell Lulu? What was going on here?

"He also says," the doorman went on, in a slightly bored voice, "that he's not leaving until you see him, and that this time he really means it."

Whoa! I stared at the intercom some more. Why did Justin Bay need to see Nikki Howard so badly but didn't want Lulu to know? I tried to remember what I knew about Justin Bay, which — beyond what I'd read in the pages of Frida's *Us Weekly*, and that he'd been horrible as Leander in the *Journeyquest* movie — wasn't much, except that he was incredibly good-looking.

Oh, and rich. Because his dad, Richard Bay, had also been an actor, star of the mega-successful *Sky Warrior* franchise when he was younger. Now he produced heartwarming family-friendly television shows on prime time and raised buffalo (why did Frida keep leaving her celebrity gossip magazines lying around where I kept finding them? Worse, why was I always picking them up and reading them?) on a huge ranch in Montana.

Maybe Justin had a surprise for Lulu. Sure, that had to be why he wanted to see Nikki and not her. Right?

"Do you want me to call the police, Miss Howard?" was the doorman's next surprising question.

"What?" I squawked in astonishment, into the intercom's handset. "No! No, that's okay. I'll be right down."

"Sure thing, Miss Howard," the doorman said. "I'll send the elevator up for you."

I hung up the handset. Okay. Great. I was going to have to talk to Justin Bay. As Nikki Howard, though, not as me, because I couldn't tell him I wasn't Nikki. It had been hard enough to convince Lulu and Brandon that I wasn't Nikki Howard. Forget Justin Bay. His portrayal as Leander in the *Journeyquest* movie had pretty much proven he was the dumbest guy on earth. . . .

Fine. I could do this. I could —

Oh, God. I couldn't do this. I didn't have *time* for this. I had to get back to the hospital. I knew, now that I had had a good night's sleep (even if it had been on a couch, in front of Lulu's demo for her new rock video — she was cutting her first album. Her singing voice wasn't that bad, actually), that I had to find out what was going on, how my parents could have done this to me, why no one had even told me what was going on, what had happened to my old body . . .

. . . and Nikki Howard's brain.

I put Cosabella down and darted into Nikki Howard's bathroom. Yeah. Nikki's face was still the one that looked back at me in the mirror. No chance that any of this had turned out to be some kind of bizarre nightmare.

I splashed some cold water onto it to wash the sleep away, then pulled open a drawer in hopes of finding a brush, found one, and was dragging it through my hair — carefully, so as not to hurt the tender sutures at the back of my head. I mean, Nikki's head — then pulled a toothbrush from the gold cup by the sink. It was Nikki Howard's toothbrush, but I used it anyway. Because, whatever — my teeth are Nikki Howard's teeth now. Right?

I rinsed, then wiped my mouth, then grabbed the first jacket my hands came into contact with — something made out of buttery soft brown suede.

I was about to walk out of Nikki's room when it hit me that I'd almost walked by her computer without checking it to confirm whether what Brandon had said last night was true. I mean, about me being dead. Sure, Justin was waiting — but Googling myself would only take a second.

And besides, if I'd really been in a coma for a month, I probably had a ton of e-mails. Sure, most of them would be spam, but it would only take a minute to check them and see if maybe Christopher had written. . . .

But when I opened Nikki's pink laptop, I saw right away something wasn't right. It wasn't just that it was a Stark-brand PC, which, frankly, wasn't what I'd buy if I were a millionaire supermodel with all the money in the world.

It was that the keyboard was sluggish, not responding to my commands quite as soon as it ought to have.

It only took a second for me see why. Every time I pressed a letter on the keyboard, the network activity light on Nikki's modem flashed.

Which, I knew perfectly well from Christopher's father's obsessive belief that all our computers are being monitored by the government, meant that someone was tracking Nikki Howard's keystrokes.

Her computer — unlike the Commander's — was totally being spied on.

Someone who didn't spend much time on computers — like, say, a world-famous supermodel — wouldn't have noticed. But to someone who basically lived on one, like me, it was totally obvious.

And deeply, deeply sinister.

I pulled my fingers off the keyboard so fast, it was like I'd been stung. I hadn't clicked on anything except Google News. I hadn't typed in my name or anything else that could have given me away.

Still. Talk about creepy. Who'd be spying on Nikki Howard?

And *why*? How interesting could a supermodel's e-mails be, anyway?

Just then I heard the elevator doors open, and I darted from Nikki's room. The elevator operator — a different one from last night — grinned at me and said, "Good morning, Miss Howard."

"Shhhh," I said, and pointed at the sleeping Lulu and Brandon. They looked so angelic. No way would you guess they were a couple of lunatics who might kidnap someone in the hopes of curing her of brainwashing by "Scientologists."

"Oh, sorry," the elevator operator whispered. He held the door open for me. "Going down?"

"Yeah," I said, with one last and final look at my "captors." And I stepped onto the elevator . . .

. . . just as a tiny white blur whizzed past me and into the car.

"Cosy," I hissed at Nikki Howard's dog, who'd plopped down onto the elevator floor as if she owned it. "Get out. You don't really belong to me. I'm not coming back. Go home."

But Cosabella only whined softly.

"Seriously," I whispered. "You can't come. I'm going back to the hospital." I scooped the tiny dog up and plopped her down onto the white carpeting just outside the elevator door. Where I commanded her to stay.

But one look at that sad furry little face — not to mention hearing her pathetic whine — and my heart melted.

"Oh," I said, realizing her desire to go with me might actually have nothing to do with her love for me and more to do with a call from nature. "Sorry. Come on, then."

And the dog leaped excitedly into the elevator after me, her stumpy tail wagging like a . . . well, I don't even know what. Thing that wags a lot.

The elevator operator smiled at me (well, at Nikki Howard) and closed the door. Then we glided down to the lobby, where he slid the door open again and said, "Have a nice day, Miss Howard."

"I'm not —" I began. But then I caught a glimpse of my reflection in one of the lobby's mirrored walls. And I realized the futility of it all.

"Thanks," I said instead. And stepped off the elevator, with Cosabella at my heels.

The strangest thing of all? Even though all I'd done was wash her face and brush her teeth, Nikki Howard still looked gorgeous. Gorgeous enough, anyway, that the UPS guy delivering packages to the mail room dropped his electronic clipboard thingie when he saw me . . . then picked it up, all flustered.

Either that, or he was just freaked out to see a celebrity of my magnitude in jeans and Skechers.

Somehow I suspect it was the aforementioned gorgeousness.

Which might sound like it's cool. I mean, being so gorgeous that you stop UPS drivers in their tracks.

But when it's just something you were transplanted into? It isn't really all that much of an accomplishment.

I hadn't really had a chance to notice the night before, having been in the middle of being kidnapped and realizing I was trapped inside someone else's body and all, but the lobby of Nikki's building was huge, with a gigantic crystal chandelier hanging in the middle of the ceiling.

Standing directly beneath that chandelier was Justin Bay, looking as if he'd just stepped out from the pages of one of my sister's teen magazines. He was dressed casually in jeans, a gray V-neck sweater, and a brown leather jacket. When he saw me coming toward him, his darkly good-looking face twitched, and his gaze darted nervously past my shoulder as if to see if anyone else was getting off the elevator with me.

When he saw it was just me, though, he seemed to visibly relax. He even broke into a grin that showed all of his white, impossibly even teeth.

"You came," he said, in that voice I recognized from the awful *Journeyquest* movie, as I approached him.

"Uh," I said. Cosabella had pranced away from me, heading straight toward the revolving doors outside. "Yeah . . . but I can only stay a minute. I have to go. Was there something you wanted me to give Lulu?"

Justin's grin vanished. "Lulu?" His handsome face looked perplexed. "Why would I want you to give something to Lulu?"

"Um, I don't know," I said. Cosabella was standing on her hind legs, dancing around in front of the revolving doors. I'd been right. She really needed to go. "I just figured that's why you wanted to see me and not her. I thought you had a surprise for her or something."

"What is this, a joke?" Justin reached out and grabbed one of my hands. And he wasn't exactly shaking it. He clung to it, while gazing down meaningfully into my eyes with his own pleading and half filled with tears — just like that scene in *Journeyquest*, the movie, when his character, Leander, pleaded with the evil sorceress not to kill his beloved Alana (played by Mischa Barton). "Nikki, where have you been, baby? I've been *dying*. You haven't returned any of my calls or text messages. It's been more than a *month*. Then I hear you're finally back, and you don't even call? What did I do wrong? Just tell me."

As I stared at him in growing horror as his words sank in, I became aware of three things at once. One, Justin Bay was in love with me. Well, not with me, but with Nikki Howard.

Two, Nikki Howard was apparently a total skank who was slutting around behind her best friend and roommate Lulu's back with her boyfriend, Justin. Not to mention behind the back of Nikki's own boyfriend, Brandon.

And three, Nikki Howard's dog was about to pee on the marble floor of the lobby of her building.

"Could you just hold that thought?" I said to Justin, slipping my hand out from his. "I just have to let my dog out."

"Nikki," Justin said, his face clouding over with frustration. "You can't —"

"Seriously," I said. "Just hold on a minute."

I hurried away from him and over to the revolving door.

"Here, Cosy," I called to the dog. "Here, girl —"

And the little dog darted after me as I pushed on the revolving door and went out into the cool autumn air. As soon as we got outside, Cosabella squatted next to one of the planters beside the building . . . and I realized she hadn't just needed to pee.

I also realized I had nothing to clean it up with.

"Oh, my God. I'm so sorry," I apologized to the doorman, who'd been standing a few yards away, flagging down a cab for another resident.

He looked at me with an expression of bewildered amusement.

"Miss Howard," he said. "I'll take care of it, like always."

Oh, my God. Nikki Howard's doormen clean up after her dog for her? How totally embarrassing. I could feel myself blushing. A detached part of me realized that it was interesting that Nikki Howard blushed so easily.

But most of me just continued to be mortified. Also, hideously uncomfortable, because of what had just gone on back in the lobby.

"Really, um," I said. "It's okay. If you just have a plastic bag or something, I'll clean it up."

"That's not necessary, Miss Howard," the doorman said, now looking at me as if he thought I'd lost my mind. Apparently, Nikki Howard *never* offered to clean up after her own dog. "It's me, Karl. I'll take care of it."

I wanted to die. I said, "Well. Okay, Karl. I'm really sorry. Look, I hate to ask, but I, um, have to go. Can you make sure Cosy gets back to the loft?" No way was I going back into that lobby and facing Justin again.

Karl nodded and went to scoop up the little dog —

Who took one look at me and began to wail.

Not just whine. Not just bark. But howl. Like a tiny coyote. With a bouffant hairdo.

What was her problem now?

Karl was all too happy to answer that question for me.

"She misses you," Karl said, all jovially. But there was an undercurrent of seriousness in his voice. "She did this the whole time you were gone last month."

Oh, my God. I was a horrible person. I had abandoned my dog for more than a month.

Then I remembered: She wasn't my dog.

And I wasn't a horrible person, either. Karl didn't know that the reason Cosabella had been abandoned was because her real owner was — I'm pretty sure — dead. Well . . . in a way. Unless Lulu was right about the whole spirit transfer thing. Which I was pretty sure she wasn't. Because such a thing wasn't physically possibly.

"Cosy." I hurried back to the doorman and took the little dog from his hands. Instantly, she stopped crying and tried to bury herself inside my jacket.

"Cosy," I whispered to her, my heart melting all over again. "I can't take you. You don't really belong to me. And I'm going back to the hospital. They don't let dogs in the hospital. Remember?"

But the dog just smiled up at me from inside my jacket, panting happily, her tail thumping against me.

And I knew in that instant that I was taking Cosy with me, come hell or high water. Whatever that expression means.

Yeah. My life wasn't getting unduly complicated or anything.

It was kind of ironic that just as I was thinking this, Justin Bay appeared, looking annoyed. He strode over to me to take my arm.

"Is this about that ring?" he leaned down to ask me in a low voice. We were standing on Centre Street, a one-way street that was still busy enough that I could barely hear him above the traffic noise. "The one I gave Lulu? Because it didn't *mean* anything, baby. I only did it to throw her off the scent, because she was getting suspicious about us. You can't honestly be holding that ring against me —"

"I don't know what you're talking about," I told him. Which was the truth. "And I really have to go now —"

His face twisted with emotion.

And the next thing I knew, he had hold of both my arms and was hauling me toward him to lower his lips over mine.

My second kiss in the past twelve hours was even more devastating than the first one. I could feel this one all the way down to my toes, which instantly curled inside my Skechers.

I used to always snort derisively when I got to the parts in Frida's romance novels when the dukes snatched up the poor but spunky heroines and molded their bodies against the front of their waistcoats or whatever. I always thought to myself, as the heroines' bodies went limp in response, "Yeah, right. Like *that* ever happens."

Imagine my surprise when my own body — or, I guess I should say, Nikki Howard's body — went limp in response to Justin Bay's kiss, right there on Centre Street, in front of Karl the doorman, a string of taxis waiting for the light to turn, a million pigeons, and everyone else who might have been looking. I nearly dropped Cosabella — who was getting smushed between us, anyway — I was so shocked.

Was this normal? Was this how bodies were supposed to react when getting kissed — especially by guys who were practically strangers to me (aside from a passing familiarity due to the pages of gossip magazines)? Or were Justin Bay and Brandon Stark just phenomenally good kissers? Because this kissing thing — seriously, I could totally get into it. Kissing *rocked*. I was loving the kissing thing. I mean, obviously it was wrong — *so wrong* — to be kissing Nikki Howard's best friend's boyfriend, especially behind Nikki Howard's boyfriend's back.

Not to mention the fact that, truthfully, I didn't even like either of these guys. I mean, I still had a monster crush on my own best friend, back home. If *he* had been the one bending my body on Centre Street, I swear to God, there probably would have been an explosion or something.

Which was why I knew I couldn't let this kissing business continue, however much Nikki's body might have wanted it to. What if Christopher came strolling up (for whatever unlikely reason) and saw me with Justin Bay's tongue rammed down my throat? He hates Justin Bay for what he did to ruin the *Journeyquest* movie with his terrible acting.

And okay, he wouldn't necessarily know it was me and not Nikki Howard.

But that's beside the point.

And what about Lulu? Supposing Lulu woke up and looked out the window and saw us? True, Lulu had kidnapped me. But she had done it out of the goodness of her heart.

It was kind of hard to say anything, though, with Justin's mouth on mine. Awesome as this felt, it just couldn't go on. It took every ounce of determination I had to wrench my lips from his and say, "Um, please stop —"

"You know this is what you want," Justin said in a thick voice — really! Just like the dukes in Frida's books! — keeping an iron grip on my arms.

The thing was, he was totally right. I did want it. Did I ever. But I wasn't going to be boneheaded enough to *say* that.

"No," I said weakly instead. "I don't. It's wrong."

"That's not what you said in Paris," Justin reminded me.

"Um," I said, keeping my still throbby mouth carefully averted from his, in case he tried to persuade me some more. "I don't know. I've never been to Paris. Please let go —"

A second later, much to my surprise, he did let go. But not because I'd asked him to. He'd let go because Gabriel Luna, of all people, appeared as if from nowhere and yanked him forcefully off me.

"I believe the young lady asked you to release her," Gabriel said to Justin, in his crisp British accent.

Whoa! This was getting more and more like one of Frida's romance novels every minute! In a totally excellent way.

"Who the hell," Justin asked, checking his leather jacket for dents where Gabriel had manhandled it, "do you think you are?"

"A friend of Nikki's," Gabriel said woodenly in response. An F.O.N.! Gabriel Luna had just called himself an F.O.N.!

To me, Gabriel asked, in a much warmer, concerned tone, "Are you all right, Nikki?"

I nodded, absently stroking Cosabella, who hadn't taken too kindly to being squashed against me and was growling at Justin with all the ferocity of a six-pound rottweiler.

"I'm fine," I said. "Just worried about — you know. Who might have seen us."

I meant Christopher — and Lulu — of course. But this caused Justin to look all around quickly, as if realizing for the first time that we were actually standing on a fairly busy street corner. Not once did he glance in the direction of the wide floor-to-ceiling windows just above us, though. The cad! Or was *scoundrel* the right word? I'd have to check one of Frida's books.

"That's right," Gabriel said mildly, noticing Justin's sudden alarm. "Paparazzi could show up any minute. I thought I saw some around the corner, actually, on my way over."

And that was all it took to cause Justin to say, "I'll call you later, babe," to me before flipping up the collar of his leather jacket and hurrying away.

I couldn't believe it! Lulu, his alleged girlfriend, he didn't give a second thought to. But paparazzi scared him so badly he took off like a shot! What a jerk. Or rake. Or whatever.

Gabriel looked at me and asked, "Are you *really* all right, Nikki?"

I blinked at him . . . then glanced over at Karl, who was staring at both of us with his mouth hanging open a little, his fingers on his cell phone, as if he'd just been about to call nine-one-one. Noticing the direction of my stare, he hastily tucked the phone away.

"I'm fine," I said to Gabriel. "Really. I just . . . I need to go. Back to the hospital. I . . . I wasn't supposed to be let out this early, and . . . I just need to get back."

"I know," Gabriel said in the same calm voice in which he mentioned the paparazzi. "I've just come from there. I stopped by to see how you were doing, and I found the place in an uproar because you were gone. Snuck out for a bit of fun last night, did you?"

I stared at him, not understanding what he meant at first. Snuck out for a bit of fun? No, actually, I was kidnapped by two F.F.B.F.s dressed as surgeons.

But then I realized what he must have walked up and seen — me in front of my (well, Nikki Howard's) apartment building, making out with Justin Bay — and how that had to have looked.

And I felt myself blush to my hairline.

"N-no," I stammered. "No, it wasn't like that! Not at all. There was a misunderstanding. It was Lulu! Lulu Collins and Brandon Stark —"

I broke off. I could tell by his expression that I was only making things worse.

"Look, I just need to get back," I said, unable to meet his gaze I was so mortified. "I'll . . . I'll see you later."

And I turned, Cosabella still in my arms, and headed for the curb.

His voice stopped me before I'd gone a single step.

"I wouldn't bother. There are no taxis."

"Hardly ever are, this time of day," Karl, who appeared to be an unapologetic eavesdropper, called from over by the door. "Everyone's heading uptown to work. Give it an hour."

An hour! I didn't have an hour! I had to get back to the hospital! Especially if what Gabriel said was true, and "the place was in an uproar." Why had I stopped to check my e-mail upstairs on Nikki's completely compromised computer? I should have looked for a cell phone so I could call my parents and tell them not to worry. Maybe Karl would let me borrow his . . . oh, whatever, I just needed to get uptown. . . .

"That's okay," I said in a voice gone suddenly shaky. "I'll just take the subway."

"You can't take the subway," Gabriel said simply.

"It'll be fine," I said, turning to head in the opposite direction, toward Broome Street. This was my neighborhood, after all. I knew exactly where I was. I didn't really think it was going to be fine, but what else could I do? "I can just grab the Six over by

Bleecker and take it to Fourteenth Street and walk the rest of the way. It's not far."

Then, as I reached into my pocket for my wallet and Metrocard, I realized it wasn't actually my pocket at all but Nikki Howard's pocket.

And it was empty.

"Oh, no," I said with a groan. I didn't have my wallet. Or my Metrocard. Great. Just great.

"It doesn't matter," Gabriel said in the same calm voice. "Because you can't take the subway anyway."

I started to say that of course I could — why couldn't I?

But no sooner was the first word out of my mouth than my arm was grabbed. Thinking it was Justin Bay (again), I whipped around, fast, expecting to have to fend off another knee-melting French kiss.

But instead I saw a group of elementary school girls, in plaid skirts and maroon sweaters, who all started screaming the minute they saw my face.

"I told you, Tiffany!" shrieked the one who had hold of my arm, an adorably freckled nine-year-old in braids. "It's her! See!"

And Braidy pointed past my face to a four-story-high mural painted on the side of a nearby building — a mural that just happened to be of Nikki Howard in a bikini, urging viewers to come to the new Stark Megastore in SoHo.

"See? I told you! It's her!" Braidy screamed, practically yanking my arm out of its socket. "Nikki, Nikki, can I have your autograph?"

"I want it, too, Nikki!" Tiffany shrieked, shoving a pen and a French notebook in my face. "Sign mine, oh, please!"

"I'm not Nikki," I cried. I tried to get away from them without outright smacking any of them. "Seriously, you guys, I'm not —"

"Girls!" A nearby nun, who was clearly supposed to be in control of the group but who had vastly underestimated the power of a supermodel over her young charges, called vainly for order. "Stop this! Stop this at once! Leave the young lady alone!"

But they wouldn't leave me alone. They didn't believe me when I said I wasn't Nikki Howard.

And why should they, when the proof that I was Nikki Howard was spray-painted as big as a building just a street away?

They were pulling at my jacket, threatening to tumble Cosabella out from under it. Who knows what they would have done if Gabriel and Karl the doorman hadn't waded in and rescued me? One minute I was being mauled by a pack of screaming schoolgirls, and the next, Karl was holding them off while Gabriel was steering me bodily away from them, one arm around my shoulders, saying in a wry voice, "Now do you see why you can't take the subway? At least, not unless you're wearing a hat."

It was a joke. Well, sort of.

Except that the situation wasn't actually all that funny. Because in a way, he was right. I was never going to be able to ride the subway again as an anonymous New York City citizen. From now on, I'd be riding the subway as Nikki Howard, supermodel. Unless I carried around a giant sign that said, I'M NOT REALLY HER. DON'T BOTHER ASKING FOR MY AUTOGRAPH.

I must have looked really crushed or something, since a second later, Gabriel gave me a little hug with the arm he'd put around me and said, with a sigh, "Never mind. I'll give you a ride."

And he gestured toward a pale green Vespa that was parked in the circular drive in front of the building.

That's right. A Vespa.

Which has to be the least cool mode of transportation in the universe. I mean, to average American guys.

But Gabriel wasn't American. And he obviously didn't care that his motorbike would be considered, by the average American male, completely effeminate.

"I have helmets," he assured me, I guess mistaking my astonishment for reluctance to ride on a scooter due to the safety issue.

"Okay," I said faintly. I just wanted to get away from Nikki Howard's screaming fans — who were still being held back by Karl and the frantic-looking nun — and Nikki Howard's crazy roommate and her boyfriend(s) and her building and the giant mural of her on the building right down the street, and back to my family.

And I didn't care how I did it.

"Here," Gabriel said, and handed me a motorcycle helmet from a compartment on the back of his Vespa. He helped me fit it over my head (or Nikki Howard's head). It didn't make my stitches hurt, which was good.

Then he helped me climb onto the bike and showed me where to put my feet. Then he got on, as well, and said, "Hang on to me."

Which I knew meant put my arms around his waist.

But of course I'd never touched a guy like that. I mean, aside from all the guys I've made out with in the past twenty-four hours. Which hadn't exactly been initiated by me.

Except before I had a chance to fully obsess over what I was about to do, some of the schoolgirls broke away from Karl and their teacher and began tearing toward us, screaming, "Nikki! Nikki!"

And Gabriel started the motorbike up. There was a lurch, and I had to grab him around the waist to keep from falling off the bike backward.

And then he said, "Here we go!"

And we went.

TWELVE

I'VE LIVED IN MANHATTAN MY WHOLE LIFE.

I've eaten dim sum in Chinatown and brick-oven pizza in Little Italy. I've been to the top of the Empire State Building and the Statue of Liberty, too. I've traced my ancestors back to their entry into this country (from England on my dad's side; Hungary on my mom's) via Ellis Island, and I've spent hours getting lost in the Strand, the world's biggest used bookstore.

I've had breakfast at Tiffany's (well, a bagel outside it on a field trip to the Museum of Modern Art) and seen the Vermeers in the Frick (hard to believe he painted them without the help of a computer).

I've ridden the subway to Coney Island, used the paddleboats in Central Park, and skated (though not well) at Rockefeller

Center. I've even been to the World Trade Center, back when it was still the World Trade Center and not Ground Zero.

But I've never, ever cruised up Fourth Avenue on the back of a cute guy's motor scooter before.

And I have to say, it's the way to travel. It completely beats my other primary modes of transportation — the subway and walking — hands down. Even though the wind was really cold and made my eyes water — and Cosabella didn't seem too thrilled about being wedged between my belly and Gabriel's back — it was super fun darting in and out of traffic, and dodging bicycle messengers, and almost running a red light . . .

. . . and best of all, feeling the warmth from Gabriel's back, coming through the leather of his jacket, and seeing him smile every time he looked back to make sure I was okay.

And even though he was smiling at Nikki Howard and not at me, I had to admit . . . I could have ridden on the back of Gabriel Luna's Vespa all day. For the first time since I'd woken up in the hospital, I actually felt . . . *good.*

Not good about the fact that someone had apparently stuck my brain in Nikki Howard's body (so not).

But good about the fact that I was actually alive and got to experience cruising up Fourth Avenue on the back of a cute guy's Vespa.

And that made me realize how very, very lucky I was. Whoever had done this — however it had happened — the fact that it had enabled me to experience something like that . . . well, I was grateful.

At least, about that part of it.

The part about all those schoolgirls wanting my autograph because they thought I was Nikki Howard?

Not so much.

Unfortunately, we reached the hospital all too soon. Twenty blocks is a long way if you're walking, but it isn't long enough if you're flying down the street on the back of a cute guy's pale green Vespa. Just fifteen minutes or so later, we were pulling into the underground parking garage beneath Manhattan General.

And I started feeling nervous about the kind of reception I was going to get inside. I mean, it was true I had been kidnapped. But I could have gotten away a lot sooner than I had. The truth was, I had kind of been mad at my family for not telling me about the whole Nikki Howard thing. What, exactly, had they been thinking?

So I'd sort of put off going back until I'd absolutely had to.

Now I had the feeling, based on what Gabriel said, that I might be in trouble when I got there.

So when Gabriel pushed the button to get a parking slip, I said, "Seriously, you don't have to come up with me, you can just drop me off." Because I didn't want him to witness the screaming I expected to ensue. I mean, even though I'm crushing on

Christopher, not Gabriel Luna, it's still embarrassing to have a cute guy see your parents flip out on you.

"After what happened outside your flat?" he asked. "Not a chance. I'm going to make sure you get delivered safely."

I felt myself flushing. "What happened back there," I couldn't keep myself from saying, "what you saw, with Justin — that wasn't — he just showed up this morning. I didn't —"

"I meant with the schoolgirls," Gabriel said.

"Oh," I said. I was glad the helmet hid my blush. Still. I couldn't let it go. "He isn't . . . he isn't my boyfriend or anything."

"Isn't he?"

I realized I'd just made what he'd seen on Centre Street look infinitely worse.

"No," I tried to explain. "He's my *roommate's* boyfriend. I think he . . . got the wrong message."

"I'd say so," Gabriel said.

Oh. God. Obviously, I just needed to keep my mouth shut.

But I couldn't seem to do so. As we pulled into a parking space and Gabriel switched the Vespa's engine off, I asked, "How did you know? When no one could find me at the hospital? To go looking for me at Nik — I mean, my apartment building?"

"Just a guess," Gabriel said, taking his helmet, which I'd carefully peeled off, from me. "A lucky one, as it happens. I suppose

I don't blame you for sneaking out, seeing as how they won't let you have any visitors. But you really frightened them, you know, running off like that — your parents, I mean. Or I suppose that's who they are — I haven't actually met them, but I saw them when I stopped by your floor this morning, before they threw me out. Your mum was crying."

I chewed my lower lip. Even though I don't *like* like him, I didn't want him to think I was the kind of girl who would run off from a hospital and make my "mum" cry, any more than I wanted him to think I was the kind of girl who'd stay out all night with a cheeseball like Justin Bay. . . .

I wanted to tell him the truth. About what had happened to me, I mean. I felt like he'd really understand. Anyone who could sing like that — well, he'd have to understand, wouldn't he?

But I couldn't tell him. Because obviously, if they hadn't even told *me*, and I wasn't supposed to be receiving visitors except my immediate family, and they kept kicking people off my floor, this whole thing was supposed to be a secret. I didn't know why — but I was going to get to the bottom of it.

Today.

"It . . ." It was so weird, the two of us, having this moment — if that's even what it was, here in this parking garage . . . the same one where, just last night, I'd bitten Brandon Stark as he'd stuffed me into a limo. "It's really nice of you to be so concerned about me," I said. "I mean, considering the fact that we hardly know each other."

"Well," Gabriel said. "After what happened that day at Stark's, I feel as if I know you, at least a little. You gave us all quite a scare. You really . . . you ought to take better care of yourself, Nikki."

I blinked at him in confusion. What was he talking about? "I — what?"

Gabriel seemed to hesitate, as if he weren't sure he wanted to say what he did next. But then he reached out and took one of my hands and said, looking down at me with that intently blue gaze, "It's just that you're so lovely . . . and so sweet. You shouldn't throw your life away on drugs and alcohol."

I think my eyes almost popped out of my head. "*What?*" I croaked again, this time in disbelief.

"I know your publicist is saying you were hospitalized for hypoglycemia and . . . what was it? Oh, right. Exhaustion," he went on. "But I was there that day, remember, Nikki? And I honestly didn't think you were going to make it. You just lay there, so completely still. I thought you were dead."

I don't think I could have spoken if I tried. He thought Nikki Howard had spent the past month in the hospital because she'd been in *rehab*? Was that what everyone thought? Oh, my

God! I was so embarrassed! I could feel my cheeks burning with shame. . . .

On the other hand, what did I care what he thought about Nikki Howard? It didn't have anything to do with me. . . .

Oh, wait. I guess it did.

"But I'm not —" I started to say.

But Gabriel just shook his head.

"You don't have to make up excuses for me, Nikki," he said, his voice as gentle as his fingertips. "I know how hard it is, living in the spotlight, having to listen to the gossip. And I'm glad you're getting the help you need now —"

"But —"

"Everything's going to be all right now," he said as he led the way to the elevators. "I'm really pleased you decided to come back to the hospital. Your parents will be happy to see you." He gave me a wry grin. "Maybe they'll forgive me now, for sneaking onto your floor the other night, when I wasn't supposed to."

"Um." Cosy and I joined him in the elevator car as it arrived. I was feeling more dazed than ever. "Yeah. About that —"

"Admitting you have a problem is the first step toward conquering it, you know, Nikki," Gabriel said, smiling down at me. I smiled back up at him because I couldn't help it.

But smiling at him turned out to be a mistake. Nikki

Howard's smile was like kryptonite to guys or something. It seemed to completely immobilize them. Gabriel seemed to totally forget where we were. The elevator doors closed, and then we just stood there for almost a whole minute, with Gabriel staring at me.

Hello. Awkward.

"Uh," I said, "I don't know what floor we're going to."

"Oh." Gabriel gave a start, then dropped my hand and hit the button for the fourth floor. "Sorry."

Before I had a chance to think of anything to say — such as, *I am not now, nor have I ever, been on drugs* — however, the elevator doors slid open to reveal a burly security guard, who said, "Sorry, folks. Access to this floor is . . ." Then his eyes widened when he got a closer look at me. "You!" he cried.

"Um, yeah," I said. My cheeks were still on fire. Drugs! Alcohol! Really. Did I ask for any of this? "Are my mom and dad around?"

And the next thing I knew, Mom and Dad were all over me with their *Where have you beens* and their *We were worried sicks*, hugging me and berating me at the same time. It really was just as embarrassing as I'd anticipated. Dr. Holcombe was hovering around, too, nervously chewing on the end of his glasses while holding a clipboard. Dr. Higgins — the female doctor who'd been wearing her hair in a bun — was beside him. Only her hair wasn't in a bun anymore. It was hanging all over the place, looking straggly, like she hadn't had a chance to fix it up, given the whole part where I'd disappeared and everyone was freaking out about where I was, apparently.

Which was going to be hard to explain, since I didn't want to rat out Lulu and Brandon, as they'd genuinely thought they were doing the right thing.

On the other hand, I did have to answer my parents' questions.

But Gabriel Luna solved the whole problem for me by cutting everyone off and saying, "I found her at her flat."

Which was when Dr. Holcombe slid his glasses back into place and asked, "Excuse me, but who is this young man?"

It was right then that Frida came around the corner, her head down and her shoulders slumped dejectedly. When she heard Dr. Holcombe's voice, she looked up, saw me, and broke out into a huge smile . . .

. . . until her gaze fell on Gabriel. Then the smile vanished, and she gasped. "Gabriel Luna!" she cried.

"*That's* Gabriel Luna?" Dad whispered to Mom, in a perfectly audible voice. "He's the one who was here asking for Nikki Howard a little while ago."

"That's the boy I saw beside her bed," Dr. Higgins said, pointing at Gabriel. "He's the one who brought her the roses!"

The glance Frida threw at me could have frozen coffee. "*He brought you roses?*"

"He brought *Nikki Howard* roses," I corrected her. Because I could see all too clearly where this was headed.

"Wait . . . Gabriel Luna from the Megastore grand opening?" Mom asked.

"Yes," Gabriel said, extending his right hand toward my parents. "Hello. I'm sorry I didn't introduce myself earlier, but you were busy having me thrown out. It's very nice to meet you."

Mom, looking like she was in a daze, shook Gabriel's hand and murmured, "Nice to meet you, too," while Dad, as soon as she was done, stuck out his own hand and, shaking Gabriel's, said, "Where have you been with my daughter?"

"Gabriel brought me back here," I explained, rushing to Gabriel's defense. "It's a long story, but I didn't exactly leave on my own, and . . . well, he sort of rescued me."

Gabriel flashed me a smile of thanks for this. Which I returned. In spite of the fact that he apparently thought Nikki Howard was a drug addict, I figured he deserved some credit, anyway.

"Well," Dr. Holcombe said, in a voice that was a little fake in its heartiness, "in that case, we have much to thank you for, then, Mr., er, Luna."

"It's nothing," Gabriel said. "Really. But I have to say, I think —"

Dr. Holcombe wasn't interested in hearing what Gabriel thought, however.

"Frida," he said, cutting Gabriel off. "Why don't you show Mr. Luna to the cafeteria and get yourselves a bite to eat while your sister and parents and I have a little talk. All right?"

Before Gabriel could say anything, Frida went from staring daggers at me to staring lovingly up at him, her pupils practically going heart-shaped, like a cartoon character's.

"Sure," she said, in a breathy voice I'd never heard before, and taking hold of Gabriel's arm, she cooed, "Here, follow me. I'll show you the way."

Which of course made me actually want to slug her, for acting so dopey. Why does my sister always have to act like such — I'm sorry to say it, but it's true — a *girl*?

Although, now that I know what it actually feels like to get kissed, I guess I couldn't really blame her.

"Uh," Gabriel said, looking back at me as Frida led him toward the elevator we'd just stepped off. "All right, then, I guess, uh, I'll see you later. . . ."

"Bye," I started to say, waving.

Before I could utter a word more, Frida had dragged him around the corner, and he was gone. For all I knew, forever.

But I had more important things to deal with just then than my sister's completely inappropriate crush on a British singer-songwriter. And that included my mother, who was looking down at my half-open jacket and going, "Oh, my God. Is there a dog in your coat?"

"It's Nikki Howard's dog," I explained.

"How in God's name," Dad wanted to know, "did you end up with Nikki Howard's dog?"

"Well," I said, "it all started when I woke up and found that somebody had put my brain in Nikki Howard's body."

Dr. Holcombe, looking very uncomfortable, opened a nearby office door and gestured for us to follow him, saying, "Please. Come in. Sit. We need to talk."

"Oh, yes," I said, following him with my head — or should I say Nikki Howard's head — held high. "We do."

THIRTEEN

"YOU HAVE TO UNDERSTAND," DR. Holcombe said as he sat behind his enormous mahogany desk, a cup of coffee cradled between his hands. "The procedure we performed on you, Emerson, was necessary in order to save your life."

"I get that," I said. "I doubt you go around doing brain transplants on people who don't need it. Although I don't know how I got lucky enough to be the first."

Dr. Holcombe cleared his throat. "Er . . ."

"Wait." I stared at him. "I was kidding. You mean . . . I'm *not* the first?"

"Oh, my word, no," Dr. Holcombe said, laughing heartily. "The youngest, definitely. But not the first, by any means."

I blinked at him. "But . . . wait a minute. I just saw a documentary on brain transplants a few months ago. It said none had ever been successfully done on a human being."

"Well, none that we've ever publicized, no," Dr. Holcombe said. "None of our recipients has ever cared to make the procedure public. Quite the opposite, as a matter of fact —"

"*Recipients?* You mean you've done this . . . a *lot?*"

"Oh, yes," Dr. Holcombe said. "My team and I perfected the procedure some time ago. We've been performing it for several years now. It's extremely expensive — and still quite rare. You came to us with injuries that, in any ordinary circumstances, would have been instantly fatal. It was pure serendipity that a viable whole-body donor became available at the same time your heart gave out."

"Viable whole-body donor?" I echoed. I was shocked. "You mean . . . *Nikki Howard?* I can't believe you just called her that. I mean, Nikki . . . she was a *person.*"

"Dr. Holcombe is aware of that, Em," my mom said quickly. She and Dad were sitting in a pair of leather chairs in front of Dr. Holcombe's desk, while I sat between them, with Dr. Higgins and Mr. Phillips, a "legal representative" of Stark Enterprises, sitting on a couch a few feet away. When I asked, "What does Stark Enterprises have to do with all this?" Mr. Phillips said, "You're actually under the care of the Stark Institute for Neurology and Neurosurgery, a division of Manhattan

General Hospital, of which Stark Enterprises is a primary donor. It's the one and only medical center in the world that performs whole-body transplants. Stark Enterprises doesn't publicize the institute's existence — or its connection with it, of course — because there are still some, er, bioethical concerns involved in the procedure."

"You mean because in order for someone to get a whole-body transplant," I said, "somebody else has to be declared brain dead, so they can snatch their body for the recipient's use?"

"Er," Mr. Phillips said, "that's simplifying the matter a bit, but . . . yes, more or less."

"Emerson," Dr. Higgins explained gently now, "Nikki Howard suffered from a rare congenital brain defect that no one — not even Nikki herself — was aware of. It was an aneurysm — basically a ticking time bomb in her head that could have gone off at any time . . . but happened to go off at almost the same moment you were so gravely injured. Because there were so many medical personnel on hand at the time — the Stark Megastore staff had requested that an ambulance, in addition to a team of paramedics, be on site throughout the day in the event the protests during the grand opening grew violent — they were able to act quickly enough to keep her — and you — alive for transport to this hospital. But once you both arrived here, it was quickly determined that neither of you had a chance to survive . . . at least, not on your own."

"Right," Dad said, his eyes looking very bright, for some reason. I was shocked to see that the brightness in his eyes was due to tears. I had never seen my dad cry before. Except during *Extreme Home Makeover*, of course. "By the time your mother and I arrived, you were on life-support machines. They basically told us to say good-bye to you."

"Until," Mom added, her eyes equally shiny, "Dr. Holcombe showed up and examined you. Then he told us there might be one way to keep you alive . . . but that it was extremely risky. And that there'd likely be . . . complications."

"You mean, like, I'd wake up in someone else's body?" I asked. "*That* kind of complication?"

"It's true you're not . . . well, *you* anymore, Em," Mom said. "On the outside, anyway. But you're still you on the inside. That's why Dr. Holcombe and his team felt it was better not to tell you right away what had happened. You had already been through so much. You just needed time . . . time to adjust —"

"Oh, God." I dropped my head into my hands. I couldn't believe this. I couldn't believe any of this was happening to me.

And that Stark Enterprises was apparently behind it.

"Look," I said, fighting back tears. How could my parents have gone along with any of this? How could they have allowed this to happen? "This isn't right. You can't *do* this. It's . . . it's *sick*."

"Now see here, young lady," Dr. Holcombe said, looking annoyed. "What's sick about it? Thousands of people are declared legally brain dead every year, and thousands more find themselves in bodies too infirm to continue living in. What is so wrong with providing those patients with a second chance at life? Besides which," he added, a little less irritably, "I honestly don't think you have any right to complain. You went into my surgery a grievously injured girl and came out a supermodel! Millions of girls would die — literally — to be in your shoes right now!"

That's when I realized that even though this man had saved my life — even though, at one time, he'd wrapped his hands around my brain, gently lifted it, and then spent hours carefully stitching it into place inside someone else's head — he didn't know me.

He didn't know me at all.

"But you didn't have my permission," I accused him.

"Ah," Mr. Phillips said. "But we had your parents' permission."

I swung an accusing look at Mom and Dad. Mom's eyes, I saw, were as bright with tears as my own.

"You were going to die otherwise, honey," she said. "You wouldn't be here if it weren't for what Dr. Holcombe and his team did."

I just looked at her. I may have had Nikki Howard's heart now, but it felt every bit as heavy as mine ever had when I was upset about something.

"Fine," I said, trying to sound reasonably adult — which wasn't easy to do, considering how high-pitched and childish Nikki Howard's voice was. "But if Stark Enterprises really wants to keep this whole whole-body transplant thing a secret . . . well, it's not going to stay a secret for long. Because people are going to notice something is up when I walk into school on Monday, and I look just like Nikki Howard, but I'm going around calling myself Emerson Watts."

Mr. Phillips cleared his throat.

"That isn't going to happen," he said calmly.

"But —" I looked from him to my parents and back again. Why did my parents look so . . . so guilt-stricken? What was going on? "Yeah, it is. I mean, I can't not go back to school."

"Emerson Watts won't be going back to school," Mr. Phillips said. "Because Emerson Watts no longer exists."

"What do you mean, I no longer exist?" I asked. "I'm sitting right here."

"Em." My dad's voice was gentle. "Look . . ."

I glanced at him. There was something about his expression — something I couldn't put my finger on.

But I knew I didn't like it. I saw that Mom, sitting next to him, wore much the same look on her face . . . sort of panicky, but sort of pleading at the same time. They both looked over at Mr. Phillips, then back at me.

Wait. Why were they looking at *him*?

"When we first got to the hospital," Dad went on, "and Dr. Holcombe here told us about the transplant, there were . . . well, there were certain conditions. Things we, as your parents, had to agree to before they would consider doing the surgery."

I looked from Dad to Mom and then back again.

"What kind of things?" I asked, wondering what on earth they could be talking about.

Mr. Phillips pulled a thick pile of papers from a briefcase beside his chair and handed me a heavy stack from the top. I looked down and saw forty or fifty pages of fine print, neatly stapled and notarized. At the bottom of each page were my parents' signatures.

"Well," Mr. Phillips said, flipping through the copy of the contract he had in front of him, "for one thing, they agreed that, in the event that your surgery was a success, you would honor all of Nikki Howard's contracts, endorsements, and licensing agreements."

My eyes bulged.

"*What?*" I looked frantically toward my parents. But both of them had their gazes glued to the floor.

"In other words," Mr. Phillips continued, apparently thinking I didn't understand what he'd just said. Except that I *had* understood. I was just hoping against hope that he was wrong. "You will continue fulfilling Nikki Howard's duties as the Face of Stark. Failure to do so will result in a full and immediate reimbursement of the cost of the surgery, and possible legal ramifications."

Now I wasn't just staring. I was gaping.

"Wait," I said. My heart was starting to hammer, hard, inside my chest. Or rather, Nikki Howard's chest. "Are you saying what I think you're saying?"

"I'm not certain what you think I'm saying, Miss Watts," Mr. Phillips said. "But if you mean, am I saying that if you do not honor all of Nikki Howard's Stark-related professional commitments, your parents will owe this hospital two million dollars, in addition to legal fees — and fines, including possible jail time, if confidentiality is also breached — then yes, that is what I am saying."

No. No, this wasn't possible. This was a hallucination. The part with Gabriel Luna? That had really happened. But *this* was unreal —

"Oh, and there was something else your parents agreed to," Mr. Phillips went on.

"There's *more?*" I groaned.

"This part," Dr. Holcombe said, "I can assure you is quite standard, Emerson. We require it of all our patients. For the protection of the institute. We can't let what we do here get out, of course. There are people — religious leaders, politicians — who wouldn't understand that what we do saves lives. If people were to leave here with entirely new bodies and faces, but still insisting they were the same person they were when they came in . . . well, as you suggested earlier, word would get out very quickly. That's why we require all of our patients to allow us to declare their previous identities legally dead."

My jaw dropped. "But I'm not dead!"

"Legally," Mr. Phillips said, "I can assure you that you are. It all comes down to the locus of identity. Just what is the locus — or perceived location — of our identities . . . our souls, as it were? Is it the brain? Or is it the heart and body? Nikki Howard's brain, it's true, is no longer functioning. Her heart, on the other hand, continues to beat."

"Her . . . heart?"

I laid a hand over my heart. Or, I guess I should say, I laid Nikki Howard's hand over Nikki Howard's heart. I felt its steady thump-thump-thump. Up until that moment, the sound of my heartbeat had always been reassuring to me.

Now it sounded . . . well, foreign.

"Emerson Watts's heart, however," Mr. Phillips continued, "stopped beating well over a month ago. If all motor function has ceased in a body, and the brain is removed, then that person, by the legal definition set in place by a landmark 1984 court decision here in New York State, is deceased. Whereas the person with the living brain and beating heart — in this case, Nikki Howard — is, legally, alive."

My eyes widened. I couldn't understand any of this. Did this guy not realize I'm only in eleventh grade? Granted I'm in all AP classes. But still. "*What?*" I asked again.

"What I'm trying to explain, Miss Watts," Mr. Phillips said slowly, as if by his taking more time to pronounce them his words would make more sense to me, "is that approximately thirty-four days ago, Emerson Watts — according to the current definition of the word as mandated by the laws of the state of New York — died."

I did not like the sound of this. I did not like the sound of this one bit.

"Wait," I said. "So according to the state of New York, I'm dead?"

"*Emerson Watts* is dead," he corrected me.

"But . . . *I'm* Emerson Watts," I cried.

"Are you?" he asked, with a little smile.

It was the smile that did it. Suddenly, I was afraid. More afraid than I'd ever been in my life . . . including when I'd seen that plasma screen television start to fall right where my sister was standing.

"*Yes*," I said, leaning forward in my chair. "*Yes*. Why are you — I mean, why are we — even discussing this? What are you trying to tell me? Are you really going to sit there and tell me that I'm dead, and that Nikki Howard is still alive?"

"Not at all. What I'm telling you, Miss Watts, is that you *are* Nikki Howard."

FOURTEEN

I WAS BACK IN MY HOSPITAL ROOM —
the only occupied patient room in the entire A wing of the
Institute for Neurology and Neurosurgery — and back in a hospital gown. Dr. Holcombe and his staff wanted to run some
more tests. How well I did on the tests would dictate how soon
I got to go home — or I guess I should say, to Nikki Howard's
loft, since that's where my home was going to be once I was
released, now that I was to resume Nikki Howard's contractual
responsibilities.

Of course, Mom and Dad told me I didn't have to go through
with it. The part about pretending to be Nikki. They said (later,
when Stark's legal eagle, Mr. Phillips, wasn't around) that they'd

find a way to pay the two million — and the legal fees and fines — if I didn't think I could handle it.

"We can always declare bankruptcy," Mom said, way too cheerfully.

Yeah. Because that's so what I want my parents to have to do for me.

I told them I wasn't worried. Not about Nikki Howard's contractual responsibilities. And I wasn't. I mean, come on. How hard could modeling be, anyway? You just have to stand there in front of the camera with your stomach sucked in, right? Look at all those models Frida's always reading about in her fashion magazines. They're not exactly rocket scientists.

But I'd already experienced enough of Nikki Howard's personal life to know it wasn't going to be easy. Nikki's love life alone was . . . complicated. To say the least.

That had my stomach twisted up in knots (although that could have been the acid reflux Lulu had warned me about).

The fact was, I was basically going to have to act like Nikki *all the time*. Only our immediate family was to know the truth about who I really was. According to Mr. Phillips, a story was going to be released to the public that Nikki had suffered a head injury when she'd fainted due to her exhaustion and hypoglycemia, and that the head injury had resulted in amnesia. This was so that when I showed up for photo shoots and didn't recognize makeup artists and stylists Nikki had worked with before, there'd be a rational explanation.

Though if Stark Enterprises really thought amnesia was a rational explanation, they needed a major reality check.

I'd told Mr. Phillips right away that there was one problem: I might have already mentioned to Lulu Collins and Brandon Stark that I wasn't Nikki Howard.

But Mr. Phillips didn't look worried. He said, "The amnesia story will take care of that."

And I realized he was right. Lulu and Brandon would totally believe I had amnesia. They were already prepared to believe I'd been the victim of brainwashing by Al Qaeda or a spirit transfer. They'd believe anything.

That wasn't what I was worried about. *Really* worried about, I mean. What I was *really* worried about was . . . well, Stark Enterprises. I mean, they already had my family in an iron grip there was no way we could squirm out of — how were two professors ever going to come up with two million dollars (and fines)?

But someone was also tracking Nikki Howard's keystrokes on her Stark-issued computer. Someone who hadn't thought Nikki — or I — would notice. And I didn't want to be paranoid or anything, but I had a pretty good idea who that someone was.

And that was her employers at Stark Enterprises.

So, yeah. I didn't want to say anything, but that was concerning me. Stark Enterprises, and their sudden omnipresence in our lives.

And one other thing. What had happened to me? The me Christopher had said so long ago was fine.

"So . . . where's my body?" I asked my parents as we sat waiting for Dr. Higgins to come and escort me to the testing lab. "I mean . . . the one I was born in?"

I saw them exchange glances. Then Mom said, carefully, "Well, honey . . . we had it cremated."

I stared at her in horror.

"We had to," she went on quickly, seeing my expression. "We had to have a memorial service. We couldn't keep what happened to you a secret, there'd been paparazzi at the Stark Megastore, following Nikki Howard around. They got the whole thing on film — it was on CNN moments after it happened. Everyone saw that plasma screen land on you. There was virtually nothing else on television for days — it was a slow news week. We had to have a service. We didn't have any other choice."

"You'll be happy to know it was very well attended," Dad said, as if this was supposed to make me feel better. "Stark Enterprises paid for Grandma to come all the way from Florida —"

Suddenly, tears filled my eyes.

"Grandma thinks I'm dead?" I asked. No more T-shirts with WORLD'S GREATEST GRANDCHILD printed on them for Christmas. No more birthday cards with twelve dollars tucked inside.

"Well, honey," Mom said, chewing the inside of her lip, "yes. I'm sorry. But you know what a gossip she is around the pool where she lives. We really couldn't tell her the truth."

I couldn't believe it. It turned out rumors of my death hadn't been exaggerated.

I was dead. Legally. Medically. Technically. In every -ally, really, except the one way that mattered: literally.

I was dead, and I hadn't even been able to attend my own funeral.

"Was anybody from school there?" I asked. "At my memorial service, I mean?"

"Of course," Dad said, sounding a little hesitant for some reason. "Christopher, and his father . . ."

Now, for the first time since I'd woken up in Nikki Howard's body, I really lost it.

"Christopher?" I gasped. "Oh, my God. You mean you didn't *tell* him? Christopher thinks I'm *dead?*"

Mom and Dad exchanged panicky glances. Suddenly, I was crying so hard, I couldn't even see them. I guess it wasn't any wonder they thought I was losing it. I saw Mom signal Dad to leave the room — no doubt to search out Dr.

Holcombe and ask him for more of those coma drugs to calm me down.

"Honey, you know we couldn't tell him the truth," Mom said, coming to sit down beside me on the bed and putting her arms around me. Cosabella, who'd been busily grooming herself at my feet, hurried over to give me a few concerned licks, as well. "We felt terrible about it, but . . . well, you heard what Mr. Phillips said."

Oh, I'd heard what Mr. Phillips had said, all right. Thanks to Mr. Phillips, the mystery of why Emerson Watts, eleventh-grader, had been saved using the incredibly rare and expensive lifesaving technology of whole-body transplant had been cleared up.

She hadn't. Stark Enterprises had used it to save Nikki Howard.

Not me.

"I know it's awful to say," Mom went on as she hugged me, "but . . . Christopher will get over it. Eventually. With time. He really will."

"G-get over it?" I wailed. "My best friend th-thinks I'm dead, only I'm not, and I c-can't even tell him — and you think he'll just g-get over it?"

Frida chose that moment to stroll into my room. Her brown eyes were practically crackling with rage, and her chin was sticking out — sure signs she wanted to have a confrontation with me about something.

But she stopped dead in her tracks when she saw that I was crying.

"What's with her?" she demanded.

"She just found out about Christopher," Mom said, gently rocking me. "You know, thinking she's dead."

"Oh." Frida stared at me. "So? Don't worry about him. I saw him in school the other day, and he was fine."

This just made me cry harder. It also caused Mom to say, "Frida!"

"Well?" Frida sauntered over to where my television's remote control sat on the bedside table and picked it up, switched on the TV, and began flipping channels. "It's true. He was a little upset at first, but he's already over it. I don't know why you're freaking out. You said he's not your boyfriend, anyway. Remember?"

Mom got up, let go of me, and snatched the remote from Frida's hand in one fluid motion.

"May I have a word with you in the hallway, young lady?" she asked briskly.

The two of them left the room. While they were gone, I tried to pull myself back together. I couldn't believe how selfish I'd been, not having given Christopher a second thought since

I'd woken up. Except for the whole wishing-he'd-been-the-one-kissing-me-instead-of-Justin-or-Brandon thing, I mean.

What could Christopher have been going through, all this time, thinking I was dead? Was he all right? How had he handled it, those moments after that TV had fallen on me, right in front of him? He must have been so freaked out. Who was he eating lunch with now that I wasn't in school? He didn't have anyone else to make fun of the Walking Dead with, or to play *Journeyquest* with, or watch surgery shows on the Discovery Channel with. Poor Christopher!

Unless . . . unless some other girl had snatched him up for herself. Only who? What girl at TAHS (besides me) had the sensitivity to look past all that long hair and see the potential hottie who lay beneath? What other girl was *fine* enough?

God. Surely there had to be one. She could be sitting down next to him in the cafeteria *right now*, complimenting him on his avoidance of the tuna salad. . . .

Suddenly, Frida was back, this time by herself. She looked sullen.

"I'm supposed to apologize," she said. Her gaze was on Cosabella, the now black television screen, the window behind me — anywhere but on my face. "So . . . sorry if what I said upset you. It's not true, anyway. Christopher's not fine. I guess.

But then . . . he was always so weird anyway, it's kind of hard to tell."

I had already dried my tears — or Nikki's tears, I guess, although Dr. Holcombe had told me not to think of my new body that way. *It's YOUR body, Emerson,* he'd said. *Not hers. Not anymore.*

Right. I just had her name. Her face. Her loft. Her boyfriend(s). You name it.

"I don't get it," I said to Frida. I still felt like crying every time I thought about Christopher and how a new girl might be getting to play *Journeyquest* — or sit around and watch surgery shows on the Discovery Channel — with him right this very minute. Although truthfully, the allure of surgery shows had sort of waned for me. But I was trying to suck it up. As Dr. Holcombe had pointed out, at least I was alive. "What's eating you?"

"Nothing," Frida said. "Gabriel left."

For a second I didn't understand what she was talking about. Then I remembered how she'd gone downstairs with Gabriel after he'd dropped me off.

"Oh," I said. Was *that* what was eating Frida? She was jealous that I'd spent time with *Gabriel Luna?* "Okay."

"He had to." Frida flopped into the chair next to my bed. "They wouldn't let him back on the floor."

"Well," I said, "I'm sure he'll learn to live with the disappointment."

"God!" Frida glared at me. "You don't even care about him, do you?"

"How can I care about him?" I demanded. "I barely know him. And besides . . ." I felt myself flush as I was about to add, *I like Christopher.* But I couldn't admit this, not even to my sister. Not even now that Christopher thought I was dead, and I was in Nikki Howard's body, and I had no chance of ever getting Christopher to like me. So I changed it at the last minute to, "He thinks I'm Nikki Howard."

"So?" Frida shrugged. "You shouldn't be so hard on him. He's a really nice guy. He thinks you're really great."

"How do you know that?" I asked her, finding this hard to believe, since I had it from the guy's own lips that he thought I was a drug addict.

"He told me, of course," Frida said. "Down in the hospital cafeteria. We split a cinnamon bun. You know, one of those ones that are as big as my head? Totally fatty, but I've been completely off my diet since your accident. It's hard to do the no-sugar thing when your sister is having a brain transplant. So what did he rescue you from?"

I blinked at her. "Excuse me?"

"You said back in the hallway that Gabriel rescued you. What from?"

"Oh," I said. "Lulu Collins and Brandon Stark kidnapped me last night and took me to Nikki Howard's loft. But you can't tell anyone, okay, Free? Because I don't want to get them into trou —"

"LULU COLLINS?" Frida was on her feet and shrieking. "You met Lulu Collins? And Brandon Stark? Are you *kidding* me? You hung out with them? Where did you go? Did they take you to Cave? Oh, my God, did you get to see *Justin Bay?*"

"Whoa," I said. "Hold on. First of all, stop yelling. And second of all, no, it wasn't like that —"

"Oh, my God." Frida stopped jumping up and down and looked at me, wide-eyed. "Brandon Stark and Nikki Howard are — used to be — dating. If he thought you were Nikki, he must have — did he try to *kiss* you?"

I shook my head. No way was I telling my little sister about Brandon's tongue dive, let alone what had gone on with Justin — or how much I'd enjoyed both.

"Of course not," I said. "He and Lulu were just worried about their friend. It really sucks, Free. I mean, that people think I'm Nikki."

Frida, to my surprise, rolled her eyes. "Oh, yes," she said, sarcastically. "Being mistaken for the world's most famous teenage supermodel? I'm sure that must suck."

"Um," I said, stung. "Actually, yes, it does. And thanks for telling me when I woke up."

"Telling you what when you woke up?" Frida cocked her head to ask.

"About how they'd put my brain in Nikki Howard's body," I said, injecting as much sarcasm into my voice as possible. "I appreciate it."

If I was concerned Nikki's voice was too high-pitched and babyish for sarcasm to come across, I needn't have worried. Frida looked immediately sheepish.

"Oh," she said. "That. Yeah, well, I wanted to. But they told me not to. They told me . . . well, they said it might upset you. They wanted to give you time to adjust first."

"Great," I said, still working the sarcasm thing. "Way to watch my back, sis."

But I saw that I'd gone too far when her eyes filled up with tears, and she said, "Em . . . I was really scared. I thought . . . these past few weeks I thought when you woke up, you wouldn't even know who I was. They *told* me that you'd be . . . you know. Yourself. But then I'd look at you, lying there, and I'd just see . . . Nikki Howard. And I thought, *There's no way.* I mean, that you'd wake up and be your old self and be mad at me for trying out for cheerleading —"

"*You tried out for cheerleading?*" I yelled. "Are you insane? Do you know what Mom's going to do to you when she finds out? Because I'm assuming you haven't told her, seeing as how you're still alive."

But Frida, instead of looking offended, burst out laughing.

"See?" she said. "It's so great that I'm hearing that . . . well, kind of great, because it's still annoying. It's just so weird that all that annoying stuff is coming out of *Nikki Howard*. I guess it's better than never hearing it again, but —"

"Hearing what again?" Mom asked, coming back into my room.

"Um," Frida said, quickly. "Nothing. We were just talking about . . . clothes."

Dad, following behind Mom, looked amused. "That's what I like to hear. Things sound as if they're getting back to normal if you two are squabbling. But *Em* was talking about clothes?"

"Well," Frida said, looking panicky, "no, not exactly. . . ."

"We were talking about school," I said quickly. "And what's going to happen now. I mean, now that I'm going to have to start working, and I'll be living at Nikki Howard's loft, and everything, I guess I'm going to be way too busy for high school —"

"On the contrary, young lady," Mom said, something like the old spark I knew so well showing up in her eye, just as I'd known it would at the suggestion that I drop out of school. "Under no circumstances will you be forsaking your education."

"Absolutely not," Dad said. He looked shocked. "You can't put off college, and certainly not high school. There's no long-term financial stability in modeling, like there is in teaching or a career in law or medicine."

"Of course," Mom said, chewing her lower lip, "with your schedule, attending regular school might be hard. We might have to look into enrolling you in one of those performing arts high schools. Or maybe getting you tutors. Perhaps Stark Enterprises could help us with that. . . ."

Much as I disliked the idea of us allowing Stark Enterprises any more access to our lives, I shot Frida a triumphant look.

"Gosh," I said. "But I just love Tribeca Alternative so much. I'd really like to be able to keep going there, if I could."

Mom and Dad looked plenty surprised to hear that. But their surprise was nothing compared to Frida's scowl. I guess she'd thought, with me out of the way, she could just do whatever she wanted — become a member of the Walking Dead, try out for cheerleading, maybe even start going out with an upperclassman.

Well, she'd thought wrong.

"Really, honey?" Mom looked stunned. "Well, I suppose we could speak to Mr. Phillips. I'm sure Stark Enterprises could arrange something with the school. There's no reason why, if your schedule allows it, you shouldn't be able to take some classes there when you can. You may not be able to graduate on time next year, but you'll still graduate . . . eventually."

"That'd be great," I said, with completely false enthusiasm.

"Nikki Howard would *never* get into a school with academic standards as rigorous as TAHS," Frida, the expert on all things Nikki Howard, chimed in quickly. "I mean, technically, agewise, I guess she'd be a junior, like Em. But she dropped out of high school her freshman year, when she got her first big modeling contract. . . ."

"I'm sure if Stark Enterprises gave a big enough financial gift to the school, they could get her in," Dad said. "If that's what you really want to do, Em. But, like Mom said, there are tutors — and other schools we could try, as well."

Frida turned toward me eagerly. "Yeah, Em. See? You don't *have* to go back to TAHS."

"Oh, no," I said, giving Frida the evil eye. "TAHS is *exactly* where I want to go. And they can't act like they don't have space. We all know there's an opening in the junior class, don't we?"

And my going back there would kill two birds with one stone . . . I could keep watch over Frida *and* make sure Christopher was okay. And, okay, it wouldn't be fair of me to make sure he wasn't dating other girls. I knew if I really loved him, and all, I was supposed to set him free. But . . . why should I, when I wasn't really gone?

And I also knew I couldn't tell him who I really was, either.

But still. Maybe we could become friends, like we were before the accident. And maybe . . . just maybe . . . more than friends. Like Brandon and Nikki were more than friends.

Only hopefully neither of us would be screwing around behind the other's back like those two appeared to have been doing.

The bad thing would be that I would always know something Christopher didn't know . . . that apparently, a lot of famous people — because only the super rich (or people like me, who had a massive corporation like Stark Enterprises paying for it) could afford a whole-body transplant — whom we've been told are dead are actually really alive, just living in a new body.

I'm not going to name names (primarily because no one at the Stark Institute would tell me for sure), but hints were dropped that a lot of famous people — some of whom had been about to be sentenced for crimes like securities fraud, and several others of whom were famous musicians, long thought to be dead by their adoring fans, and still others of whom were members of certain British and European royal families — who supposedly "died" are actually alive and well and just living in different bodies under assumed identities, while their family members go around pretending to this day like they're all sad about them having passed away.

But the joke's on us, because they aren't dead at all.

In other words, Christopher and I were right all along: There really *are* Walking Dead.

The problem?

Now I'm one of them.

FIFTEEN

THE PRESS RELEASE WENT OUT THE next afternoon.

I couldn't go online to Google News to read it, of course, since I was still lacking a computer (although, given the state of Nikki's computer, this was probably just as well). But I saw it on the running scroll at the bottom of CNN and then again, later, on the evening news.

Then, next thing I knew, it was the lead story on all the entertainment news shows.

It turns out Kelly, Nikki's publicist, didn't mess around when it came to her most popular client.

"The fashion and beauty industry breathed a collective sigh of relief this evening when a statement was issued from representatives of Nikki Howard," chimed *Entertainment Tonight* as photos of Nikki Howard flashed upon the screen, "assuring her fans that the teen supermodel would be back at work this week after a month-long absence from the catwalk and the New York City club scene. Fashionistas worldwide have been alarmed by reports that Nikki was suffering from exhaustion and hypoglycemia, which are said to have been responsible for that now famous fall she took at a Stark Megastore grand opening last month, giving her a concussion and a bona fide case of *amnesia. . . .*"

The next photo to flash across the screen was one that caused me almost to choke on the bag of wasabi peas Frida had smuggled in for me at my request, and which I'd been inhaling (yes, I know. I used to hate them. Now I love them. Dr. Holcombe says it's normal for patients to find themselves with tastes quite unlike the ones they used to have, in their previous bodies).

It was a grainy cell-phone photo of me (well, of Nikki Howard) on the back of Gabriel Luna's green Vespa. Both of us were looking back at the photographer with slightly alarmed expressions on our faces — though I don't remember anyone taking my picture that day.

The alarmed expressions were of course due to the fact that we were being pursued by a herd of stampeding fourth-graders.

But of course it looked as if we were upset over the fact that we were being photographed together. A fact the television news "journalists" were only too quick to point out.

"Perhaps amnesia is the excuse Nikki will give on-again, off-again boyfriend Brandon Stark for this photo snapped yesterday of the model taking a joyride on a motorbike belonging to hot new British singing sensation Gabriel Luna. The pair met at the same SoHo Stark Megastore opening at which Nikki suffered the fainting spell responsible for her head injury, and at which a young fan was killed during a melee caused by E.L.F. protesters."

I waited in horror for the reporter to show a picture of me — the old me.

But I should have known they wouldn't. I was yesterday's news. Why report about a girl being killed by a falling TV when you could show pictures of Nikki Howard on red carpets with her dress slit up to her belly button?

"Representatives for both Howard and Luna had no comments on the photo. But perhaps Nikki can tell Brandon she just 'forgot' that she already had a boyfriend. . . ."

Oh, my God. I couldn't believe it. I could barely breathe, I was so upset.

But the story didn't even end there.

"Stark Enterprises founder and CEO Robert Stark has issued a statement," the reporter went on, "expressing get-well wishes for Howard — whom many refer to as the Face of Stark."

The camera panned toward an older, craggy-faced version of Brandon Stark — his father, dressed casually in an open-collared shirt — who said, "We here at Stark Enterprises respectfully request that the press, during this period of recovery for Nikki, afford her the privacy she needs. For the next few weeks, at least, Nikki will be spending slightly less time in the limelight. She even told me she's considering going back to school —" He grinned as this statement provoked chuckles from the press corps, as if the idea of Nikki Howard attempting to get her high school degree was the funniest thing in the world. "— a decision we here at Stark Enterprises are behind one hundred percent."

What? I'd never told Robert Stark any such thing. I'd never even met the guy. And great. My own boss — well, Nikki's boss, anyway — thinks she's too stupid to make it through high school. Nice. Thanks for the support. He probably thinks that because he's been reading her e-mails.

"But high jinks like *this*," the reporter went on to say, flashing the photo of me on the back of Gabriel's motor scooter onto the screen again, "may just get this *model student* detention!"

Then a new reporter came on to talk about the current celebrity divorce scandal.

I couldn't believe it. I couldn't believe one of those schoolgirls had snapped a photo of me and Gabriel . . . and sold it! Was this what my life was going to be like from now on? Being stalked by paparazzi, my most innocent activities being spread all over the tabloids?

I was so busy staring at the television screen above my bed in horror, I didn't even see the person who came into my room a minute later.

"Nikki?" The eyes looking out at me over the top of the surgeon's mask were huge . . . and not just because they were rimmed in black kohl.

Lulu Collins had sneaked onto my floor again. This time she'd added to her ingenious disguise by carrying around a medical clipboard.

I know. The mind boggles.

Well, it was late, and most of the staff — among them my father, whose turn it was to spend the night at my bedside — were gathered in the lounge, watching some kind of sporting event. I didn't know which one, because I couldn't have cared less.

So it hadn't been hard for Lulu to slip past the security guards posted at the doors. Especially in her current ensemble.

"Hi, Lulu," I said, a little glumly.

"You remember me?" Lulu lowered the mask, her face breaking out into an enormous smile. "Oh, Nikki . . . when they said you had amnesia, I *knew* they were making it up."

"No," I said quickly. "Sorry, Lulu. I really . . . I mean, I just know you from before. Remember? When you kidnapped me?"

"Are you sure?" Lulu asked, her tiny shoulders sagging. "It's just . . . well, I saw the thing on TV, and I started thinking, you know, maybe you guys had swapped back. You and that Em girl. Because hopping onto the back of that guy's scooter? That was such a totally Nikki thing to do. Brandon is soooo mad!"

I paused. "Brandon? Angry? At me?"

"Well, sure," Lulu said, coming over to plop herself down at the side of my bed. "I mean, I don't know where Brandon gets off thinking it's okay for him to dance with whomever he wants all night long, but not okay for you to get a ride on some other guy's Vespa. That's a total, like, whadduyacallit."

"Double standard?" I offered.

"Yeah, I guess. But anyway. When I saw the picture, I got totally excited. I thought maybe you were back. I mean, that Nikki was back. The real Nikki. Cosabella is missing, too, so I thought maybe you'd come home and taken her —"

"Lulu," I said, "Cosabella's here." I pushed back my sheets to reveal the ball of fluff sleeping at my side. "I'm sorry. Back at your place yesterday morning, she was crying, and . . . well, I just didn't have the heart to leave her behind."

"Oh." Lulu's voice sounded small. "Okay. No, that's good. Cosy did miss you. I mean, Nikki. I mean . . . oh, I don't know what I mean. So I guess that was you on the back of that guy's bike? Not . . . the real Nikki?"

"Yeah," I said. "That was me. Listen, Lulu. About the whole spirit transfer thing . . ."

"Yeah?" Lulu sounded congested. Had she been crying?

I had no time to worry about her tears now. Any minute, my dad or one of the nurses — or worse, Dr. Holcombe himself — might come into my room and figure out whom I was talking to.

And somehow, I didn't suspect any of them would be very thrilled. All their talk of fines and jail time — well, Stark Enterprises seemed dead serious about keeping this thing a secret. And I didn't want Lulu to get in trouble. In spite of what a space case she was, she still seemed really sweet.

"Lulu," I said. "There was no spirit transfer. It turns out I, um, hit my head. And now I have amnesia. So that's why I didn't remember you. Or Brandon."

Silence. Lulu stared at me with eyes as wide as a Precious Moments figurine's. Then she let out a slurpy, "No way."

"Um," I said, "yeah. That's what happened. Everything they've been saying on the news. It's true."

"I don't believe you," Lulu said. "Or the news. I know that's what Kelly is going around saying now. But it's not true."

"Lulu," I said, feeling desperate. I had to make her believe me. I couldn't risk having my parents pay two million dollars. Or, rather, file for bankruptcy, since they didn't have two million dollars. "It *is* true. Why don't you believe me?"

"Because even if she had amnesia," Lulu said, "Nikki would never do *that* to her nails."

And she reached out and grabbed my hand.

I looked down, following the direction of her gaze, and saw what she meant. During that meeting with Dr. Holcombe and Mr. Phillips, I'd bitten off all the carefully manicured tips, until they were ragged . . . just like my old nails had been.

"Nikki would never, ever do something to hurt her body or make herself ugly," Lulu went on, sounding almost savage in her conviction that what she was saying was true. "So I don't know who you really are . . . but you aren't Nikki. So don't even try with the amnesia thing. It might work with everyone else. But I was Nikki's best friend. I know everything about her. And I know she would never, *ever* do that."

I stared at her and the grim set of her tiny little mouth. Lulu *didn't* know everything about her alleged "best" friend, Nikki. She didn't, for instance, know that her best friend, Nikki, had been screwing around behind her back with Lulu's boyfriend, Justin.

But over my dead body — literally — was I ever going to let Lulu know about that.

Still, Lulu deserved the truth — what truth I could tell her without hurting her — if anyone did.

And so I said, "Okay, Lulu. You're right. I'm not really Nikki Howard. The truth is, the doctors here stuck Emerson Watts's brain into Nikki Howard's body. And I'm not supposed to tell anyone, or my parents will owe two million dollars — which they don't have — to Stark Enterprises, who paid for the whole thing, I guess to keep their spokesmodel alive after Nikki suffered a fatal aneurysm that day at the Megastore opening."

Lulu blinked back at me. Once. Twice.

Then she burst out laughing.

"Yeah, right," she said. "Good one!"

I blinked back at her.

"I know," I said. "It sounds like a made-for-TV movie or something. But you know, they have this new Nikki Howard beauty and clothing line coming out, and I guess they spent a lot of money on it or something, and they want me to pretend to be her so they can keep on —"

"Right!" Lulu interrupted. She was practically rolling off the bed, she was laughing so hard. "Like, if they were really going to do something like that, they'd pick someone as clueless as *you* are to take her place!" She reached up to wipe away tears of laughter. "Um, no offense, or anything. I'm sure you're nice. But Nikki's job is really hard. I mean, do you even have any modeling experience?"

I tried not to laugh. I mean, at the *Nikki's job is really hard* part.

"No," I said, drily. "But I think I'm going to be able to handle it."

"Oh, right," Lulu said again, laughing even harder. "Do you even know what a Manolo tip is?"

"Well," I said, thinking back to all those copies of *CosmoGIRL!* Frida left lying around. "A Manolo is a type of shoe, right?"

Lulu made a delighted noise. "Oh, God," she cried. "I can't believe this. This is going to be great! Nikki's going to laugh her ass off when she hears about this. You know you're not going to last a minute out there, don't you?"

"Well," I said, slightly stung, "that's why they made up the amnesia story. So if I screw up, we can blame it on that. Why? What *is* a Manolo tip?"

But Lulu ignored the question.

"God," she said. "This is hilarious. I can't wait to tell Brandon —"

"No," I cried, reaching out to grasp her spool-thin wrist. "Lulu. You can't. I told you. It's a secret. I mean, I'm going to be coming to live with you — in Nikki's place — and everything. We're going to be roommates — or loftmates or whatever. But seriously. You can't tell *anyone*. Or my parents will get into big trouble."

She stared at me, suddenly serious.

"Okay," she said gently. "Okay, Nik — or whatever your name is. Listen." She swung her tiny feet, in four-inch stilettos, above the floor. "Do you want me to call Bliss? Because I could totally set up an appointment for you with an emergency nail repair technician."

"No," I said. "That's okay. Listen, Lulu. When I was at your place — *our* place — I noticed something about Nikki's computer."

Lulu looked instantly bored. She studied her cuticles. "Yeah? What?"

"Someone's spying on Nikki's e-mails," I said. "Basically anything she types or looks up on it. In real time, from a remote location. Do you have any idea who'd do that?"

"No," Lulu said. "That's a brand-new computer. Mr. Stark gave it to her. He gave me one, too. They're pink."

"Yes," I said, "I know it's pink. Mr. Stark gave you one, too?"

"Uh-huh. They're the newest models from Stark Enterprises. Or something." Lulu blew a bubble, then skillfully popped it. "What do you mean, spying on Nikki's e-mails?"

It was at that moment that one of the nurses came in, holding my patient chart.

"Er, hello," she said, when she saw Lulu perched on the end of my bed. "Do I know you?"

"Oh, no," came Lulu's airy reply, as she hopped off my bed and glanced busily down at her own (stolen) chart. "Just making rounds. You know."

The nurse, who was clearly no one's fool — perhaps recognizing that most of the staff wore Crocs, not stilettos — narrowed her eyes. "Excuse me," she said. "But where's your pass for this floor?"

"Oops, there's my beeper," Lulu said. "Gotta go, bye!" She scooted out of the room while the nurse rushed after her, crying, "Wait! You, there!"

I totally hoped she escaped.

It was weird. If someone had asked me just a month ago what I thought about Lulu Collins, I'd have replied that I thought she was another shallow celebrity, obsessed with clothes and partying.

And I *still* think that about her.

Except . . . I think I'm starting to like her.

So what does that say about me?

SIXTEEN

AND THE NEXT THING I KNEW, I WAS
being released.

I guess I shouldn't have been surprised . . . that they were
releasing me, I mean. They'd completed every test under the
sun that they could conceivably do on me. The strangest part
was that, well . . . I'd passed them all.

And these were mainly *physical* tests. Let's just say that I've
never performed well in tests of my physical endurance. I've
never exactly aced PE. I've always been the last person chosen
for teams in volleyball and basketball. I've always made a point
to play outfield in softball, so that in the unlikely event a ball
ever *did* come my way, I had plenty of room to get out of the way.
I was crafty about coming up with excuses as to why I had to sit

out from bowling or swimming or even Rollerblading. I've just never *liked* physical exertion. I prefer reading. Or playing video games.

So naturally some of the results from my tests astonished even *me*. I mean, I was required to run on a treadmill for ten minutes straight — and I could actually do it . . . even after having been in a coma for over a month! In my old body, I wouldn't have lasted more than a minute, maybe two, at a slow jog. I'd have hyperventilated, or worse.

Nikki Howard, however, had kept her body in superb condition. It wasn't actually hard to see why, since fattening foods upset her stomach, and anything processed seemed to taste like chalk on her tongue, forcing me to radically alter my former diet of chips and sweets in favor of healthy stuff I wouldn't have touched before in a million years, like fish and vegetables. Which my new stomach found comforting and my new tongue found delicious.

I know. I was kind of depressed about it, too.

The thing was, Nikki could run, swim, even *jump rope* for up to half an hour at a time before even starting to feel tired.

What's more, in her body, it was even *pleasurable* to do these things. For the first time, I got what they meant when they talked in PE about runner's high. I felt good after exercising. Finally, I *got* it . . . about the whole exercise-being-fun thing.

Too bad I'd had to get a whole new body before I did so.

Once I'd passed all the tests Dr. Holcombe sent Dr. Higgins to do on me, he signed my release papers and said I could go home . . . but that I would, of course, need to come in for more tests from time to time, as well as periodic checkups.

Even though I'd been unconscious during most of my stay with them, the staff lined up to say good-bye to me on my way out . . . only I had to leave down the service elevator, of course, because once Nikki's publicist, Kelly — who had arrived to pick me up and take me to my first assignment, a photo op with Robert Stark himself, to show the world that Nikki Howard might have amnesia, but she was fine! Just fine! — had issued her press release about Nikki Howard's amnesia, the front lobby to the hospital had been jammed with press, eager to get a shot of Nikki leaving the place.

I shook hands with Dr. Holcombe, Dr. Higgins, and the rest of the doctors and nurses and orderlies who had cared for me. Dr. Higgins and a few of the nurses broke protocol and hugged me, accidentally squashing Cosabella a little in the process, then laughing about it.

I stopped laughing, though, when it came time to hug Mom and Dad good-bye. Because they were not taking the whole letting-their-baby-go-even-though-they-had-no-choice-in-the-matter thing well. In fact, they had already insisted on issuing me a Stark-brand cell phone on which I was to check in with them three times a day (and on which they'd be calling me approximately every five minutes, judging from the look on Mom's face).

They weren't the only ones who were worried. I'd never lived away from them — except for a few weeks last summer when Frida and I had worked as counselors at sleepaway camp. I was trying to put on a brave face about it, but I was basically terrified — and also the tiniest bit angry. I know they hadn't had any choice and all, but really. . . .

A *supermodel?* For Stark Enterprises?

Frida I wasn't so worried about missing. She and I had already shared a "special moment" alone in my hospital room while I'd been packing my (admittedly few) things to leave.

"God," she'd said, "I can't believe you had Nikki Howard's entire closet to choose from, and what you've got on is what you picked. Those Skechers are so pathetic. If you wear them to school, I'm going to die of embarrassment."

"Frida," I'd snapped, particularly stung by her tone because I was already so worried about everything else. "No one knows I'm even related to you anymore, okay? So you don't have to worry. And could you give me a small break? I'm stressed enough as it is, I don't need you ragging on me about my fashion choices."

"Oh, please tell me again," Frida had mock-begged, "about how you don't know how to handle it because you're so beautiful now. . . ."

"What I don't know how to handle," I'd said through gritted teeth, "is the fact that my own sister tried out for cheerleading."

"I didn't just try out for cheerleading," Frida had bragged. "I made the squad."

I'd gaped at her. I go into a coma for a month, and my own sister becomes a member of the Walking Dead (only not literally, like me)? Her assimilation was almost complete! She was just one spray-tan away!

"No," I'd said, refusing to look at her. "You're just saying that to get a rise out of me. I don't believe you."

"Believe it," Frida had informed me. "Just because you hate our school and have zero school spirit, Em, doesn't mean I do. And don't think you're showing up there as Nikki Howard is going to intimidate me. Because it's done. I'm on the squad."

"Frida." I hadn't known how to explain it to her . . . especially since Mom had already tried so many times and evidently failed. "Cheerleading is . . . well, it's *evil*."

"Cheerleading is a SPORT, Em," Frida had shot back. "If I wanted to try out for the basketball team, would you be giving me a hard time?"

"Well," I'd admitted, "no. Because you don't have to wear a skirt and HALTER TOP when you play it."

"Look, I have news for you, Em." Frida had looked more serious than I'd ever seen her. "Cheerleading is something I've been wanting to try for my whole life. I was really lucky to make the team . . . even if it's only JV — and I don't intend to let you or Mom spoil it. I know I'm not pretty and little like the other girls on the squad . . . I know they only let me on because I'm a good spotter and I can hold up my end of a pyramid. I can't do a back handspring or even that great of a cartwheel. But I'm going to work hard and take TAHS to the tumbling championships this year. And then both you and Mom will be sorry you looked down on something that brings so much pleasure to so many people. Especially me."

I'd just stared at her. Until she'd added, "And if I'm not mistaken, in some of the ad campaigns Nikki Howard's contracted for, and that you're going to be doing now, you're going to be wearing *a lot less* than a halter top — hello, *Victoria's Secret model.* And you can walk in there and tell the art director how sexist his ad campaign is, but guess what? They'll just hire some other girl to replace you. So you better get over yourself."

At which point she'd turned on her heel and stalked from my room, right past Mom and Dad.

"What's eating her?" Dad had wanted to know.

But I hadn't told him. I had bigger things to worry about than Frida — who had lately more than proved she could take care of herself — just then. I was minutes away from officially starting my new life as Nikki Howard on the outside and Em Watts on the inside.

I hadn't exactly been given any guidelines, of course, as to just how I was supposed to accomplish this. Dr. Holcombe and his team were scientists, not social workers, and they had no idea what to tell me about being Nikki Howard. Their job was over: I was alive.

Granted, I was living someone else's life. But what I did with that life, apparently, was up to me . . . and Stark Enterprises.

Still, I was really, really hoping that I wouldn't screw it up for my family. And myself.

Standing in front of Mom, Dad, and Frida now, I wiped the nervous sweat off my hands — Cosabella's fur was proving excellent for this — and said awkwardly, "Well. So. I'll come by as soon as I have a night off." The truth was, I didn't want to commit to a particular night for dinner with my parents in front of Mr. Phillips, who was standing right there, watching. I figured Stark Enterprises knew enough about my personal business.

But Mom didn't catch on. I probably should have just told my parents about Nikki's computer. But the truth is, they're both so un-tech-savvy, they'd probably think spyware is something you eat with.

"Friday for sure, no excuses," Mom said firmly, standing on tiptoe to kiss my cheek. She'd never had to stand on tiptoe to kiss me before. "We'll go to Peking Duck House on Mott Street. That was always your favorite."

I rolled my eyes in Mr. Phillips's direction. He was tapping on his BlackBerry. Interesting that he didn't carry a Stark-brand handheld personal organizer.

"Maybe," I said. "I'll call you." But not on this Stark-brand cell phone, I wouldn't.

"Friday," Dad said, giving me a squeeze that caused Cosabella to grunt in protest as she was squashed. "You heard your mother."

"Call us as soon as you get there," Mom said, fussing with my jacket. "I wish you had a warmer coat than this. I should have brought you something from home."

"Mom," I said.

"Surely Nikki has warmer coats than this," she said, picking at the slim jacket I'd plucked from Nikki's closet. "Promise you'll find something warmer to wear tomorrow."

"Mom," I said.

"It's November," Mom said. "Here, take my scarf, at least." She wrapped her scarf around my neck.

"Mom," I said as she twined the woolly scarf around my neck tightly enough to strangle me. "I'm just getting straight into a limo and then out again when I get there. I don't need —"

"Don't forget to call," Mom said, hugging me again. Then she let me go as suddenly as if she'd had to force herself.

Both Cosabella and I felt a little bruised by the time we got to Frida, to whom I said awkwardly, "So. See you in school tomorrow?" Mr. Phillips had succeeded in securing me a place at Tribeca Alternative, and I'd gotten permission to start there whenever my schedule permitted. Which I was hoping was going to be tomorrow.

Frida shrugged. "Yeah. Whatever," she said. We gave each other wary pats on the back — although hers was more on my waist because she was so much shorter than I was — and then I turned around, barely able to see due to the sudden tears in my eyes. I think it was the scarf that did it.

That's when a redheaded woman in a bright green skirt suit, with one of those headsets in her ears, stepped forward and, escorted by two armed security guards, took me by the arm and began steering me into the elevator, going, "Yeah, yeah, we got her," into the mouthpiece. "We're on our way. ETA to Stark Corporate, fifteen minutes."

One of the security guards stabbed the B button for basement, and then as the elevator doors slid shut on the tearfully smiling faces of my family, the woman in the green skirt suit turned to me and said, switching off her Stark-brand headset and smiling in a very fake way, "Nikki, darling." She smelled of expensive perfume. "I'm so glad you're feeling better. I was so worried! Oh, right, I forgot, you don't remember me. Kelly Foster-Fielding." She held out her hand to shake mine in a grip so firm, I thought my own would be crushed. "I'm your publicist. How are you feeling, honey?"

I blinked at her. Did she really not know, or was this a put-on for the security guards? Did Stark Enterprises not tell her? I mean, that I wasn't *really* Nikki Howard?

But Kelly didn't even wait for a response from me. Instead, she whipped out a BlackBerry from her oversize tote and, pressing buttons on it so quickly her thumbs were a blur, went, "I'll be trying to give you a little breathing room this week so you can ease back without getting completely slammed — and I get the school thing, I really do — but there are a few people I haven't been able to put off. *Cosmo* wants you for their January cover and won't take no for an answer. I'm telling you, Nik, this amnesia thing is pure gold, since they want to do a piece on you, too. But I'm not promising them anything, because I've also got requests for both covers and pieces from *Vogue, Elle,* and *People* — well, we can scratch *People,* I don't know who they think you are, an *American Idol* winner? But this is the big news: Larry King. Right? You and Larry dishing the dirt? I'm trying to put them off until you've actually got something to hock. It's a complete waste otherwise. Listen, I'm fielding offers from three publishers for a book deal . . . a roman à clef, tell-all, how-I-overcame-losing-my-identity . . . whatever you want, they don't care, they'll hire a ghostwriter, all you have to do is let them slap your photo on the cover —"

The elevator doors slid open, and taking my arm again, Kelly dragged me quickly toward the waiting ink-black stretch limo, while both the security guards flanked us. We'd barely gone two feet before a half-dozen paparazzi leaped out from the shadows and, shouting Nikki's name, began to snap pictures of me, their long telephoto lenses so close, they would have jabbed me in the eye if the security guards, saying calmly, "All right, guys, let the ladies through," hadn't shoved them out of the way and guided us into the waiting car.

Once we were safely inside the cool leather interior of the limo and the door had been shut behind us and the car was on its way, Kelly went on, as if she hadn't even been interrupted, "Anyway, all of this is great news. If we can time the release of the book so it coincides with the release of the new clothing and beauty lines — sister, you can't PAY for that kind of publicity. And they'll be paying US! Oh, and of course all the usual places want you, the morning news shows and Ellen and Oprah and *The View* and so on. I'm holding them off as best I can, but you're going to have to do one of them —"

I, meanwhile, was collapsed against the seat opposite her, completely stunned by the incident that had just taken place, Cosabella clutched to my chest, her little heart fluttering against mine. I didn't know which had shocked me more — the paparazzi, what Kelly had just said — or the fact that Brandon Stark was sitting across from me, his arms folded in front of his chest. He appeared to be fuming about something, if the curl of his lip was any indication.

"Um," I said, tentatively. "Hi?"

He looked pointedly away. Kelly, meanwhile, continued her rapid-fire speech, which I could barely follow. In her mid- to late thirties, with her bright red hair cut into a pageboy that perfectly framed her pale, expertly made-up face, she seemed as put together as any woman I had ever seen. There wasn't so much as a single snag in her misty black hose, and the heels of her patent leather pumps had to be four inches at least. I had no idea how she walked, let alone how she'd run from the photographers back there.

"I'll admit, Oprah's not exactly your target demographic," Kelly went on. "But it can't hurt. Nemcova did it after that whole tsunami business, if that's how we want to model this. But it doesn't matter because — big news. Are you ready for this? *Sports Illustrated* called."

I could tell by the way she'd said it that I was supposed to react somehow. But I didn't know what to say. I hate *Sports Illustrated*. It's all about . . . well, sports.

"That's great," I said. Wow. This modeling thing was going to be a bit harder than I'd thought. "Right?"

"Nikki!" Kelly looked as if she were about to throw her BlackBerry at me. "You've only been after me for two years to get you *SI*. Well, they finally called. And they want you. For the next swimsuit issue. Could you DIE?"

She accompanied the word *DIE* with a shove to my shoulder. I slumped over onto the seat. What I really wanted to say was, "Actually, yeah. I *could* die. In fact, I already did."

But what I said instead was, "Wow. That's great. Thanks."

Kelly looked at me for a full second. Then she went, "You could summon up a *little* bit more excitement for me, couldn't you? Just a little bit? It's *SI*, honey. There's a chance you could end up on the cover. In fact, I *know* you will. I can feel it in my bones — Brandon, no, no more Red Bull, you're cranky enough."

Brandon slammed the limo's refrigerator door and sank back into his seat, looking churlish.

"So?" Kelly looked at me expectantly. "Aren't you excited?"

"I'm super excited," I said. Though the truth was, all I felt was a growing dread. "So . . . I'm going to have to pose for this in a bathing suit?"

"A bathing suit." Kelly laughed. "God, you really do have amnesia. It's called a swimsuit, honey. Okay? And, oh, my God, *what* have you done to your nails?"

She seized both my hands and sat there looking down in horror at my fingernails. Or I guess I should say Nikki Howard's fingernails, which I'd bitten down almost to the quick.

"I — I guess I bit them a little," I said, in a small voice.

"A little?" The next thing I knew, Kelly had flung my hands

back into my lap and put her headset back on. "Yes, Doreen? Hi, it's Kelly. We're going to need some emergency nail tips. Yes, I know it's last-minute, but what am I supposed to do, I just saw them. Hideous. No, I know she's never had problems before, but we're dealing with a whole new ball game here. You would not believe . . . great. See you then, hon."

Kelly hung up, then looked at me in a very disapproving way. "You're only hurting yourself, Nik," she said to me, shaking her head. "You're only hurting yourself."

Inexplicably, my eyes filled up with tears.

I know! I was crying over fingernails.

"I'm sorry," I said. "I'm really sorry. But I don't understand anything. I thought I was going to a photo shoot. What do my fingernails have to do with anything?"

"You're going to take part in a photo shoot with Mr. Stark," Kelly said sharply. "For a profile *Vanity Fair* is doing on him. You're the face of the new Stark — the young, vibrant Stark — so of course he wants you in the shoot. You and Brandon, of course."

Brandon's scowl had, if anything, only deepened at the sight of my tears.

"But," I said. I couldn't believe I was crying. I really couldn't. I don't cry. I mean, except over important things, like Christopher thinking I'm dead.

This whole time, through this whole thing, I'd never once

cried . . . except about Christopher. Not over the loss of my former body. Not over the loss of my former life. Not even over the loss of my former self.

Because up until that moment, I hadn't felt as if I'd lost my former self.

All it took, apparently, was one publicist yelling at me about my fingernails, however, to make me realize how very, very lost my former self really was.

It wasn't just the fingernails, of course. Part of it was what had happened just before the fingernail abuse. The whole thing where I'd had to say good-bye to my parents, and how I'd left things with my sister, with whom I'd had a little fight — why hadn't I just been supportive about the cheerleader thing? In retrospect, it wasn't that big a deal. Maybe cheerleading *is* a sport. They have gymnastics in the Olympics, after all — and then I'd come out of the hospital and been besieged by photographers, all screaming someone else's name but pointing their cameras at me, and gotten into a limo with a guy who couldn't have been meaner to me and a publicist who seemed to think everything I did and said was wrong. . . .

This photo shoot was going to be a disaster. I could already tell.

"I can't do this," I said, trying to hold back my tears. I didn't mean I couldn't do the Nikki Howard thing. Obviously, I couldn't do that.

And I *definitely* couldn't do *this*, what Kelly wanted me to do. Because suddenly, I'd remembered something. Something really important. And that was Lulu asking me if I knew what a Manolo tip was. And I realized I didn't. I had no idea. Modeling, easy? How could I have been so arrogant? *Why hadn't I read Frida's issues of* CosmoGIRL! *more carefully?*

"I — I don't remember how to do this!" I wailed.

"Well, you better damned well remember how," Kelly said, in a hard voice. "Because your future is riding on it. Not to mention mine . . . and about thirty makeup artists, stylists, art directors, photographers, lighting technicians, and personal assistants, all of whom are waiting for you . . . and that's not including whoever they're bringing in to cater. You better get over whatever it is you're going through, missy. People's jobs are depending on it. We've been plenty patient this past month while you've been going through whatever it is you've been going through, but it's time to get back to work. Brandon, I told you, you leave that Red Bull alone. You know how you get."

"We're here," Brandon said, pointing out the window. "And we've got company."

Kelly turned her head to look out the window. Then she swore and turned on her Stark-brand headset.

"Yeah, Rico?" she barked. "Get security outside of 520 Madison. We've got protesters. *Again.*"

I had no idea what she and Brandon were talking about. The truth was, I didn't really care. I was still trying to absorb what Kelly had just told me. I'd had no idea so many people depended on Nikki Howard for their livelihood. Sure, I'd known it was important to Stark Enterprises that she continue as the Face of Stark.

But I hadn't even begun to comprehend just what that entailed.

Until now.

Two million dollars? That was how much they'd paid for my brain transplant to keep Nikki alive? I was starting to think they'd gotten off cheap. . . .

Then Kelly was saying, "Go. Go, go, go, go," and she was shoving me out of the limo . . .

. . . and into the arms of a waiting security guard, who was trying to shield me from the hordes of protesters gathered in front of the entrance to the massive Madison Avenue skyscraper we'd just pulled up in front of.

"Hey," I heard someone scream. "It's her!"

A second later, my shoulder was seized, and I was spun around to face a woman holding a sign on a stick that said STARK ENTERPRISES KILLS!

"It's NIKKI HOWARD!" The woman — whom I now saw was wearing combat fatigues and a beret — blew a whistle, and all the other protesters surged toward me. The minute they saw me, their faces contorted with anger.

"How do you justify being the public face of an orga-
nization that is putting the small business owner out of
work?" a man in overalls screamed at me, while a woman pushing a baby in a stroller yelled, "You're what's wrong with
America!"

I actually thought this was a little harsh, and not just because
I wasn't who they thought I was. Well, technically.

But I didn't get a chance to tell them this, because the burly
security guard was already hustling me away from the hands
that were reaching out, trying to clutch me. He more or less
barreled through the crowd, using his elbow as a battering ram,
until we ducked through a revolving door, into a vast green
marble lobby, where we were joined a few seconds later by
Brandon Stark and Kelly Foster-Fielding.

"Good Lord," Kelly said, brushing herself off like a cat whose
fur has been ruffled. "They get worse every day."

"Good to see you, Miss Howard," the burly security guard
who'd shielded me from the protesters' wrath said, with a nod
to me. "Been a while."

I smiled at him tremulously, my tears forgotten in my shock
over what had just happened. "Th-thanks . . ."

"Martin," he said to me, with a toothy grin. "You really *did*
lose your memory, just like they said on the news!"

I was about to assure him I really had when Kelly grabbed

my arm and said, "Enough chitchat, people, we're running late as it is. Let's go."

And then I was being dragged toward an elevator. And I realized I was about to meet Mr. Robert Stark himself.

Which was a relief. Because I realized I had a thing or two I wanted to say to him.

SEVENTEEN

EXCEPT THAT I DIDN'T GET TO. SAY WHAT
I wanted to say to Mr. Stark, I mean. At least, not right away.

That's because the minute I stepped off the elevator into
Stark corporate headquarters, a swarm of hair stylists, makeup
artists, and wardrobe assistants descended on me. Kelly snatched
Cosabella away, assuring me she'd look after her for the duration
of the shoot. And then I — not my dog — was the one swept
away for grooming.

At first I didn't know what was happening. All I knew was
that these total strangers were coming up to me and this
one guy kept pulling on my hair and going, "Honey, what happened? They run out of product . . . *on the entire island of
Manhattan?*"

And a woman kept peering into my face and being like, "So . . . we're going for the natural look, are we?"

And this other woman grabbed my hand — this was all as I was being pulled down a hallway — and went, "Yeah, it's as bad as Kelly said. Get the drill file!"

Drill file? And were those *product* and *natural look* remarks of a snarky nature?

They were. Soon I was being berated by Norman for my hair-care technique ("So we fall and bump our heads and lose our memory, and suddenly we don't know how to deep condition anymore?"), as well as my skin-care regimen by Denise ("Honey, what happened to that exfoliant I got you last month? You have to *use* it for it to actually work."), and, of course, my nail-biting ("No! Oh, for the love of God, no. Why would you *do* this? Why, why, why?") by Doreen. It wasn't until Norman gave my hair a bit too hard of a tug that I did something about it. I was, like, "Ow!" and he was, like, "Oh, did the widdle baby get an owie?" with all this fake sympathy, and I went, "Yeah, actually, I did," and I grabbed his hand and ran it along the raised scar at the base of my skull.

After that, he got very quiet . . . and much gentler. I don't know if Norman said something to the others — he must have — because they stopped picking on me, too. They also started explaining to me what they were doing. Like the makeup lady — Denise — told me how it's important to wash your face every night and every morning and to use a gentle astringent to really get out the dirt. Then, if your skin is flaking, to use a moisturizer . . . which of course I've never used before in my life, because my old skin never flaked, it only broke out from too much oil.

But apparently I have *dry* skin now.

And then Norman told me it was probably better not to wash my hair every day . . . that it was easier to style and more manageable if I only washed it two or three times a week. And he gave me some powder I was supposed to sprinkle into my hair every morning and comb through, so it wouldn't ever look greasy.

And Doreen the nail lady applied a paste to each one of my nails that quickly hardened to a fake nail that she filed short, then painted black. Then she went, "Bite them. Go on. Try."

And when I stuck my nail into my mouth, I nearly broke a tooth on it.

"You'll never bite them again," she said, "so long as you wear these. You'll come see me twice a month so I can fill the gaps as they grow."

And then drops were being put into my eyes to get the red out (and I was being gently chastised for crying) while the whole team tried to think of things to tell me that I might have forgotten, like that my skin is too sensitive to wax (like this was actually something that was going to happen), so I have to shave unwanted body hair (including my bikini line, about which Norman said to me, "You have to use a BRAND-NEW RAZOR every time," which, hello, was totally embarrassing. But also incredibly useful, considering what Kelly had told me in the car about the swimsuit issue thing), and that processed foods aggravate acid reflux (like I hadn't noticed), and that (more interestingly) Brandon and I were fully breaking up before my accident because I was sick of him catting around with Mischa behind my back (fortunately, they told me this while Brandon wasn't in the room). None of them seemed to know that Nikki had been catting around behind Brandon's back with her roommate's boyfriend (thank God).

All of this made the time pass very quickly, so I barely noticed my eyelashes were being curled, and my hair flat-ironed, and my toenails painted black to match my new fingernails, and that they were even bleaching my arm hairs (yes).

Then they went, "Okay, off to wardrobe," and I was sent to a (barely) curtained-off area of the room where three tiny girls, each about a foot shorter than me, started taking off my clothes (without even asking!) and making me put on new things . . . things I couldn't even figure out HOW to put on, so it was a good thing they were there, actually, to help.

Then they would look at what I was in and one of them would take a Polaroid and run out of the curtained area and then come back with a yes or no. Finally, they settled on this diaphanous white dress that was so low cut it would barely stay on, and these silver stilettos, and no earrings, and finally I was let out of the curtained area and led down a long, plushly carpeted hallway, past a lot of stylishly dressed people who stared at me — *up* at me, mostly, since I was so tall in my stilettos — and a few of whom said, "Hi, Nikki." I tried to say hi back, but whenever I did, I'd get a shocked look. I guess Nikki wasn't known for being particularly friendly while on a shoot.

Which I could sort of see why, considering how people poked and pulled her.

Then finally, I was led up to a door that had the words ROBERT STARK CEO written on them in silver letters. And the door was thrown open, and I was in Mr. Stark's office at last.

Except that Mr. Stark's office was in total chaos because of the photo shoot. There were power cords running crisscrossed all along the carpet, and giant klieg lights set up all over the place, shining down hotly on everyone, and skinny guys in black shirts and jeans everywhere, and girls in ponytails, wearing fancy glasses, holding cups of latte, and big blackout cloths draped over the floor-to-ceiling windows that must have offered a panoramic view of Manhattan.

And in the center of it all was a huge mahogany desk at which sat Robert Stark in a white shirt unbuttoned about six inches to reveal a lot of gray chest hair. And behind him stood his son, also wearing a white shirt open to reveal his completely hairless chest. Both men looked tanned (thanks, I knew from Denise, to bronzer, which she'd also smeared all over me — and I mean, *all* over . . . there is apparently no room for modesty in modeling) and handsome in the lights. Robert Stark, though, looked impatient, while his son just looked bored.

I was getting ready to go up and introduce myself and ask if we could have a word together in private — because maybe if Mr. Stark met me and saw what I was like, he might reconsider the whole making-my-parents-pay-back-the-two-million-dollars-if-I-didn't-honor-Nikki's-contract-with-Stark arrangement . . . and also might tell me why he'd given Nikki a computer that was loaded with keystroke monitoring software.

But just as I was about to take a step in Mr. Stark's direction, someone grabbed me and wrapped me in a fierce hug.

"There you are!" cried a woman's voice — gravelly, and big, to match the hug. "Oh, my God, I can't believe how long it's been! I wanted to come see you in the hospital but they had those damned family-visitation-only restrictions! *But I'm her agent! I'm family,* I told them. No deal. Well, let me look at you."

I was held at arm's length while a dark-haired middle-aged woman, whippet thin, in a cream-colored skirt suit, examined me from head to foot.

"Gorgeous, as always," she concluded when she was done checking me out. "Couldn't be more gorgeous. Oh, but you don't have the foggiest idea who I am, do you? You really *did* get a bump on the head!"

"Um," I said, glancing past the woman, at Robert Stark, who was complaining to someone about the cuff links on his tuxedo shirt, which appeared to keep coming undone. "You're Rebecca, my agent?"

"That's right, that's right!" She flung her arms around me again. "Rebecca Lowell! Thank God you're all right. If anything had happened to you . . . well, I don't know what I'd have done!"

"Run straight back to that trailer park in the Ozarks to see if she could find someone else to pluck from obscurity," said a man in leather pants with a pencil mustache drily.

"Oh, hush," Rebecca said to the leather-pants man. To me, she said, "I know this is probably all very overwhelming. But you've always been a natural and I know you'll snap back in no time. And speaking of being a natural . . . how excited are you about *SI?* Oh, Nikki, when I heard, my heart . . . well, I just thought I'd cry!"

"Step away from the talent, Rebecca," Pencil Mustache said. "Now that she's here we can finally get to work."

"Oh, I'm sorry, Raoul," Rebecca said, still hanging on to me. "It's just that when I think how close she came to death —"

I wondered how she'd react if I told her her client Nikki really *had* died. Just not legally in the state of New York.

"Yes, well, I'll take good care of her for now, Bec." The man she'd called Raoul took me by the arm and said, "We've met before, Nikki, but you don't remember, I see. Which is a crushing blow from which I doubt I'll soon recover. Never mind. Hop up onto this desk here so Pete can check the lighting —"

Obediently, I hopped up onto the enormous mahogany desk — after first checking to make sure my diaphanous dress was covering everything it was supposed to be covering. Which it wasn't doing the world's best job of. My nipples were kind of showing. . . .

"Yes, yes," Raoul said, totally noticing what I thought I was doing so subtly. "Never mind that now, we've all seen it before. Now roll over and stick your heels in the air — elbows up, chin in your hands — Norman, hair." Norman darted forward to arrange my hair as I let Raoul twist me into a completely uncomfortable — even painful — position on the desk. "Yes, that's better. All right, gentlemen, places."

I couldn't see what was going on behind me, because I was trying to hold my painful pose. But I suppose Mr. Stark and his son went back to their places, since Raoul said, "Good, good. Let's take some Polaroids."

Well, I thought to myself as the photographer, Gwen, started snapping away. *This isn't so bad.* Why had Lulu laughed so much when I asked how hard modeling can be? It's not exactly difficult . . . although my neck kind of hurts. And I think there's some mascara in my eye. And —

"Nikki, Nikki," Raoul said. "Can you try not to look like you're in pain? I know you are, darling, but don't think about it. Think about lovely things, will you? Lovely thoughts, lovely face —"

I realized with horror that I'd been grimacing. I immediately plastered a huge smile onto my face.

"Not quite that lovely, Nikki," Raoul intoned. "This isn't a Sears portrait studio. Relax your mouth. Think dewy . . . Denise, can you make her lips more dewy? There. There. Now, a few more —"

And then Raoul and everyone gathered around to look at the Polaroids as they developed. So I started to sit up. Now, I thought, would be the perfect time to speak to Mr. Stark —

"Nikki, darling," Rebecca called sweetly, from somewhere beyond the circle of white light thrown by the kliegs, so I couldn't see her. "Where do you think you're going?"

"Um," I said. "To change back into my real clothes?"

"The shoot's not over," I heard Brandon say, with a smirk. "It hasn't even begun."

"But . . ." I looked at the dozens of Polaroids now being dropped indifferently to the floor.

"Test shots," Brandon said. "God. What, did you get a little too much wind between your ears riding around on the back of that scrub's scooter?"

I bristled. "For your information, Gabriel Luna is a very hard-working singer-songwriter and *not* a scrub . . . unlike some people I could mention."

Brandon stuck out his chin. "Hey," he said. "For *your* information, I've got several production deals in the works right now . . . not to mention, I'm recording my own album."

Yeah, I wanted to snarl. *With your dad's money.* But I didn't dare, with his father standing right there. Checking his e-mail on his — non-Stark-brand — BlackBerry, but still. He could have been listening.

Knowing what I knew about Nikki's computer, I didn't doubt that he was.

"No bickering, children," Rebecca called from the darkness beyond the desk. "And Raoul will tell you when you can relax, Nikki."

And that's when I began to realize why Lulu had laughed at me when I'd said modeling was easy.

There is nothing easy about it.

Unless you think it's easy trying to look *dewy* and *think lovely thoughts* while twisting your body into the most uncomfortable position possible at the same time you're trying not to mess up your makeup or expose a nipple while wearing five-inch-heel shoes and not notice how incredibly hot your jerk of an ex-boyfriend is.

Because allow me to assure you, it's not.

Especially when you're doing it for the first time, and in somebody else's body.

EIGHTEEN

IT WAS NEARLY TWO HOURS LATER
before Raoul got enough shots he thought he could use. I had to
do a bunch more different poses. Some of them involved me biting into a big red apple. That was fake. And tasted like dirt.

Another pose I had to do involved hanging off Brandon
Stark's shoulders like I was one of those baby rhesus monkeys
clinging to its mother. I said I thought that pose was kind of
misogynistic, because it implied that women are helpless and
need a big strong man to support them.

I mostly just said that because draping myself over Brandon
that way reminded me of how fun kissing him had been and
made me want to kiss him again, which, considering how mad
he was at me about Gabriel — and the fact that I'm crushing

on someone else entirely — didn't seem like it would be the best idea.

Raoul didn't take my advice, anyway, though. And Rebecca took me aside and asked if I had a fever.

"Because normally you know better than to criticize an art director's vision," she said.

I pointed out to her that the media is notorious for infantilizing women in their images of us and asked if it didn't bother her, as a feminist, that she was partly contributing to that.

She looked at me and went, "Are you taking any kind of medication for your head injury? Because if so, they need to up the dosage."

I could sort of see her point. I mean, if I didn't do the pose, they'd just hire some other model to do it as Frida had pointed out.

Still, it was totally embarrassing having to smush my boobs up against Brandon like that. Not that he seemed to mind . . .

That was the problem. My embarrassment aside, I didn't mind much, either.

And I think Brandon started to get over his being mad at me about the whole riding-on-the-back-of-Gabriel-Luna's-Vespa thing, because after about a half hour into my smushing my boobs into his back, he whispered, "Hey. What are you doing after this?"

I was caught totally caught off guard, and asked, "Who? Me?"

"No," Brandon said very sarcastically. "I'm talking to Pete, the lighting guy. Of course you."

"Oh," I said. "I don't know. I guess I'm just going back to the loft. Why?"

"Cool," Brandon said. "Maybe I'll stop by."

I felt myself starting to blush. I didn't know a whole lot about guys, but I knew what *Maybe I'll stop by* meant. Or at least I was pretty sure I did. Considering where my boobs were.

I had a good idea where they'd be later, too. I was positive I wasn't going to be able to stop them from being there. Not if I knew Nikki. Or at least how she got when guys started kissing her. They tossed the word *wanton* around a lot in those romance novels Frida — and, okay, I have to admit, I — liked to read.

Well, *wanton* pretty much summed up how Nikki got whenever a guy stuck his tongue in her mouth.

Okay. *My* mouth.

But what about Christopher? I mean, he was the one I really loved, and I'd never even once managed to get within kissing distance of him. . . .

Oh, God. This was all so confusing.

I tried to think up some excuse as to why Brandon shouldn't stop at the loft later and finally seized upon a perfect one.

"The thing is," I whispered, "I'm going to bed early. I've got school in the morning."

Brandon made a face — until Gwen, the photographer, asked him to please stop.

"*School?* You're kidding me, right?"

"No," I said. "Tribeca Alternative High School. My first day. I want to be nice and well rested. And, well, you know. What with the accident and all . . ."

"I thought the school thing was just a PR stunt," Brandon said.

I jerked my boobs off him in shock. "A *PR* stunt? Who said *that?*"

"Nikki," Gwen called. "Don't move, please! Pete's just adjusting the lighting —"

"Well," Brandon said, "that's what people are saying —"

"Education is necessary for anyone to grow as an individual," I said. "I'm going to school so I can go to college someday, not as a PR stunt." And not just so I can check up on my best friend, whom I happen to be crushing on, and make sure he hasn't found some other girl, either.

"Kelly," Gwen yelled.

"Nikki," Kelly called to me. "Could you get back in your place, please?"

I got back in my place, draped over Brandon's back. But I wasn't happy about it. People were saying Nikki Howard was going to high school as a PR stunt? That was *terrible!* And so untrue! I could see I needed to speak to Brandon's father, now more than ever. He couldn't keep the truth about what had really happened to Nikki to himself now. He just couldn't. It wasn't fair.

But it was really hard to get Mr. Stark's attention, because every time he wasn't posing for the cameras, he was on his (non-Stark-brand) cell phone yelling at someone, or telling one of the many people in the room to get him someone else's phone number or an espresso. Finally, after what seemed like another five hours — my feet were throbbing, and my mouth muscles twitching from smiling so much — Raoul said, "That's a wrap, people! You can all go home!"

And Mr. Stark said, "Thank God," and started taking out his cuff links. I was sitting right on the desk in front of him, so I just went, "Mr. Stark? Can I talk to you a minute?"

And he looked down at me and went, "No."

Seriously! Just like that!

But I'm not a straight-A student — and haven't gotten to level forty-five in *Journeyquest* — for nothing. I mean, I'm no quitter.

And not even a billionaire corporate executive who also runs an underground brain transplant clinic is going to thwart me.

"It's just," I said, in a low voice, as everyone around us was gathering up power cords and taking down the blackout curtains, "don't you think what you're doing is wrong? I mean, about Nikki."

He looked right at me. His eyes, I noticed, were brown, with tiny ruby glints in them. Or maybe that was just the way they looked in the klieg lights, which were being turned off, one by one.

"Don't get me wrong," I went on quickly. "I'm *totally* grateful for what Dr. Holcombe did for me. And I am totally willing to go through with my end of the contract. But don't you think Nikki's friends — her family — deserve to know the truth? So they can mourn her properly? I mean, some people even think she was in rehab last month. How *unfair* is that? I'm sure once they understand your issue with the whole thing, they'll get it. It's just that you can't go around *replacing* one person with a completely different one, you know. It's not right. I know Nikki might have been a model and all, but that doesn't mean she didn't have a unique personality and people who loved her. And I'm not sure you're aware of this, but someone loaded that computer you gave her with keystroke tracking software —"

"JESSICA!" Mr. Stark startled me by yelling.

One of the ponytailed girls in the fancy glasses came scurrying up. "Yes, sir?"

"Jessica, get my coat. Is my reservation at Per Se all set?"

"Yes, sir," Jessica said, trailing after her boss as he strode away from me. "And your car's waiting downstairs —"

It was only then that I realized: *Robert Stark was walking away from me!* He was just walking away from me, as if I hadn't said anything! As if I were just . . . not even there! As if I were just . . . just . . .

An airhead model.

"But — Mr. Stark!" I called after him.

But Robert Stark just kept going, walking out of his office without so much as a second glance at me. I couldn't believe it. I couldn't believe how he'd just walked away like that. The one person I thought could help me — or not even me so much as Nikki — and he'd just completely ignored me, as if I were a fly. Or a busboy.

Or a *girl*.

"Don't even bother," a deep voice behind me advised.

I turned around and found myself looking up at Brandon. Brandon was staring after his father with a look I can only describe as . . . well. Not very friendly.

"He doesn't speak to the talent," Brandon informed me.

I stared at him in confusion. "The talent? You mean . . ."

Me. I'm *the talent*.

"Or to me," Brandon added bitterly, "if he can help it. He's much too busy and important."

"But." I shook my head, not sure I understood. "He's your *dad*. Of course he can't be too busy for you."

Brandon gave me a strange look. Then he said, "You really *do* have amnesia, don't you?"

And with that, he turned around and walked away before I could say another word.

I was on my way back to the changing area to slip into my own clothes when I ran into Rebecca and Kelly.

"Darling, you were fabulous!" Rebecca cried.

"I wasn't," I said to her. My neck still throbbed from the way Raoul had made me arch it. "I didn't know what I was doing. And Mr. Stark hates me." Although, truthfully, I wasn't sure that was such a bad thing. . . .

"So you're a little rusty," Rebecca said, with a shrug. "You hit your head! We should all look so good after a concussion. And Bob Stark hates everybody. Uh, this is ringing —" She held out the cell phone my mom had given to me. It was flashing my home number. My mom was calling, no doubt about dinner. I realized I hadn't followed her directions and called as soon as I'd gotten to the photo shoot.

I let it go to voice mail. "I'll call her back," I said. I didn't think I could handle my mom and all her questions and concerns just then.

"Great," Rebecca said. "Now, Kelly and I want to take you out for dinner to celebrate the *SI* gig. We got your favorite table at Nobu. We'll make it a ladies' night . . . unless Brandon wants to come?"

I glanced over my shoulder at Brandon, who was already on his way to the elevators.

"Uh, Brandon's got other plans," I said. "And actually, I'm really tired. I think I'm just going to head back to the loft and crash, if that's okay. I mean, I just got out of the hospital this morning, and I've got school in the morning —"

"Say no more," Rebecca said, with a smile. "We'll do it another time. Tomorrow afternoon, after the *Elle* shoot, perhaps."

"Tomorrow?" I stared at her. "We have a shoot tomorrow?"

"Honey, you are booked solid all this week," Kelly said, thrusting Cosabella into my arms. "You are on fire, you're so hot right now. Are you sure you don't want to reconsider this going back to school thing? Because it's really cutting into your availability —"

"No," I said. "I mean, yes. I mean, I have to go to school." I *wanted* to. How else was I going to find out if Christopher was still unattached? Oh, and get an education?

Kelly shook her head. "This school thing's gonna kill me," she grumbled. And a second later, she was barking into her headset, "No! I told you! She's not available until after three P.M. What part of three P.M. did you not understand?"

"Well, I think it's great," Rebecca said to me. "Christy Turlington ended up studying comparative religion and Eastern philosophy at NYU, you know. If she can do it, you can.

Although, how smart could she be if she thought Fashion Café would ever take off?"

"Um," I said, because I had no idea what she was talking about. "I should go. . . ."

"Of course you should." Rebecca took me by the arm and started steering me back to the changing area. "Girls! Nikki has to go!"

And like magic, a few seconds later, I had been stripped of my ethereal dress and stilettos and was back in my own clothes, in a limo headed back downtown — by myself, this time. And in my lap — besides Cosabella — was something Rebecca had handed me on my way out.

"Oh," she'd said. "Here. I've been meaning to give you this."

And she passed me a bronze leather tote marked PRADA that caused my shoulder to sag, it was so heavy.

"What's this?" I'd asked curiously.

"Hon," Rebecca said, with a laugh, "it's your purse! You dropped it the day of the accident. I've been holding it for you. Your life is in there. Your Sidekick, your cell phone, your credit cards . . . hold on to it this time, all right, honey?"

Now, in the limo, I dumped the contents of Nikki Howard's purse into my lap and marveled at what I found there.

I'd suspected before. But now I knew for sure.

I was rich.

Nikki Howard had a platinum American Express card, two gold Visas, a gold MasterCard, a platinum Chase bank card for quick ATM withdrawals, tons of cash (four hundred and twenty-seven dollars' worth), and a bank statement that said she had three hundred thousand, sixty-six hundred, thirty-two dollars, and eleven cents in her savings account, and twenty-two thousand dollars in her checking account.

And that was just what was in her bank accounts. Who knew what she had invested? Because I found a business card for a Goldman Sachs investment adviser that was tattered and looked well used.

I was freaking loaded. Not enough to buy myself out of my Stark contract. But I could help my parents out if they ran into problems. This was *awesome*.

The first thing I did (after admiring Nikki's neatly balanced checkbook) was check out her cell phone. But, like the one my mom had given me, it was Stark-brand. Same thing for the P.D.A. The batteries of both were dead from having gone without charging for so long, so it wasn't like I could turn them on to check (and even if I had, I'd have been unable to tell. Only the Commander would have been able to know for sure). But I suspected they, like Nikki's laptop, might have been tapped.

Maybe I was just being paranoid. But waking up in someone else's body can do that to a girl.

The rest of Nikki's purse seemed to contain only makeup and half-empty containers of acid reflux medication. But it was comforting to know I had some money, at least. All I wanted to do when I got to the loft was order some takeout for dinner (which I could now pay for — and I didn't feel guilty about using Nikki's money, because after that photo shoot, I felt like I'd earned it), strip off my clothes, take a long, hot bath, maybe watch some TV, and go to bed.

And now I could pay the delivery guy. And pick up a bagel or whatever for breakfast on my way to school in the morning.

But when I arrived at the loft five minutes later, I saw my plan for a quiet dinner and a nice bubble bath in Nikki's Jacuzzi go down the drain . . . pretty much literally. Because when the elevator doors opened to let me and Cosabella out into Nikki's place, a dozen people — including Lulu and Brandon — yelled, "Welcome home, Nikki!," threw streamers, popped champagne corks, and rushed to hug me.

Yeah. I was surprised, all right. Especially since the person hugging me the hardest turned out to be Justin Bay.

✳ NINETEEN

WE WERE AT A CLUB CALLED CAVE. IT was called Cave because it was in the bowels of New York City, in a part of the subway system that the city had planned and then abandoned due to lack of funds nearly a century earlier. Someone had installed spotlights along the rock walls in strategic places, strung a sound system through it, put a couple DJs in place, and now it was the hottest dance spot in Manhattan. There was a line out the door that went halfway around the block, even on a Wednesday night. You couldn't get in unless you were somebody.

Nikki Howard, it turned out, was somebody. Even though she was only seventeen and not legally allowed into bars.

But it was all right, because Nikki didn't drink. I found this out from the bartender when I wearily approached the bar, parched from so much dancing, and he said, "Hey, Nikki, long time no see. The usual?"

"I have amnesia," I said. It seemed to me I'd been saying this to people all night long as they approached me and cried, *Nikki, it's me! Don't you remember me? It's Joey/Jimmy/Johnny/Jan from Paris/Denmark/East Hampton/Los Angeles!* "Didn't you hear? I don't know what the usual is."

The bartender took a long-stemmed cocktail glass, filled it with water, added a curled piece of orange peel, then slid it toward me. If you didn't know it was just water, it looked exactly like a martini, only with orange peel instead of an olive.

"We call it the Nikki," he said, with a wink. "Only the bartenders in town know it's just water. You can't drink alcohol because of your stomach problems, remember? And because you're not twenty-one, of course," he added piously.

I grinned. I was kind of starting not to be so annoyed with Nikki Howard . . . something I wouldn't have thought earlier in the day.

"Thanks," I said gratefully, and sipped Nikki's signature drink while I surveyed the dance floor. I couldn't believe it was so late — nearly two in the morning — and the club was still so crowded (and only getting more and more crowded) on a weeknight. Of course, I had never been to a place like this before.

Maybe they were always like this. Here at the bar there was barely a seat available. I had only gotten mine because a gallant fan had surrendered his (in exchange for an autograph, of course. The first time someone had asked, I had almost written Em Watts, but changed it to Nikki Howard at the last minute. I'd been so swamped by autograph seekers all night, I'd actually gotten almost used to it).

Out on the dance floor, bodies were gyrating to hypnotic techno, and different colored flashes of lights and thick clouds of dry ice made it impossible to tell who was who. I knew Lulu was out there somewhere, along with both Brandon and Justin and a ton more of Nikki Howard's "best" friends (she'd collected more and more as the evening wore on). We had begun the evening at the loft, then moved on to a boisterous dinner at one of Bobby Flay's restaurants (and the Food Network chef had actually been there and come over to our table to wish me — I mean, Nikki — a speedy recovery from my amnesia), then ended up at Cave.

Lulu had been so excited about the surprise party she'd thrown together for me, I hadn't had the heart to tell her I wasn't exactly in the mood for a party. I'd tried to go along with the whole thing, even letting her drag me off into Nikki's closet and choose an outfit for me to wear for the evening.

Which was why I was sitting at one of the many bars in Cave in black spike-heel ankle boots, a low-cut black top, and a gold lamé miniskirt. I looked just like a hooker I'd seen once down on the West Side Highway. Though I hadn't wanted to hurt Lulu's feelings by saying so. Especially since the hooker had been a man.

"Aren't you having *fun?*" Lulu bounded up from out of the dry ice smoke to ask me suddenly. She was in a contrasting outfit of gold lamé ankle boots and top and black skirt. She'd teased both of our hair to stand about five inches out from our heads. She was calling it Eighties Night.

The only problem was, we were the only two in the entire club in eighties attire.

"I sure am," I told her. Then I added, "But, you know, I have to go home soon, Lulu, because I have school in the morning."

Lulu's tiny mouth popped open like a baby bird's.

"Oh, my God," she cried, "I forgot! That's right, you're doing that school thing. You must, like, totally hate me."

"I don't," I assured her. The truth was, out of all the people I'd met since waking up in Nikki Howard's body, she was my favorite. Brandon was still acting angry with me over Gabriel, and Justin, of course, was giving me the cold shoulder because Lulu was around (for which I was grateful. I didn't want to talk to him, anyway). I didn't know who the other people were — Lulu had introduced them, but their names and how Nikki was supposed to know them had gone right over my head. None of them had turned out to be having secret affairs with me (or rather, Nikki), much to my relief. . . .

But while they all seemed pleasant enough, they just kept talking about people I didn't know, and I mostly just felt left out and . . . well, pretty lonely, despite all the autograph seekers (and the fact that my mom kept calling, even though I was still sending her calls to voice mail. Why did she have to be so clingy? I was sixteen and a half, I could take care of myself) and people who evidently knew and adored Nikki Howard, who kept coming up and gushing over her.

Being adored was great. It really was.

But it had been a long day, and I just wanted to go back to the loft and get some sleep.

Was that so wrong?

"What's up with this school thing, anyway?" Lulu wanted to know, smiling flirtatiously at a guy who surrendered his barstool for her — seriously, it was amazing what guys would do for a pretty girl. It was a whole different world, being gorgeous, a world with which I was entirely unfamiliar — then hopping onto it and signaling the bartender for a drink. "I mean, why do you want to go to school so badly?"

"Because," I said. No way was I telling her about Christopher, and I decided it would be wiser to keep my mouth shut about Frida, too. "I want to go to college someday."

"College?" Lulu made a face. "What for?"

"So I can get a job," I said. "Teaching, probably. Both my parents are professors, and I'd like to be one, too." Then, realizing what I'd said, I blanched. "I mean —"

But Lulu just waved my statement aside. She was still convinced her spirit transfer explanation, not my amnesia story, was the correct one for Nikki Howard's bizarre recent behavior.

"'Teaching what?" The bartender had brought her a drink without her even specifying what she wanted. Lulu's signature drink was something yellowish that had green leaves floating in it and some crystals all along the rim. When I tasted one that had fallen on the bar, I found that it was sugar.

"I'm not sure," I said. "I like a lot of subjects. That's another reason why I want to stay in school. To figure it out." Then I had an idea. "Hey, you should come with me!"

Lulu nearly choked on her drink. "Wh-what?"

"You should," I said, getting excited by the idea. "I'm sure your dad could get you in. He's super famous. TAHS would be excited to have you. Come with me tomorrow!"

Lulu made another face. "Um . . . thanks, but no, thanks."

I shook my head. "Lulu," I said, "you're only seventeen. You should be in school. You shouldn't even be living by yourself. Why *do* you live alone, anyway?"

She looked up at me, her elfin face twisted with confusion.

"I don't live alone," Lulu said. "I live with you."

"I know," I said. "But I mean, why don't you live with your parents?"

"Because my mom took off with my snowboard instructor and wants nothing to do with me, silly," Lulu said cheerfully, "and my dad's new wife is five years older than I am. How stoked would *you* be to live at home in that situation?"

And with that, she polished off her drink, jumped off the stool, and jetted back off to the dance floor, leaving me alone at the bar.

Only not for long, because a second later, Justin Bay slithered onto the stool she'd vacated and went, "So you honestly expect me to believe you don't remember anything — *anything* — about us . . . and Paris?"

I looked at the bartender, and he slid another Nikki special toward me.

"You shouldn't be talking to me," I said to Justin. "You're Lulu's boyfriend. And no, I don't remember anything. That's what the word *amnesia* means. Memory loss. It's Greek for forgetfulness."

"Oooh," Justin said, wrapping his arm around my waist and leaning his face down to nuzzle my neck. "One bang on the head, and you're Miss Smarty-Pants, aren't you? And you know good and well that I can trigger your memory, if anyone can. . . ."

It was amazing. My body's reaction to his warm lips on my neck was instantaneous. I felt like an electric current went up and down my spine. Only it was not unpleasant.

The thing was, Lulu was dancing not twenty feet away.

What happened next was as instantaneous as the reaction of my skin to his lips.

And that was that I dumped the contents of the cocktail glass the bartender had just slid toward me onto Justin's head.

All the people around us hooted with surprise as Justin sputtered and leaped off the barstool. To say he seemed startled would be an understatement. He looked completely horrified — the more so when he licked his dripping lips.

"You're drinking *water?*" he cried.

"It's called a Nikki," I said grandly, slipping off my barstool. "I don't do alcohol. Or other people's boyfriends. And don't you forget it."

I stalked away to the sound of applause.

I found Lulu dancing with three other girls, all of whom were dressed in the height of eighties chic as well. It was if she'd sent out some secret coded message before we'd even left the loft. Here I was, one of the world's hottest supermodels, and I still didn't get how girls did that. Figured out what to wear, I mean.

"Lulu," I shouted at her, to be heard over the incredibly loud music. "I'm going home. You can stay if you want, but I just wanted you to know I'm leaving."

Lulu stopped dancing and stared at me.

"No," she said, shaking her wild-looking hair. "We *never* leave without the other person. If you're leaving, I'm leaving, too. Let me just go tell Justin."

"Uh," I yelled. "Justin's kind of . . . mad right now."

"Oh," Lulu said, comprehension dawning instantly. "Has he been hitting on you?"

Now it was my turn to stare. "You *knew*?"

Lulu rolled her huge eyes. "Duh. I know Nikki has a problem saying no to boys when they start kissing her . . . and also that boys have a problem saying no to kissing Nikki. But I thought that first part might have been cleared up by the spirit transfer."

"Well, I said no," I said, uncomfortably. "And now he's mad."

I felt absurd standing there on the dance floor, having this conversation . . . especially since some guy who was wearing a ton of gold chains and very big pants that showed off a lot of his underwear danced up and started grinding on me.

"Aren't you Nikki Howard?" he asked me.

"No," I said to him. Then I turned back to Lulu. "You mean, you knew this whole time?"

"I suspected," Lulu said, with a shrug. "But look, it's not like Justin and I ever had this big love connection. He just always gives me really nice presents whenever he hooks up with someone else. And ever since you got back from the shows in Paris, there've been a lot of really nice presents."

"I'm so sorry," I said, meaning it. I felt terrible. Even though it wasn't my fault. It was Nikki's.

And I wasn't Nikki. Or at least, I hadn't been at the time she'd done the terrible things that had hurt Lulu.

"You are too Nikki Howard," Big Pants insisted, dancing up on me again. "Damn, girl! You are one fine piece —"

I turned, placed my hand in the center of his chest as he ground his pelvis against my leg, and pushed him down.

"It's all right," Lulu said, stepping neatly over Big Pants as he sprawled across the dance floor. "You really can't help it. It's like you're powerless over kissing. Anyway, if we're leaving, we should probably get Brandon. Last time I saw him he was — oh, there he is. See, this isn't good."

Lulu pointed. Brandon was in the DJ's booth, arguing with the DJ about something.

"I'll get him," I said, and hurried over just in time to hear Brandon saying, "You never want to play *my* songs, man. Why is that?"

The DJ's reply was calm but brutal. "Because your songs suck."

Brandon pulled back his arm as if he were going to punch the DJ in the face. I flung myself forward and grabbed his arm, throwing all my body weight onto it so that he staggered backward with me.

"What're you doing?" he demanded, his words drunkenly

slurred. "Did you hear what this guy just said? I'm gonna take him out."

"No, you're not," I assured him. "We have to go now."

"I can't go now," Brandon said, trying to shake me off. "I gotta kill this guy first."

"No," I said, digging my stiletto heels into the grout of the tiled floor to keep him from moving forward. "Brandon, you can't. We gotta go. The limo's waiting for us —"

"Good," Brandon said, dragging me inexorably forward. "I'll be there in a minute. Soon as I've killed this guy."

Not knowing what else to do — but knowing I had to distract him somehow — I gave a sort of leap, keeping one arm wrapped around Brandon's arm and throwing the other around his neck, and clamped my mouth over his.

As I'd hoped, Brandon's reflexes weren't too badly affected by alcohol for him not to catch me the moment I leaped into his arms. And he became too preoccupied with kissing me to remember his animosity toward the DJ. Kissing really is wonderful that way. I almost forgot myself that I was doing it just to get Brandon to quit wanting to fight . . .

. . . until, that is, someone standing close by cleared his throat, and I dragged my lips away from Brandon's and saw Gabriel Luna standing there staring at us, holding a CD in his hand and looking vaguely bemused.

"Oh," I said, color rushing into my face. I was, after all, being held in the air by Brandon Stark. Although at least this time he hadn't slung me over his shoulder, firefighter style, like when he'd stuffed me into the limo the night he and Lulu kidnapped me. "Hi."

"Uh," Gabriel said. "Hello. Everything all right?"

"Oh," I said, trying to sound breezy. "Yes. We were just leaving. Brandon, you can put me down now."

"No," Brandon said sullenly as he stared at Gabriel, apparently recognizing him from the grainy photo of the two of us on Gabriel's Vespa that had been all over the place the day before.

"Ha." I gave a nervous laugh and tried to smile my dewiest at Gabriel. "He's kidding. Put me down now, Brandon."

"No," Brandon said again.

I closed my eyes briefly, praying there wouldn't now be a fight between Gabriel and Brandon.

But I needn't have worried. Because of course Gabriel doesn't like me that way, considering the fact that he thinks Nikki Howard is a recovering addict and all. When I opened my eyes again, he was still gazing at me with that same bemused expression.

And Lulu had come up behind him and was scowling.

"God, what is taking so long?" she demanded, in a surprisingly loud voice. She looked like a five-foot-tall angry general. "The car's waiting, you guys. Move it or lose it!"

Obediently, Brandon followed her, not seeming to notice that he was still carrying me. Not knowing what else to do, I waved good-bye to Gabriel from over Brandon's broad shoulder. Gabriel waved back — then seemed to catch himself and lowered his hand, looking around as several people standing nearby cried, "Oh, my God — that's Nikki Howard!" One or two rushed up to ask for my autograph, but Brandon just grunted and kept walking, not pausing even for a moment.

Being carried out of the hottest dance club in Manhattan at two in the morning by Nikki Howard's on-again, off-again boyfriend wasn't too embarrassing. Especially when we encountered about nine thousand paparazzi on the sidewalk between the front of the club and the waiting doors of our limo. That was especially nice. I mean, not.

"Great," I said, after Brandon had dumped me inside the car and I'd straightened out my skirt, which had hiked up past my hips. "You know what that looked like, right?"

"What?" Lulu asked blearily, as she reapplied her lip gloss.

"Like I was too drunk to walk and Brandon was carrying me out of there."

"So?" Lulu admired her own reflection in the Swarovski crystal–encrusted compact she was holding. "You didn't know any better than to drink too much. You forgot. You have amnesia. Remember? God, that's the perfect excuse for everything."

She looked up from the compact. "Oh, no, wait . . . how could you remember that? You have amnesia."

Brandon, who'd piled into the limo after us, chose that moment to collapse on top of me.

"Your place or mine?" he asked my stomach.

"Oh, my God, get *off*," I said, giving him a shove. "I'm not going to your place, and you're not staying at mine. I don't even like you that way. I only kissed you to keep you from getting your face smashed in by that DJ. You're in no condition to be fighting anyone."

"You're nice," he said, not moving an inch and, in fact, snuggling more deeply into my lap. "You're much nicer than you used to be, before you hit your head and scrambled your brains. You were so *mean* before. Remember, Lulu? When Nikki was so *mean* all the time?"

Lulu snapped open her purse and put her lip gloss away, cocking her head to study me thoughtfully. "She *is* a lot less bitchy," she said. "It must be because of the spirit transfer."

"I don't care why it is," Brandon said, sighing happily as he hugged my belly. "I'm just glad she's back. And so much *nicer*." A few seconds later, he let out a gentle snore.

I threw Lulu a helpless look, like, *What am I supposed to do* now?

"Just push him off when we get home," she said, with a shrug of her razor-sharp shoulder blades. "He won't wake up. Tom'll take him back to his place on Charles Street. It's not like he'll remember any of this tomorrow. He never does."

"He does this a lot?" I asked, glancing down at Brandon's handsome, peacefully dozing face.

Lulu looked at me blankly. "He likes to party," she said.

I could see that she had no idea what I was talking about — also that she was beginning to nod off herself, every bit as tired as I was. I was going to have to get to the bottom of the Brandon problem someday soon, I knew.

But not tonight. Tonight, I just wanted to go to bed.

Which I did, the minute we got home, carefully setting Nikki's alarm for seven o'clock — giving me a grand total of four hours' sleep — so I could get to school on time.

Well, I guess no one had said it was going to be easy, this balancing high school with a full-time modeling career. I had no idea how I was going to pull it off.

All I knew was that I had to, if I was going to establish any kind of normalcy in my new life.

Normalcy. When I had Nikki Howard's face and Emerson Watts's brain. Right. Because that had been working out just great so far.

TWENTY

I COULD SEE THAT THE WALKING DEAD
were in fine form when the cab I'd been lucky to snag let me
off in front of TAHS the next morning. They were all leaning up against the chain-link fence around the construction
site across the street (because why have a high school if it isn't
across the street from a former thread factory they've imploded
to make room for more condos, so you can listen to the *beep,
beep, beep* of trucks backing up all day?), text messaging one
another.

All but Whitney Robertson and Jason Klein. They were
making out.

I felt some throw up come into my mouth, just looking
at them.

But it might have been the Danish I'd snagged at the deli near the loft and made the mistake of trying to eat for breakfast. It turns out Nikki Howard's digestive system and Danish? Not so much.

I just hadn't had time to make myself a decent breakfast. I hardly believed it when the alarm went off. It seemed like I'd only just closed my eyes, and it was time to wake up again. I wanted to die when I saw what time it was. One thing I knew for sure — no more going out on a school night. Not for me.

And then, as I'd lain there, staring at Nikki Howard's plain white walls — a housekeeper or someone must have come to clean, because Gabriel's roses were gone. I guess they'd finally wilted and died — with Cosabella licking my face, eager for breakfast and a walk, it had occurred to me that I didn't *have* to go. Really. No one was making me. Nikki Howard was an emancipated minor. She didn't have to go to school if she didn't want to. I could roll over and go right back to sleep — lovely, delicious sleep. The limo wasn't coming to pick me up for the *Elle* shoot until three. I could stay in bed all day if I wanted to.

It was tempting. So tempting. Especially because I'd been too wired to go right to sleep when I'd gotten home last night and, after listening to Mom's messages — seven of them, each one more aggravated than the last — had finally gone to Lulu's room and checked her laptop while she slept and found that hers, too, had the same keystroke tracking software on it that Nikki's had.

I'd disconnected the modems to both and found the keyboards worked perfectly when I plugged them back into the modems again.

It was true I still had only a Stark-brand PC . . . but once it was functioning without spyware, who needed school? I'd have to set up a whole new online identity for Nikki, since I knew my parents had canceled my old ones (too much temptation, they'd told me, especially since I was supposed to be dead). But it was going to be so good to be online again! I could play *Journeyquest* and IM Christopher —

Oh, no, wait. I couldn't. Because how would Nikki Howard know Christopher Maloney? In order for her to get to know him, she was going to have to go to school today. . . .

Which, I will admit, is the only thing that sent me stumbling out of bed, grabbing blindly for clothes, pulling on the first things my fingers came into contact with, which turned out to be some kind of high-waisted dress I was supposed to wear over black leggings with these cowboy boots and a lot of long necklaces (Lulu had laid them out for me last night, giggling about how I needed to look good on my first day of school).

The ensemble actually turned out to be surprisingly comfortable. I mean, for something that wasn't a T-shirt and jeans.

And after I'd brushed my teeth and washed my face and run a brush through my hair (careful of my still-tender surgery scar), I noticed in the mirror that . . . I actually looked kind of good.

Who knew you could look good and actually *feel* good at the same time? I mean, obviously, you always feel good in sweats. But hardly anyone *looks* good in them (at least, according to Frida). Not that I have ever let that stop me from wearing them to school, except on the occasions Frida spotted me and made me turn around and change into something else.

But when she didn't, the Walking Dead would often stop and stare at me, because I so didn't match their uniform of pressed khakis and collared shirt . . . never a drawstring at the waist!

Maybe that had something to do with why, when I got out of the cab and started heading up the steps for the main office, every single person loitering in front of the school stopped what they were doing and simply . . . stared at me.

Then I heard the whispered words *Nikki Howard* and remembered that it wasn't me, Em Watts, they were staring at, or the fact that I was wearing a non–standard issue Walking Dead uniform, but the fact that I was actually wearing a celebrity's body.

Oh, yeah. That's right.

A second later, I saw one of them detach itself from the nest and slink over. It took a second for me to register that it was my sister, Frida. That's how much she'd been assimilated to resemble all the others.

"Uh, Nikki?" she said, pretending like she didn't know it was actually me.

I stopped in my tracks and stared at her. That's because she was wearing a red-and-gold TAHS cheerleading uniform.

And looked totally adorable in it.

"Did you change into that when you got here?" I blurted. It was the first thing that popped into my head. Fortunately, we were far enough from everyone that there was no way anyone could overhear us. "Because Mom would never have let you out of the house in that. Does she even know you made the squad?"

"I changed when I got here," Frida said impatiently. "And no. And you're supposed to act like you don't know me."

"I *don't* know you," I said, taking in the short pleated skirt. "But . . . it looks . . . it looks . . ."

"Don't even say it, Em," Frida said, her eyes narrowing.

". . . cute."

Frida's jaw sagged. "Wait . . . did you just say what I think you said?"

"I think Nikki is catching or something," I said, shaking my head. "I'm starting to like all kinds of things I used to hate."

"Like Brandon Stark?" Frida wanted to know. "Because there was a picture of you on TMZ this morning being carried out of Cave last night by him. Also one that showed you with your legs spread apart as you fell into the limo, and you could see your —"

My blood went cold. "Mom didn't see it, did she?"

"Like she checks Perez Hilton first thing in the morning. She's too busy trying to call you. Are you *ever* going to answer that cell phone she gave you? All I can say is, good thing you were wearing panties. Oh, my God," Frida said to me, under her breath. "Don't look now, but, like, *everyone* is checking you out. They're *all* staring — I said, DON'T LOOK. But they're all looking. They're — hey. Where did you get those necklaces?"

"I don't know," I said. "They're Nikki's. I think they're from her Stark clothing line. I can get you some, I think —"

"That'd be awesome. Just look at them," she said with relish, glancing back at Whitney and the other dead-eyed wannabes. "They're trying to figure out what I'm doing talking to you. I said, DON'T LOOK." Then she added, "Oh, my God, Whitney is looking over here. WHITNEY ROBERTSON IS LOOK-ING OVER HERE — this is amazing. Whitney Robertson is actually looking at me. ME. She's never looked at me before, ever. This is the best day of my life."

"Yeah, well," I said, brushing by Frida to head to the doors of the school, so I could get to the administration office. "Welcome to Nikki Howard's world, Frida. Good to know someone appreciates it."

As I slipped through the doors I glanced over my shoulder and saw about thirty people rush up to Frida, all clamoring to know what she and I had talked about. Frida played it cool, shrugging and playing with her hair.

But it was clear she was in heaven.

Too bad that, for her to get that way, I was going to have to go through hell.

They assigned me my old locker.

I should have known that they would, of course. It's not like anyone else had dropped out midsemester.

So it wasn't any wonder that I ended up with my old locker . . . and in many — though not all — of my old classes.

There was apparently some concern that Nikki Howard wouldn't be able to keep up in the AP courses Em Watts had originally been enrolled in . . . especially in light of her alleged amnesia. I had to do some fast talking back in the admin office but did manage to get Nikki Howard enrolled in AP English, Bio, and Trig (I assured them that if I couldn't keep up with any of my classes, I'd drop out of them).

Of course, having missed a month's worth of school, there was a very good likelihood I actually wouldn't be able to catch up . . . but I was willing to try, if it meant I could be in some classes, at least, with Christopher. How else was I going to strike up a friendship with him?

It was weird pretending I didn't know my combination so that my student guide, this freshman I'd never met before, wouldn't think I had ESP or something.

The freshman, Molly Hung, was totally freaking out over the fact that she was showing Nikki Howard around her school. She was really shy, and I saw her fingers shaking as she showed me how to spin the combination lock. After she'd let me try the combo myself a few times to get used to it — and after I'd pulled the locker open and seen, to my dismay, that all my stuff was gone (although, of course, I should have expected that) — she finally worked up the courage to ask a question.

"Do you really go out with Brandon Stark?" she wanted to know. "B-because I saw a picture of you with him once . . ."

"Uh," I said. "Yeah. I mean, we're kind of keeping it casual. I had, um, an accident, and I —"

"Oh!" Molly flung a hand up over her mouth and looked horrified. "Right! I forgot! You can't remember. I'm so sorry! Really. God, I'm so stupid."

"It's okay," I told her. "Don't worry about it."

But she went around looking like she wanted to kill herself, anyway.

She walked me to my first-period class — I'd been lucky enough (sarcasm) to get back into Public Speaking — and, at the door, she said, "Um . . . I know how hard it must be, starting at a new school where you don't know anyone. So if you want to sit with me at lunch, that — that would be cool with me."

"Uh," I said. I hadn't even thought about the crucial lunch-seating situation. Whom would *I* be sitting with, anyway? I had just assumed I'd sit with Frida, but I realized now that would be absurd. Why would Nikki Howard sit with some girl with whom she'd had a casual conversation on the steps in front of the school? The truth was, Nikki Howard would probably go out to lunch, anyway.

Oh, who was I kidding? Nikki Howard would never have been in a regular high school in the first place. Except as some stunt for a reality show.

"Thanks," I said to Molly. "If I have lunch in the caf, I'll try to look for you."

"Well, have a good class," Molly said, blushing with pleasure. "And if you need me, here's my cell. Call me for anything. ANYTHING. Okay?"

"Okay," I said, and smiled at her.

To my surprise, Molly blushed even harder. Then she hurried away giggling and looking really . . . well, pleased is the only way I can describe it.

Can I just say it's totally weird to smile at someone and have them seem so excited about it? After all, it was just a smile. No one *ever* used to react like that when I smiled at them back in my old body. But in Nikki's body, when I smile, everyone practically seems to have a heart attack.

Except Brandon's dad.

And I knew things were only going to get weirder when I walked into Public Speaking — late, thanks to all the forms I'd had to fill out in the office and the fact that I didn't know stuff like Nikki Howard's Social Security number. Every time someone asked me for it, I had to look it up (I'd remembered to charge her Sidekick), but that was okay, though, because I was supposed to have lost my memory anyway.

I walked into Public Speaking, interrupting an oral presentation McKayla Donofrio was giving on the importance of reading to your children. She stopped dead when she saw me and just stared. Soon the rest of the class woke up and did the same thing. It took a second or two for Mr. Greer to notice no one was talking and to open his own eyes and see me standing there.

"Oh," he said, pretending he'd been awake the whole time. "Right. They told me to expect you. Nikki Howard, right?"

"Right," I said, holding out my late pass and admission slip. "Hi."

"Great, great," Mr. Greer said, taking both slips and not even looking at them. "Class, this is Nikki Howard, she's a new student who'll be joining us for the rest of the semester. Nikki, grab an empty seat . . . I think there's one over there. . . ."

He pointed to my old seat. Of course.

I went toward it, my head ducked, pretending I couldn't hear all the whispers as I slid into my old seat. Christopher, I'd noticed, when I'd risked a glance at him, was awake for once.

And that wasn't the only thing about him that had changed.

He'd cut his hair.

I didn't mean to suddenly stagger to a standstill and stare at this guy who was supposed to be a stranger to me, but it was pretty hard not to, since I hadn't — ever — seen Christopher with hair above his neck. Gone was the long blond curtain that had swept past his shoulders for as long as I could remember — certainly since middle school and all through high school. He now wore his hair in a cut indistinguishable from Whitney Robertson's boyfriend's, Jason Klein. In fact, if I'd just glanced in Christopher's direction, I might even have mistaken him for Jason Klein, that's how close the resemblance was now. There was nothing at all to tell him apart from the rest of the Walking Dead. He was even wearing what appeared to be a pale green *Polo* shirt with his jeans.

What had *happened?* I know it must have been upsetting and all, watching me die (sort of) right in front of him, and going to my memorial service, and all of that.

But upsetting enough to have turned him *preppie*?

"So, Nikki, just to get you up to speed," Mr. Greer said, startling me from my full-on openmouthed astonishment, "we're doing five-minute persuasive arguments on a topic of the student's choice. I won't expect you to have anything ready for this week, but if you feel up to it, you can try next week."

"Okay," I said quickly, tearing my gaze from Christopher and sliding into my seat. I automatically flipped open my brand-new notebook — anything to take my mind off what had happened to Christopher — and stared blindly straight ahead.

But it was really hard to concentrate on what McKayla was saying. I couldn't stop thinking about Christopher and his hair, even though, now that my back was to him, I couldn't see him anymore.

What had happened to him? Had the Walking Dead assimilated him, just like they had my little sister? How could this have happened in such a short time? I realize I'd been gone a month, but still! How could he have cut his hair like that? He'd resisted the Commander for so long —

And then I died, and bang . . . resistance was suddenly futile? No! No, that was just so wrong!

Not that his haircut looked bad. Quite the opposite, actually. Even Frida would have to admit Christopher looked good.

Really good. This was an alarming development I wished she'd warned me about. Supposing Christopher, now that he had this new look, was actually attracting female attention? I mean, besides mine.

No. It wasn't possible. The only female attention Christopher had ever attracted before was mine, and he hadn't even been aware of it (or at least, that I'd been female).

But he looked really, really good now. I mean, I always thought he looked good. But now *everyone* had to have noticed how good he looked. What if he was going out with someone? Oh, why hadn't I thought to ask Frida what was going on with him, romantically? A lot can happen in a month — obviously. I mean, look at me. Talk about makeovers . . . I had a whole new body. Not to mention a new face, name, Social Security number . . .

As if the fact that I suspected my best friend might be cheating on me with other girls (only not really, because he never knew I'd liked him that way in the first place, plus, he thought I was dead) wasn't bad enough, I kept getting the feeling that everyone in class was looking at me.

I was probably only being self-conscious.

But a quick glance up from the doodles I was making in my new notebook confirmed it: I wasn't imagining things . . . everyone *was* staring at me. The minute I looked up, every head in the room swiveled quickly away from me.

Except, I noticed, when I pretended to drop my pencil and swung down to pick it up and swung a quick look in his direction, Christopher's.

Christopher's gaze was fastened on McKayla.

He hadn't even noticed me! What was up with that? Why was he even awake, anyway? He *always* slept through first period. Was Christopher going out with McKayla? No way. McKayla was head of TAHS's business club. *Business club*. No way could he like her. All she could talk about was how after she graduated from Harvard, she was going to revolutionize Wall Street. Christopher couldn't like her. He couldn't possibly. . . .

I could see I was going to make a lot of progress thinking in that direction.

Frustrated, I began doodling harder. I drew a tiny poodle, this one like Cosabella. Lulu had promised last night to look after her while I was in school all day. The poor thing had whined and yelped when she'd seen me leaving the loft without her. I didn't know much about dogs, but this didn't seem like the most stable behavior. Had Nikki really taken her dog *everywhere* with her? Because Cosy certainly acted like it was a federal offense if she was left behind.

I was dreading the mess I'd find at home when I got back. I highly doubted Lulu was the most responsible dogsitter. I was fairly certain there'd be some major carpet scrubbing to do tonight.

Oh, well. Nikki's fingers needed limbering up anyway. They were basically useless. I couldn't draw a thing with them . . . not even a measly poodle. What had Nikki Howard done with her hands all day, anyway? You can only put on so many layers of nail polish, right?

"Psst."

I looked over my shoulder, hoping Christopher was the one psssting me. Only it wasn't. Whitney Robertson smiled at me.

Yeah. Whitney. Smiled. At me.

The next thing I knew, a folded-up piece of paper sailed in my direction. Instinctively, I caught it.

When I unfolded it, I realized it was a note.

A note from Whitney.

I didn't know what to do. Whitney had never thrown me a note before. I saw her fellow Walking Dead member Lindsey twinkle her fingers at me. Like, *hello!* She was smiling, as well.

Instinctively, and before I could stop myself, I smiled back. Wait! What was I doing? *Smiling* at the Walking Dead?

Ducking my head so that Nikki's hair fell down to hide my face, I looked at the note.

Hi! it said, in curlicue writing with a flower dotting the i. *Welcome to TAHS! We're so excited to have you here. I'm Whitney Robertson. I know you probably get this a lot, but seriously — I'm your biggest fan. I know a lot of people say that, but in my case, it's really true. I've been an admirer of your work since you first started back in print ads.*

Anyway, I know it must be weird for you, starting a new school and all. So I just wanted to say Hey! And if you have period B lunch, there's totally a place for you at our table! We're by the salad bar. XXXOOO Whitney

Then she had put her cell phone number.

I stared at that note for a long time. A lot of different responses went through my head as I read and then reread it. I thought about crumpling it up and throwing it back in her face.

Then I thought about writing a response and saying that I'd heard all about Whitney, and how mean she'd always been, and that I wouldn't sit with her and her friends at lunch if they were the last people on earth.

But I didn't end up doing either of those things. Because — and I know this sounds bizarre — I really didn't think Nikki Howard would do either of those things.

Not that I was actually trying to *be* Nikki Howard, of course. At least, not at school.

But since I *was* her, I just . . . I don't know. I just couldn't see Nikki Howard — what I knew of her, anyway — caring about what some twerpy girl like Whitney wrote to her in a note.

I guess that's because, when I looked deep down within myself, I just couldn't be bothered to care about Whitney anymore, or her stupid one-upmanship. I had too many other problems.

Like that my best friend couldn't even bring himself to make eye contact with me.

Still, I knew if I didn't acknowledge her note at all, she'd feel slighted. And I didn't need to make a new enemy my first day. Even if she wasn't exactly a *new* enemy.

So I flipped my hair back, turned in my seat, and smiled at her.

And something extraordinary happened.

Whitney Robertson blushed.

Seriously. I never thought I'd live to see the day. But her cheeks turned bright pink with pleasure, and she smiled back at me and waved, and Lindsey, behind her, waved, too.

And Whitney mouthed, *Call me!* And pantomimed making a phone call.

I smiled again to acknowledge her, then turned back in my seat. This being Nikki thing was easier — in some ways — than I'd thought it would be.

Whitney was all over me the minute class ended. Which wasn't cool, because I'd just been about to turn to Christopher and make a little comment as a sort of icebreaker, like, *Is this class always this boring or what?*

Only I couldn't, because the Prom Queen From Hell was on me like ketchup on a steak.

"How *are* you?" she hurried over to ask me as soon as the bell rang. "I saw on *Entertainment Tonight* about your . . . *you know.* It must be so awful, not being able to *remember* anything!"

"I can remember some stuff," I said, as I gathered my things. For instance, I could remember all the times Whitney and her friends had laughed at my underwear in the girls' locker room, because they were Hanes Her Way briefs and not Victoria's Secret thongs, which is what they all wore.

"Oh, that's good," Whitney said. "Well, like I said, I'm Whitney, and this is Lindsey —"

"Hi!" Lindsey cried. "I'm, like, totally your biggest fan. I loved that spread you did in *Vogue* in July, with the gold accessories, and the tiger —"

"— and we're just so excited to have you here at TAHS," Whitney went on, speaking right over Lindsey, as if she hadn't said anything. "It is such an honor that out of all the schools in New York, you chose ours —"

"Are you guys going to move anytime soon?" Christopher, who was standing behind us, inquired. "Because some of us need to get to our next class."

Whitney glanced at him over her shoulder, then rolled her eyes and moved out of the way.

My heart swooped at that eye roll. Because it meant that, haircut or not, Christopher hadn't been accepted by the Walking

Dead. He wasn't one of them! He may have looked like he was, but he wasn't. He was still safe! He was still *him*!

"Thanks," Christopher said, as he walked by.

"See you later," I said to him.

He threw me a distracted look over his shoulder — as if he'd heard someone speak but wasn't sure who — before disappearing into the throng in the hallway.

Beside me, Whitney sneered and said, "Sorry about that. Don't pay him any mind. One of our resident freaks. So, you know, if you have any questions about TAHS or need anyone to show you around, I'd be more than happy to help. What are you doing for lunch, for instance? You definitely don't want to go to the caf. The food there completely reeks —"

"Is that the new Marc Jacobs hobo tote?" Lindsey interrupted, pointing to the bag slung over my shoulder. "Because I'm on the waiting list for one —"

"I don't know," I said. "I just found it in my closet this morning." Waiting list. Ha! "Well, I have to get to Spanish. So if you'll excuse me . . ."

"Me, too!" Lindsey squealed. "I think we must be in the same Spanish class! Room six eleven? Oh, my Dios! Here, let me show you where it is."

"God, Lindsey, calm down," Whitney said crabbily. "I'm sure Nikki can find her own way."

"That's okay," I said, turning to look Whitney square in the eye. "Lindsey's being a great help. Well, bye, Whitney. It was nice to meet you."

And I walked off arm in arm with Lindsey, conscious of being the recipient of a hundred envious stares as we made our way down the hall — Whitney's the most envious of all.

But this time, it didn't bother me.

Because for once I was having too much fun to worry about it.

TWENTY-ONE

I FOUND FRIDA WHERE SHE ALWAYS WAS just before lunch: the ground floor ladies' room the freshman girls tended to haunt, carefully applying her lip gloss.

There were any number of other freshman girls in there with her, but one look at me and they fled as if someone had pulled a fire alarm. I'm sure, given Nikki Howard's reputation, they thought I'd gone in there to do drugs. You'd have thought they'd have stuck around to watch, maybe snap a cell phone pic of me wiping my nose to sell to the *Enquirer* for some extra cash.

But TAHS's freshman class had never had a reputation for being that enterprising. Besides, the truth was much tamer: I was in there to pump Frida for information.

"Why didn't you tell me Christopher cut his hair?" I demanded, lowering myself onto the sink beside the one she was leaning against.

"What?" She puckered at her reflection as she reapplied. "Oh, yeah. Christopher cut his hair. News at eleven. Whatever. He did it for your memorial service. His dad made him."

I stared at her reflection in shock. "That's terrible!"

Frida simpered in the mirror. "You think so? I thought it was sort of respectful. You know, of your memory. His long hair was gross. And besides, Christopher didn't put up much of a fight, from what I heard. He's been like a zombie since you croaked. He doesn't seem to care about anything."

I perked up at hearing this. "Really? Did he cry? At my funeral, I mean?"

Frida shot me an annoyed look. "God, you are so vain now."

"I am not!" I hopped off the sink and glared at her. "I am totally the least vain person you know. How can you even say that? All I want to know is if Christopher seemed sad after I died. That's not vanity. That's just curiosity. If *you* had died, you'd probably expect the city to shut down and name a day after you —"

"I would not," Frida said, with a sniff. "And I suppose Christopher might have seemed sad. But I don't even know why you care. I thought you two were *just friends*, anyway. And you can do *way* better than Christopher now. And besides, you already have Brandon Stark — and Gabriel Luna, probably, unless that Vespa ride was a fluke. How many boyfriends do you need, anyway?"

I ignored her. "Who does Christopher eat lunch with now?" I asked her. "I mean, now that I'm dead?" *Not McKayla Donofrio. Please don't say McKayla Donofrio. . . .*

"I don't know," Frida said, grumpily. "I never see him in the caf anymore. Someone said he's been eating in the computer lab. You know he works there as a TA."

"Thanks," I said, and started to hurry off to find Christopher — but not before I heard Frida shout after me, "You better come eat with me, Em — I mean, Nikki! I already told everybody you were going to! Don't you dare stand me up!"

But I didn't have time to worry about my sister's reputation among the junior varsity cheerleading crowd. I only had forty minutes before lunch was over and I had to get to my next class. I raced down the hall toward the computer lab (fortunately not running into Molly Hung, who might have wondered how I knew my way around TAHS so deftly after her extremely short tour). . . .

And there he was, exactly where Frida had said he might be, in the empty computer lab, eating a sandwich in the glow of a solitary game of . . . *Madden NFL?*

But Christopher *never* played sports-related video games. Christopher *hated* sports. What was going on here?

Still, I really don't think I'd be exaggerating if I said that, though he was doing something extremely bizarre (based on his old patterns of behavior, anyway), Christopher *looked* adorable with his short blond hair totally rumpled. He clearly hadn't bothered combing it before letting it air dry after his shower on his way to school. The collar of his green Polo shirt was slightly askew in the back, and bits of sandwich crumb had spilled down the front. He'd never been one for working out, so his biceps, disappearing into his short sleeves, weren't ridiculously huge looking, like Jason Klein's. But they weren't nonexistent, either.

"Um," I said, since he was so involved in the game he didn't notice me standing in the doorway. "Excuse me?"

He glanced over, then nearly choked on the mouthful of soda he'd swigged. Then he couldn't say anything at all, because he was too busy coughing.

"Sorry," I said. Whoa. I probably should have rehearsed this a little better. What was Nikki doing in a computer lab, anyway? What was my excuse for seeking Christopher out going to be? "I just . . . I was wondering —"

"The administrative offices are down the hall," Christopher said, having recovered himself.

Then, to my utter astonishment, he turned around in his chair and returned to his game. Of *Madden NFL*.

Oh, yes. Christopher Maloney had just blown me off. For a video game.

And not even a *good* video game. And he hadn't even blown off *me*, either, but Nikki Howard. He'd just blown off the hottest teen supermodel on the *planet*.

What was wrong with him? I knew he liked Nikki Howard. I'd seen for myself how he'd stared at her that day at the grand opening at Stark's. What was going on here?

And why hadn't I figured out before what I was going to say to him? Why did talking to people have to be so *hard*? This would have been so much easier if I could have just IMed him.

Wait . . . e-mail . . .

"I know this isn't the administrative office," I said quickly. "They said in the administrative office that I could sign up for a student e-mail account here."

This wasn't even a lie. That was the most glorious part of all.

"Oh," Christopher said. He looked away from his computer screen reluctantly. "Sure. Yeah. I can set you up with one, if you want."

"You can?" I rushed over and sank down into the computer chair beside his. "Wow, that would be so great. Thanks."

I smiled at him.

And he completely ignored me.

It's true I'd only been Nikki Howard for a couple of days. But I had already learned in that short time what Nikki's smile did to people. Especially guys. It rendered them completely helpless. Guys turned to total Jell-O when Nikki smiled. They would do anything — *anything* — Nikki wanted when she smiled. There was only one guy who had seemed immune to Nikki's smile, and that had been Brandon Stark's father.

And now the only other guy in the world who I actually cared about impressing: Christopher Maloney. He wouldn't even look me in the face. He kept his gaze firmly on the computer screen in front of me as he drew up the school's e-mail database.

How was I going to get through to Christopher — as a person, not as Nikki Howard — if I couldn't even get him to look me in the eye and see that there was someone in here, behind the mascara?

"So," I began, feeling desperate. "You like . . . computer games?"

Oh, my God, could I sound more lame? If I'd been in the computer lab (I mean, as Em Watts), listening to this conversation between Nikki Howard and Christopher, I'd be laughing my butt off round about now.

"Some of them," Christopher said, tapping away at his keyboard.

"Me, too," I said. "Have you ever played *Journeyquest?*"

That got his attention. Finally. He turned his stunned gaze toward me. "*You* play *Journeyquest?*" he asked incredulously.

"Sure," I said, my heart giving a happy double thump, despite the fact that I probably should have been insulted. I mean, what was so weird about Nikki Howard liking *Journeyquest?* What, she was too stupid to play a tactic-based RPG?

Oh, who even cared? He'd looked at me! He'd looked me in the eye! It wouldn't be long now until we were friends again! He'd ask me over, and soon we'd be eating Doritos and watching surgery shows and getting yelled at by the Commander, just like old times. Everything would be normal again. Everything would be just like it used to be. I was so happy! Happier than I could remember being since I'd looked into that rearview mirror and seen Nikki Howard's face looking back at me.

"Level forty-five is only as high as I've gotten, though," I said.

Level forty-five, Christopher! It's me, Christopher! Em! Look at me, Christopher! Look into my eyes! Do you see me? Hi, it's me, Em! I'm looking right at you!

Christopher studied me a moment longer, and I could have sworn he saw me. I really thought he had.

But then he completely crushed me by looking away.

"I don't play that game anymore," was all he said, and he went back to typing.

Wait. What? What just happened? What did he mean, he didn't play *Journeyquest* anymore? No one just stops playing *Journeyquest*. It's not just a game. It's a lifestyle.

And what about me? Me, Em? Had he seen me or not? He hadn't. He couldn't possibly, right?

Or he wouldn't have looked away.

"Yeah," he said. "So your new e-mail address is going to be Nikki dot Howard at TAHS dot EDU. It should be effective right away."

What was going on? Why was he just ignoring me like this? Guys just don't ignore Nikki Howard. Em Watts, yes.

But even gay guys ask Nikki what kind of moisturizer she uses (not that I know the answer).

"Okay," I said, not knowing what else to say. "Thanks."

Okay. Christopher didn't want to talk to me. I mean, Nikki Howard. I could take a hint.

No. No, actually, I really couldn't.

"You know how to set up your e-mail account at home?" Christopher asked me. "Right?"

I knew how to set up my own e-mail account. I'd been setting up my own e-mail accounts since I'd gotten my first one in the fifth grade.

My mom, the women's studies professor, had always urged Frida and me never to act dumb just to try to win over a guy.

But this was one case, I felt, where she'd have understood.

Because suddenly, I realized I had an excuse to talk to Christopher again tomorrow. And I really, really needed one. Because it didn't look as if he was going to be asking me over for Doritos and surgery shows anytime soon.

"I really don't know how to do that setting up thingie," I said. I was practically batting my eyelashes, I was hamming up the defenseless female thing so much. My mom would have had a coronary.

Christopher stared at me. "You don't?" he said. He didn't sound too surprised.

"No," I said. "Is it hard? Do you know how to do it?"

"Yes," he said. "It's not hard. Do you have something in your eye?"

I quit batting my eyelashes.

"No," I said, dropping the defenseless female thing. Dang, why did flirting have to be so difficult? Why couldn't he just grab and kiss me like Brandon and Justin had? I was good at kissing! Or, at least, Nikki was. "If I just bring in my laptop tomorrow, will you set me up?"

"Sure," he said. I couldn't believe he hadn't fallen for the eyelash thing. Which, by the way, I was pretty sure would have made Justin Bay fall over. In a coma. "That'd be fine."

"Great." I smiled at him. I put it at full wattage, the kind of smile that had caused Raoul, the art director, to say yesterday,

Nikki, could you tone it down a little? We aren't selling used cars here.

But I didn't want to tone it down any more. I wanted to do whatever I had to in order to get a reaction from Christopher.

Not that it appeared to be working, since he continued to just stare at me blankly.

"I'm Nikki, by the way," I said, still smiling. "I mean, I know you know that. But . . ." I stuck out my right hand.

Christopher didn't smile in return.

"I'm Christopher," he said, taking my hand and shaking it. "Maloney."

His grip was firm but strangely lifeless. I don't know how to describe it, except that . . .

It was like shaking hands with a dead person. I mean, someone who really *was* dead only still walking around.

Which made no sense, since *I* was that person.

His fingers were warm, like mine. I knew he wasn't dead. Not really. It was like something inside him had just . . . given up. Like with his battle over his hair with his dad. He'd just . . . surrendered, after all these years. He honestly didn't care anymore.

What was going on with him? What was *wrong* with him?

And how was I going to get close enough to him to find out, when I could barely get him to look at me, to see that I was here, inside Nikki Howard?

I didn't want to let go of his hand . . . and I didn't think it was because of Nikki's wantoness, either. I mean, a hand is different from lips or a tongue. It just felt so good to be close to him again, to be in his presence, even if he didn't know it was me.

But I knew I had to let go, because you can't sit around in a computer lab holding hands with some guy you just met. Even if you were best friends with him in a past life, and you *are* a teenage supermodel now.

So I dropped his hand . . . just a second after he tugged on it to release it from mine. Clearly, he thought I was a crazy person. I half expected him to wipe his hand on his jeans. But he restrained himself.

"So," I said, ducking to gather up my Marc Jacobs tote in an effort to hide my mortification. "I'm headed down to the cafeteria for lunch. Do you want to join me?"

I knew what he was going to say before he said it.

"Uh, no, thanks," Christopher said, giving me a strange look. "But enjoy yourself. Stay away from the tuna salad."

It was the first remotely humorous thing he'd said. I realized how much I'd missed his sarcastic remarks. Almost as much as I'd missed him.

"Thanks," I said, with another smile.

But once again it seemed to have no effect on him. He returned to his computer screen, going back to *Madden NFL* without another word.

And I slunk from the lab, embarrassed, hurt . . . and more than a little confused.

"Oh, my God, there you are," Frida cried, rushing up to me in the hallway. "I've been waiting for, like, ever. Where *were* you?"

"I went to see Christopher in the computer lab," I said. "I told you —"

"God," Frida muttered. "Why are you hanging out with that geek when you could be with *Gabriel Luna*?"

"Gabriel Luna thinks I'm a drug addict," I pointed out, remembering last night's embarrassing social gaffe. Which are all I seem to have, apparently, where cute guys are concerned.

"Well, whatever," Frida said, grabbing my arm. "Come on. I told everyone on the JV squad you were sitting with us at lunch today."

"And just how, exactly," I asked, as she propelled me along, "are you and I supposed to have met, Frida, and become so chummy that I'm sitting with you at lunch now?"

"We met outside the school on the steps this morning," Frida said. "Remember? Everybody saw us together."

"Great," I said, rolling my eyes. "Frida, what's wrong with Christopher?"

"He's a freak," Frida said, as she dragged me toward the cafeteria. "He always was. You're just noticing it now because you're finally normal."

"No, I mean . . . what *happened* to him? He's . . . different. He doesn't even like *Journeyquest* anymore. He plays *Madden NFL*. Christopher *hates* sports. And he . . . I can't really explain it. But it's like he — I went in there to get an e-mail address for Nikki, and he'd barely look at me."

"Oh, and I suppose you thought he'd be all over you," Frida said, with a snort, "just because you're Nikki Howard now."

"Well," I said. I didn't want to sound snotty. But . . . "Yeah. I mean . . . he's a guy, right? And guys are usually all over Nikki. Unless they're gay. So what's wrong with him?"

"What do you want me to say, Em? I mean, Nikki. I told you, he's been weird ever since you croaked. I mean, weirder than usual. I guess he was just always in love with you but didn't realize it until you were gone, and now that you're dead, he's wasting away. Is that what you want to hear?" She flung a glance at me over her shoulder, saw my expression, and let out a bark of laughter. "God! It is! Get over yourself. You can have any guy you want now. Why do you have to like the one guy who liked you better when you were just average, like the rest of us?"

We'd reached the cafeteria doors. Frida turned to confront me with her hands on her hips. I stared down at her with tear-filled eyes.

"Oh, my God, Frida," I said, with a little sob. "Do . . . do you really think that's it?"

Frida stared up at me. "Oh, my God. You really like him, don't you? Listen . . . how am I supposed to know? I'm just saying. It might make sense. But I could be totally wrong. Look, Christopher is the least of your problems right now. You are about to enter the Tribeca Alternative High School cafeteria. Only it's a whole new ball game than a month ago. You're hot now. Do you understand? You have got to get Christopher out of your head and put on your game face. You're Nikki Howard, supermodel. Not Em Watts, weirdo. Got it?"

I nodded. But I wasn't really listening. I kept thinking about what she'd said. Was it really possible? *Could* Christopher have realized, after I'd died, that he'd loved me? Was that why he didn't want to play *Journeyquest* anymore? Because it reminded him of me? Was that why he'd finally consented to cut his hair? Because nothing mattered to him anymore, now that I was gone?

Oh, God! That was the most romantic thing I'd ever heard!

But what was I going to do about it? How was I going to get Christopher interested in Nikki Howard if he was busy pining away for a dead girl? Who, by the way, happened to be me?

And, no offense, but you would have thought he'd have been a little nicer to me back when I'd been alive, if he'd been so madly in love with me.

But he'd never even so much as tried to kiss me.

Wait . . . maybe *that's* what he was feeling so bad about!

Oh! That was even *more* romantic!

But before I had a chance to really digest that, Frida was yanking me on the arm, and we were in the caf . . .

. . . where the volume of the conversation, already at an ear-splitting din, increased tenfold at the mere sight of me in the doorway.

"There she is!" The murmur rippled through the entire cafeteria.

And not just the Walking Dead were saying it. The geeks, the goths, the skaters, the druggies . . . all of them were saying it. "There she is!"

I felt myself turning red. . . .

"I don't know about this, Free," I said, as Frida herded me toward the hot food line and thrust a tray in my hands.

"Trust me," Frida said. "Even supermodels have to eat, don't they?"

Maybe so. But it might have been easier simply to get something out of the vending machines down the hall, acid reflux or not. I was excruciatingly aware of being the center of everyone's attention as I made my way down the food line. My selections were buzzed about as if I'd been Tiger Woods lining up a game-winning putt.

"She's going for the tofu patty," I heard them whispering. Then, seconds later, "An apple! She took an apple!"

I wanted to throw down my tray and run from the room — run out of the school and all the way back to the hospital and up to the fourth floor and to Dr. Holcombe's office. "I need a new body! I can't be in this one a second longer! I can't be Nikki Howard! I just want to be someone normal!"

Instead, I stepped up to the cashier to pay for my food. Then I followed Frida to her table . . .

. . . where the entire junior varsity cheerleading team was sitting. They all stopped talking as Frida and I approached. I fully expected them to say, "What are you doing, trying to sit at our table, loser? The geek table is over THERE."

But I'd forgotten. I'm not Em Watts, geek, anymore. I'm Nikki Howard.

And Nikki Howard is apparently welcome everywhere (except the computer lab).

"Oooh!" a dark-haired girl cried, scooting her tray over. "I'm so glad you came over here. Sit by me! Sit by me, I'm your hugest fan!"

Frida took the place the girl was offering, though, after giving her a severe look. "Now, Mackenzie," she said, sternly, "remember what I said."

"Sorry!" Mackenzie turned beet-red. "Right, no gushing. Sorry. Sorry."

The other girls, all smiling up at me, scooted over to make room. I felt a little uneasy. I couldn't quite believe I was being *welcomed* at a table belonging to the Walking Dead.

But it soon became apparent our table was *the* table to be at. Especially when, no sooner had Frida made introductions (none of which I retained, since all of her friends appeared to be called either Taylor, Tyler, or Tory), a familiar voice cried, "There you are!"

And I turned my head to see Whitney Robertson standing there with a tray of salad and diet soda, Lindsey and several other key Walking Dead members from the junior class — including one from the senior class, Jason Klein — right behind her.

"Oh, my God," Whitney said, "I've been looking all over for you."

And next thing I knew, she was shoving red-and-gold uniforms aside to make way for herself, her boyfriend, and her best friend.

"Thanks muchly," she said to Frida's friends, who hadn't so much moved as been pushed out of the way. "So, Nikki, how are you enjoying your first day here at TAHS?"

"She's liking it a lot, Whitney." Frida, who'd apparently appointed herself my spokeswoman, looked enormously pleased.

I guess it's not every day a freshman gets graced with the presence of the most popular girl in school at her lunch table. "Aren't you, Nikki?"

I took a swig of my milk (Yeah. Nikki likes milk. Two percent. She's got acid reflux, not lactose intolerance).

"Yeah," I said, after I'd swallowed.

"I was telling Nikki today in Public Speaking," Whitney said — then added, as an aside to everyone else at the table, "Nikki and I have Public Speaking together —"

"Me, too!" Lindsey cried. "I'm in Nikki's Public Speaking class, too! Also her Spanish class. And I'm on the waiting list for that Marc Jacobs tote. . . ."

"— that we feel so fortunate that she decided to attend our school, out of all the schools in the city," Whitney went on, as if Lindsey hadn't interrupted. "Wasn't I, Nikki?"

"Yeah," I said, after swallowing a bite of the salad I'd gotten to accompany my tofu patty . . . which tasted fantastic and not at all like the cardboard box I'd been expecting it to taste like.

"I just wish we'd had more advance notice of her enrollment," Whitney went on, to everyone at the table. "Because then we could have organized a proper welcome for her."

All the girls nodded in agreement. Jason, I noticed, was staring at my boobs. I'm not even kidding.

"Wow," I said. "Thanks. That's really great. But I feel plenty welcome enough."

"Well," Whitney said, "I'm going to be sure to get you a list of extracurriculars, in case you decide you might want to join some of the fantastic clubs and organizations our school has to offer. I, for instance, am president of the junior class, as well as captain of the Spirit Club."

"Really," I said. "The Spirit Club. What's that?"

Not that I didn't know. I just wanted to see if she'd describe it the way Christopher and I used to: as the Society for the Lame.

"Oh, well, the Spirit Club makes an effort to foster school spirit among the student population by promoting events in and around Tribeca Alternative, such as pep rallies, health fairs, can drives, casino nights, weekend carnivals —"

"Casino nights," Lindsey chimed in.

"I said that already," Whitney said, giving Lindsey a dirty look. "Really, what it's all about is —" Whitney lowered her voice, as if she were afraid of being overheard — "*some* people who go to this school don't appreciate all the fantastic programs and opportunities it has to offer. So the Spirit Club does its best to get students excited about these events, such as games, community service programs . . . things that will look great on their college applications."

I blinked at her. "Why are you whispering?"

She glanced around, then seemed to realize that the school's two worst malcontents — Em Watts and Christopher

Maloney — weren't within hearing distance. "Oh, I don't know. It's just that *some* people think having school spirit is silly. But I don't think there's anything silly about wanting to take as much advantage as possible of what, for me, at least, have truly been some of the best years of my life!"

Whoa. If high school was supposed to be the best years of my life — at least so far — I was truly destined to have a sucky adulthood.

"Wow," I said again. "That sounds . . . great."

"Enough about this school crap," Jason Klein said, leaning forward so that his massive — and, to me, revolting — biceps swelled beneath the sleeves of his pink Polo. "What clubs can you get us into?"

"Jason!" Whitney lady-slapped him on the shoulder while she giggled. "Stop! Don't pay any attention to him. He's so bad."

Jason ignored her. "I saw you got into Cave last night," Jason said. "Can you get us into Cave?"

"I don't know," I said. "Maybe."

"Maybe, what?" Jason demanded. "Can you get us in or not?"

"If it's Jerks Who Interrupt Their Girlfriends Night," I said. "Then I can probably get you in."

Whitney gasped. Lindsey let out a giant horselaugh.

But what surprised me most was that quite a few of the JV cheerleaders turned around and high-fived one another, impressed by the fact that I'd dissed Jason Klein. If this, I realized, was the kind of company Frida was keeping, then I had been quite badly underestimating the TAHS JV cheerleading squad — and possibly cheerleaders everywhere. They were a fun bunch.

Frida, however, just glared at me. I mouthed *What?* and shrugged. I really don't see what else she'd expected me to say.

Jason, however, took it good-naturedly.

"Okay, okay," he said, smiling sheepishly. "You got me. I'll shut up."

Which was just another sign of how different life is when you've got a supermodel's face as opposed to just a normal one. If I had said something like that to Jason back when I'd been in my Em Watts body, I'd never have heard the end of it . . . especially from Whitney.

But since I was Nikki, and not Em, all was forgiven. In fact, as we were putting our trays away, just before the bell rang, Whitney sidled up to me, and to show there were no hard feelings, said, in a low voice, I guess so the others wouldn't overhear, "Listen, Nikki, if you're not doing anything after school, maybe you could come up to my place, and I could help you out with some of your homework. I know it must seem like you're never going to catch up at this rate — plus, I know it's been a while since you were last in school. So I just thought —"

"Gosh," I said. "Thanks. But I have a shoot."

Even if I hadn't, no way would I waste any of my precious time going to Whitney Robertson's penthouse so she could show me the wrong way to compute the area of a triangle. Or try on different-colored sparkly eyeshadows, or whatever it is the Walking Dead do in their spare time.

"Some other time, though," I added with a smile, when I saw her face fall.

As soon as she saw the smile, Whitney smiled back.

"Great!" she gushed. "Well, toodle-ooh!"

Seriously. That's what she said to me. *Toodle-ooh.*

I kind of wished Cosy had been with me, because I could have looked down at her and gone, "Well, Toto. I guess we're not in Kansas anymore."

Except that I've never actually been to Kansas.

Although I'm fairly sure Nikki has. Nikki's been everywhere.

Except where I most want to be.

TWENTY-TWO

THE *ELLE* SHOOT WAS A SNAP COM-
pared to the *Vanity Fair* shoot the day before. For one thing, I
at least had a *little bit* of an idea what I was supposed to be doing
now. Plus, I didn't have to smush my boobs against anyone this
time or wrap myself around anyone else's physical person (such
as Brandon Stark's). This time, it was just me.

Don't get me wrong. I still had to smile just the right way, but
it was more important that the gowns I was wearing flowed
right. I swear, every two minutes, I heard, "Wait — hold on,"
and someone was running over to adjust a fold or smooth a
wrinkle. It was a little maddening.

And even though I don't particularly care about fashion,
I sort of get it now. I mean, why other people care about

it, and why it's interesting and sort of important to some people.

The truth is, fashion can be sort of . . . well, fun.

I know! I never "got" fashion before. Clothes were just things you threw on to keep from being naked or cold.

But the dresses — I mean, gowns — that were at this shoot were so gorgeous, I actually caught my breath when I saw them on me. I can't even imagine where you'd *wear* a bright red long dress with a neckline that plunges to your sternum and is trimmed with dyed black ostrich feathers. I mean, except maybe to the Oscars.

However, I couldn't help but be curious about who'd designed them — which surprised the people at the shoot, because they said I should have known without asking, just by the feel and look of them.

But then Kelly reminded them quickly of my head injury (which the hair stylist, Vivian, had already found). And then they all wanted to talk about that (my interview was going to run in the same issue, but I wasn't meeting the journalist who was doing it until Saturday).

Anyway, they all took great pleasure in telling me about the designers who had gowns at the shoot and other favorite designers of Nikki's, as well. And I have to admit, their stories were kind of interesting. Like, even my mom would have gotten a kick out of the story of Miuccia Prada, a feminist mime who took over her grandfather's leather goods company in 1978, making "Miu Miu" one of the thirty most powerful women in Europe (according to *The Wall Street Journal*), with an estimated fortune of 1.4 billion dollars.

And Coco Chanel, who popularized the little black dress for women and founded a fashion empire, becoming the only fashion designer to make *Time* magazine's 100 Most Influential People of the 20th Century.

All of this — plus the lecture the makeup guy gave me about the dark circles under my eyes, thanks to my lack of sleep, and the fact that my mom would *not* stop calling (but I couldn't exactly pick up in the middle of a fashion shoot), my employer is maybe (okay, probably) spying on me, and the tugging and wrenching and holding my breath required to get me into the corsets I needed to squeeze into some of the gowns — was enough to keep my mind off what had happened in school earlier that day with Christopher. The fact that I nearly passed out several times, the corsets were so tight, and that I could barely move helped, too.

The truth was, I don't know how Nikki did it. I was supposed to stare off into the distance as if I were gazing at a far-off star (when really what I was looking at was a piece of paint peeling off the rafters on the ceiling) while *not* thinking about how I couldn't breathe and my feet hurt and how tired I was . . .

. . . and, oh, yeah, how everyone saw me being carried out of

Cave last night like I was the drunk one, not my so-called boy-friend, and that the guy I'd actually *like* to be dating, by the way, doesn't know I'm alive?

No, I mean, *literally doesn't know I'm alive.* He thinks I'm dead, and I can't tell him I'm not. And he isn't too impressed with the new body I'm in. In fact, he might just be the only guy on the planet who's not.

How can anyone concentrate on looking beautiful when all that is going on around them and inside their head, as well? Modeling isn't easy. Modeling is actually really hard. Modeling is *acting*. You have to *act* like you're actually enjoying yourself when the truth is, every single inch of you is hurting and uncom-fortable . . . most of all your heart.

I mean, if you're me.

I was almost sagging with exhaustion when the art director, Veronica, said, "I think that's all we need, Nikki. You can go now."

I swear I nearly ripped that last couture gown off, I wanted to get out of there so badly.

"You've got the *Vogue* shoot tomorrow at three —" Kelly was telling me as I ran down the steps to the limo.

"I know," I yelled over my shoulder.

"And don't go out tonight," she shouted at me, as I collapsed into the backseat. "You need to get some sleep! You looked awful today."

"I won't!" I slammed the limo door behind me. Finally! We didn't have much time.

"We're making a stop before we go to the loft," I said to the driver. "The computer store on Prince and Greene."

The driver looked at me skeptically in the rearview mirror. "It's almost eight o'clock, Miss Howard."

"I know," I said. "The store is open late on Thursdays."

I sank back against the leather seat and watched as we glided along Park Avenue, making our way downtown. I'd realized as I'd been standing there, "gazing at a far-off star," that I couldn't bring Nikki Howard's Stark-brand hot-pink laptop to school tomorrow for Christopher to set up my e-mail account on. For one thing, it was just too embarrassing. I mean, seriously — hot pink?

And for another, how could I be sure it didn't have some other kind of tracking software built into it with which Stark Enterprises could watch my every move online? No. I needed a whole new, non-Stark computer. Just like I needed a new, non-Stark cell phone on which to talk to my parents.

I'd pick up both on the way home. Thank God the Apple store was open until nine on Thursday nights.

And I had Nikki Howard's platinum American Express card.

There were perks to being rich and famous, after all.

Especially when you're rich, famous, and have your face plastered all over a Stark Megastore a few blocks away from the computer store, and everyone in there recognizes you the minute you walk in. Even late as it was, there was a line. But when you're Nikki Howard, I'm sorry to say, you get treated differently from everyone else. A salesperson came right over to me, almost before I'd gotten ten feet into the store and heard the usual buzzing that started everywhere I went. He asked if he could help me, and I told him what I wanted.

And he told me to wait right there while he went and got it.

As much as being Nikki seriously sucked sometimes, it could seriously rock at other times. I had my new laptop and phone and was out the door ten minutes and fourteen autographs later.

It was as I was waiting for the limo driver to swing around and pick me up (he'd been forced to circle while I shopped due to the number of mounted cops in the area) that I heard a voice behind me say, "Nikki?" and I turned around expecting to see another autograph hunter . . .

. . . and was shocked to see Gabriel Luna instead.

"You!" I cried.

He looked as surprised to see me as I was to see him.

"Are you stalking me?" he asked, in that adorable British accent. But he was smiling, so I knew he was joking.

"I think *you're* stalking *me*," I said. "What are you doing here?"

"I live just up the street," he said. "I'd ask what you were doing here, but it's obvious." Always the gentleman, he took hold of the enormous boxes I was carrying. "Here, allow me. Are you trying to find a taxi again? You'll never get one at this corner, you know."

"No, I have a ride," I said. "He's just circling. But thank you."

"Oh," Gabriel said. "So you've recovered from last night?"

Remembering in a rush the last time I'd seen him, I said, sticking out my chin, "That was . . . I wasn't even . . . Gabriel, I don't even *drink*. Seriously, you can ask any of the bartenders. Next time you go to Cave, have them pour you a Nikki."

He blinked at me. "A *what?*"

"A Nikki. It's just water. And I was trying to get Brandon out of there. I mean, Brandon's just — we're just friends."

"Oh." Gabriel stared down at me. He looked confused. "I see."

"I'm not who you think I am, Gabriel," I said. I could see the headlights of the limo sliding toward us. It was stuck behind a traffic light but coming inexorably closer. Still, there was something I needed to get off my chest. "My idea of a fun night is playing computer games. I didn't even *want* to go out last night. I just did it because Lulu threw a surprise welcome home party for me and I didn't want to hurt her feelings because she's been really sweet to me. I'm going to go home tonight and do homework. That's my wild, crazy life. Really."

"Look," Gabriel said, his expression unreadable. "Don't be angry. I know I come off as a bit of a prat sometimes. It's just . . . well, it's like those girls we ran into the other day. The ones who were chasing us. They look up to you. I worry you don't realize that."

"Well, I do," I said. Was that traffic light ever going to turn green? Then I shot him a suspicious look. "Wait a minute. What were *you* doing at that club at two in the morning, anyway?"

"Oh," Gabriel said, looking embarrassed suddenly, "I was giving the DJ a copy of a new song I wrote the other day. To see if he thought it would work as a dance mix."

"Oh," I said, smiling. "And? Did he like it?"

It was hard to tell in the glow from the windows of the computer store. But I think Gabriel was actually blushing a little. "He loved it, actually. He played it on the spot. It brought the place down. Everyone adored it."

The limo finally pulled up in front of me, and the driver sprang out from behind the wheel.

"I'm so sorry, Miss Howard," he said. "I got caught behind one of those tour buses. . . ."

"That's okay," I said. "Could you take this?" I took the huge boxes from Gabriel and handed them to the driver, who hurried to put them in the trunk. Then I turned back to Gabriel and said, "Well, here's my car."

"I can see that," Gabriel said, taking in with raised eyebrows the long black limousine. It had attracted the attention of quite a few people on the sidewalk, many of whom had stopped to stare at it, and me, as well.

"I owe you a ride," I reminded Gabriel. "So if there's anywhere you need to go . . ."

"Not tonight," Gabriel said, with a funny little half smile. "But I'm going to hold you to that."

He could not have shocked me more when he leaned over and kissed me — on the lips, but lightly, barely brushing my mouth with his — and whispered, standing just inches from me, "Don't you want to know the name of my new song?"

"The name of your new song?" I stared up at him, my mouth still tingling from the fleeting kiss. Even though he wasn't touching me, it was as if I were bolted into place.

"Right," he said. "It's called 'Nikki.'"

And then he was gone, disappearing into the hordes of people who'd gathered on the sidewalk to stare at me and my limo.

TWENTY-THREE

DRAGGING MYSELF AND MY BOXES
with Karl's help from the limo when it finally pulled up in front
of my building, I took the elevator up to the loft, expecting to
find it empty, since it was after nine at night. I thought surely
Lulu would be out on the town, doing whatever it was Lulu did
when she was left unsupervised.

So you can imagine my surprise when I stepped from the
elevator and heard her call my name.

"Nikki!" cried a voice from a ghostly figure stretched out
across a massage table in the middle of the loft's living room.
Lulu was — mostly — under a white sheet, while a stern-
looking woman in a white uniform kneaded her shoulders.

"Uh," I said, even more confused than usual. "Hi?"

"Hi," Lulu said, popping her head up from the hole at the top of the massage table. "Oh, yeah. I forgot. Nikki, this is our housekeeper, Katerina. Katerina, this isn't Nikki. I know it looks like her, but it's not. She had a spirit transfer, and now she's someone else. But you can still call her Nikki."

Katerina stopped kneading Lulu's shoulders and stared at me. "You say this is not Miss Nikki?" she demanded in a heavy accent.

"No," Lulu said. "Well, I mean, it is. But it isn't."

"Yes, it is, Lulu," I said, frustrated. "It's still me. I just don't remember anyone. Because I have amnesia, remember? Hi, Katerina."

Katerina stared at me for a little bit longer. Then she shrugged and went back to massaging Lulu. "You girls," she said. Only it came out sounding like "gels." "I give up with you and your silly games a long time ago."

"I know it was your turn to get massaged by Katerina, Nik," Lulu went on, plopping her face back down into the hole in the massage table. "But I just got back from a meeting with my record label, and it was such hell. They say I have to sing these two reject songs from Lindsay Lohan's album — *as if* — and I was still *such* a wreck from last night, I must have had fifteen mojitos and a box of Milk Duds, and I knew only Katerina could whip me back into shape. And, oh, my God, Nik, Brandon has been calling, like, all day. He says your cell's not on, and all his messages have been going to voice mail. What's up with that? Like, turn your cell on. Also, he is, like, totally sorry about last night. He's been talking about getting his dad's jet for this weekend and taking us to Antigua, and you know he only does that when he's suffering a major guilt trip. Just FYI. Oh, and I had to lock Cosy up, she was jumping all over me, I couldn't take it, she's in my room, she's been such a nightmare —"

I put down the boxes and crossed the loft to Lulu's bedroom door, which I swung open. Cosabella careened out of it like a shot, leaping against my shins and yapping happily, her tongue lolling. I scooped her up and went to sit down on the couch with her cradled in my arms while she lapped at my face.

"She's already had her walk." Lulu popped her head up to look at me again. "Karl took her. And I fed her. Oh, my God, *what* is on your face?"

I blinked at her above Cosy's fluffy head. "Where?"

Next thing I knew, Lulu had swung down off the massage table and, still clutching the sheet around her, marched up to me, reached across, and scraped a fingernail across my cheek.

"Ow!" I cried, leaning away from this five-foot lunatic.

Lulu looked down at her fingernail, and said, "I knew it. It's a dead skin flake. Your skin is dry. What have you been using on it?"

"Look," I said, still clutching my cheek, "I appreciate your help, looking after Cosy while I was in school and at the shoot and all. But you can't just go around *scratching* people —"

"What. Have. You. Been. Using. On. It?" Lulu demanded, shoving her finger in my face to show me the dead skin flake.

"God," I said. "Soap. What else?"

Lulu looked horrified. "Soap? SOAP? You've been washing your skin with SOAP?"

"Well, what else would you use on your skin?" I asked.

Lulu shook her head, still staring at me. Then she said to the housekeeper, "Katerina. My robe. We have a crisis that needs to be dealt with. STAT."

Katerina nodded gravely and lifted Lulu's robe. Lulu, still holding the sheet in strategic locations, slipped her arms into the robe's sleeves . . . then let the sheet drop to the floor, once she was safely covered.

"Look," I said, "I don't know what's going on here, but I do not need any kind of beauty intervention, if that's what this is about. I have a lot on my mind right now, and I just want to —"

"I beg your pardon," Lulu said. "But Nikki Howard gave you her body — she donated it — as a GIFT, with the expectation that you would take care of it."

"I *have* been taking care of it," I insisted. "I've been eating nothing but freaking green tea and tofu since I *got* this body, since that's the only stuff that doesn't appear to make my stomach churn —"

"But what are you washing your hair with?" Lulu demanded. "And how long are you letting it deep condition? And what kind of exfoliant are you using? Don't answer that, I already know: none. It's true that Nikki Howard was a natural beauty. But she didn't just GET that way. She CULTIVATED it. With a careful and diligent beauty regimen. WHICH YOU ARE NOT FOLLOWING."

"Look," I said, glancing toward Katerina for help but finding none in her direction. That's because she'd found the universal remote control, which apparently controlled not only the flat panel TV above the fireplace, but the fireplace — the flames suddenly leaped and danced as she pushed buttons — the windowpanes (you could deepen the shade of the glass to purple opaque or brighten it to clear), the stereo, and even the security camera in the elevator, and she was trying to enhance the mood by making the lighting softer. "I have a lot worse problems right now than dry skin, all right? In case you aren't aware of it, someone is spying on us. Not just me, Lulu. You, too. Your laptop was loaded with spyware. And I don't want to alarm you, but I'm pretty sure it's Stark Enterprises. I don't have any proof, of course . . . but who else would it be? It's okay now, I fixed it. But you might want to get a new, non-Stark-brand laptop. I did. And as if that's not bad enough, Gabriel Luna — remember, the guy from the scooter and the Stark Megastore grand opening where the, um, spirit transfer took place? Well, he's written a song about me. And I don't even like him. He thinks I have drug and alcohol issues. And the guy I *do* like —" Suddenly, I was fighting back tears. Just like that. "— wouldn't even *look* at me today at school, okay? So it doesn't matter if I have dry skin, or moist skin, or *no* skin. I mean, I don't even know what the point of all of this is. What is the point of being beautiful when you can't even get the guy you like to *look* at you?"

Lulu sucked in her breath. Then she looked at Katerina and said, "Better call for backup."

Katerina nodded, laid down the remote, and reached for her cell phone. Observing this, I grabbed the nearest pillow and smashed it over my face.

"Oh, no," I wailed. "No more makeovers. *No, no, no, no!*" I smacked the pillow with each *no* . . . not something Dr. Holcombe, I was sure, would recommend.

"Relax," Lulu said. The next thing I knew, she was plucking the pillow off my face and sitting down beside me. "Katerina's ordering banana splits from the deli down the street. That's what I meant by backup. We always order banana splits from the deli when we have guy problems. Not good for your reflux, but you can take one of those pills of yours before you eat it. Now. What is this about Stark Enterprises, Gabriel Luna, and some guy not looking at you?"

Astonished that I wasn't about to be given a head-to-toe exfoliation, I told Lulu first about her computer, then about Gabriel, and then about Christopher, and the way he'd barely spoken to me in the computer lab. When I was done, she shrugged and said, "Well, first of all, I never use that computer. I just think it's pretty. And Gabriel's easy, too. He's in love with you."

I nearly choked on some of my own spit.

"Lulu! No . . . that's —"

"And it's obvious what's going on with that Christopher guy," she went on.

"Really?" Startled, I stared at her, wide-eyed. "What?"

"He's frightened of his passion for you. So he's just had to shove it way, way down, so it won't show."

I blinked. "Lulu. He doesn't even *know* Nikki Howard. How can he feel passion for her?"

Lulu put both her tiny bare feet up on the coffee table and rolled her head around on the back of the couch until she was staring at the ceiling. "Oh, my God. I can't believe I have to give you this speech again. It seems like I just gave you this speech last month. I *did* give you this speech last month. But now I have to give it to you again because of the spirit transfer. But here goes. Okay, Nikki. Pay attention this time, will you? Straight guys only feel three ways about girls." She held up three fingers and put one finger down each time she ticked off a point.

"First, either they love you, and they show it by writing a song about you, like Gabriel, and asking you out, and everything is nice and fun like it should be. Second, they love you, but they're scared of their passion for you because it's so strong, like your boy Christopher, so they stuff it way, way down and ignore you, or do stupid things like make fun of you because they don't know how to express it any other way, because they're immature little babies and are too shy to, say, write a song about you. Or third, there's something wrong with them, and they start out nice and loving and then turn around and do stupid things like sleep with other girls behind your back, like Justin Bay. But we'll never figure out what went wrong with them, and neither will they, so it's not worth thinking about. Okay? That's it. The end."

She put down her hand. "Any questions?"

I stared at her. She looked serious. But it was kind of hard to tell, considering it was Lulu. So I figured I'd ask to make sure. "Um . . . yeah, I have a question. Are you *serious*?"

Lulu sighed. "Okay, I can see I didn't quite get through to you. Nikki, please don't tell me your mother never told you this."

I shook my head. "Um . . . no. I can't say she ever —"

"God!" Lulu rolled her eyes some more. "That makes me so mad! How could she not have said anything? That is so irresponsible! I mean, how can mothers send their daughters out into the world to just walk around making boys fall in love with them all day, without the slightest idea of what they're doing? Didn't you see *Spider-Man?* 'With great power comes great responsibility'! We women can't just go walking around being so awesome and not have to be careful not to make guys fall in love with us all over the place. Right, Katerina?"

"Yah," Katerina said, nodding fiercely as she bundled up Lulu's sheets for the laundry.

"My mother — much like Katerina's mother, I wouldn't doubt," Lulu went on, "sat me down when I was eleven and said, 'Lulu, the truth of the matter is, every heterosexual boy — and probably some gay ones, too, so look out, because *that's* just going to end in disaster — you ever meet is going to fall madly in love with you. He may not admit it, but it's true. So you have to take responsibility for that and not do things to encourage him — unless, of course, you *want* him to fall in love with you. Because it's cruel to play with boys' emotions in that way, because no matter what anyone else says, men are the weaker sex.' Didn't your mother tell you that?"

Completely stunned by this bit of motherly advice — my mom's own advice had always been more along the lines of, *Never go anywhere without enough money for a cab home,* and *Don't have sex, but if you do, always use a condom* — I shook my head.

"Well," Lulu went on, "it turns out, even though my mom was wrong about a lot of things — like giving me snowboarding lessons for Christmas when I turned twelve, when it turned out she was only going to run off with my instructor — she wasn't wrong about that. Every heterosexual guy I've ever met — and a few gay ones — *has* fallen in love with me. At least a little bit. Oh, not like they all want to marry me or anything . . . sometimes, like in the case of my snowboard instructor, it turns out they've wanted to marry *her*. But they've all *thought* about it. And it's true they don't always *stay* in love with me, the way they ought to — but that's usually because the love they feel for me frightens them so much, because I'm just so incredible they feel inadequate and end up running away . . . like Justin."

I just stared at her. Seeing this, Lulu said, "I'm serious. Wait and see. When the delivery guy comes with the banana splits? Just watch when I go to pay him. He'll probably ask me out."

Not sure how else to respond, I said, carefully, not wanting to hurt her feelings, "Well, Lulu . . . thanks. I mean, for the warning? But, while I'm certain it's true that every straight guy *you* meet falls in love with you, with me that's not really been the case. At least, in my past life. The thing is, in the real world, most girls don't have to go around worrying about every guy they meet falling in love with them. I could see how, now that I'm Nikki, I'll have to worry, but —"

Lulu sucked in her breath, looking outraged.

"Oh, yes, they do!" she cried. "If girls aren't worried about this, they're just kidding themselves! And playing with fire. This is true of *all* girls. Right, Katerina?"

Katerina nodded as she was folding up her massage table. "Oh, yah," she said, sounding tired. "You should meet some of my ex-husbands."

"See?" Lulu said fiercely. "It doesn't matter how old you are, or how you look — no offense, Katerina. Whether you're pretty or plain, or skinny or round. Guys can't help it. If you're a girl, it's just the way it is. Guys may not want to *admit* that they like you. They may act like total buttholes *instead* of admitting it —" This made me think, inexplicably, of Jason Klein. "— but everything my mother said is *totally* true and applies to *all* girls. And it's *a lot* of responsibility for us. I mean, we have to be so, so careful all the time not to break men's hearts. Men's hearts are very fragile. Our hearts aren't nearly as delicate. Are they, Katerina?"

"*Nein*," Katerina said, banging the massage table closed. Hard.

"Now, I don't know what's going on with your little Christopher friend," Lulu said. "But I'm guessing maybe he's just pushed his love for you way, way down because he's so frightened of it . . . that happens a lot. Can you think of a reason why he might have done that?"

I looked at Cosabella, who'd curled up in my lap and was contentedly sleeping. I really had no idea how I'd even ended up taking part in this lunatic conversation.

But there was something about Lulu — something so vulnerable and sweet — that made me *want* her theory to be true. It was certainly a very *nice* theory, and one that would boost the self-esteem of any girl whose mother sat her down and told it to her. Who knew? Maybe it *was* true. Lulu certainly seemed to believe it.

And I had no doubt that every guy she met *did* fall in love with her, at least a little.

I believed it was probably a little true for Nikki Howard, too . . . except where Brandon Stark's dad was concerned.

But then there was what had happened that afternoon with Christopher. How could I even begin to explain how weird that had been?

"I don't know," I said, slowly. "My sister said something about Christopher maybe having been in love with, um, Em Watts. You know, the girl who died at the Stark Megastore grand opening? Only him not having realized it until it was too late, and she was . . . dead. I don't know if this is true. She was probably wrong. But they were best friends before she died. And, you know, he was there when she was killed. And my sister thinks maybe now his heart is broken."

There was a pause as this soaked in. Then Lulu flattened a hand against her chest and looked at me with her huge Bambi eyes suddenly filled with tears.

"That," she said, "is the most romantic thing I have ever heard." She looked over at the housekeeper. "Katerina. Isn't that the most romantic thing you've ever heard?"

Katerina had her massage things packed up by then and was now cleaning out the refrigerator, throwing out expired containers of yogurt. "Yah," she called over her shoulder.

Lulu turned back to me. "Listen," she said, reaching out and taking my hand. "All is not lost. The important thing you've got to do now is make a connection with him. Show him that you understand what he's lost. That you *feel* his loss."

I shook my head. "But, Lulu . . . how can I do that? I'm a stranger to him now. Worse . . . I'm a *supermodel*, who represents Stark Enterprises, the company that pretty much is responsible for killing his girlfriend — and represents everything else evil in the world. I'm everything that Christopher hates. Christopher and I used to *laugh* at people like Nikki Howard. How can I make a connection with him when I'm someone he can't stand? I'm telling you, it's totally hopeless."

"Nothing is hopeless where true love is concerned," Lulu said, giving my hand a squeeze. "Haven't you heard a word I've said? You've just got to give him time. He's experienced a terrible loss.

His heart has been torn in two. It's going to take love and patience to bring him back among the living . . . like it took love and patience to bring *you* back to me . . . even if you *are* a little strange now. Strange," Lulu added, hastily, "but much nicer than you used to be."

I sighed. "I don't know, Lulu. I want to think you're right, but . . . maybe, if your theory is right, and with great power comes great responsibility, the kinder thing to do would be to just leave him alone."

Lulu looked searchingly into my eyes. "What does your *heart* say, Nikki?"

I felt tears fill my eyes. Because I couldn't help remembering what Mr. Phillips had said that day in Dr. Holcombe's office: *What is the locus — or perceived location — of our identities . . . our souls, as it were? Is it the brain? Or is it the heart and body? Nikki Howard's brain, it's true, is no longer functioning. Her heart, on the other hand, continues to beat.*

I remembered now how I'd laid my hand over Nikki Howard's heart and felt it beating. It had felt so foreign to me. I'd wondered then if it would ever feel like my own heart.

But it felt like my own heart now. It felt like my own heart now because nothing but my own heart could hurt so much. It felt like my own heart, because the truth was?

It was breaking.

"My heart says that I love Christopher," I said miserably.

"But it's so hopeless, Lulu. The chances of my ever getting him even to be friends with me the way we used to be are nil . . . let alone the chances of us ever being anything else."

The intercom buzzed, causing us both to jump.

"I will get," Katerina said, and she shuffled off to do so.

"Listen," Lulu said, giving my hand another squeeze. "If the delivery guy asks me out, will you believe me that you have a chance with Christopher?"

I slipped my hand out from hers in order to wipe away my tears. "Lulu. You're in a fluffy robe and slippers. The delivery guy isn't going to —"

"The delivery guy is *going* to ask me out," Lulu said. "I told you, we women have an awesome power that we have to wield with responsibility. So this isn't fair of me, because I'm not even interested in dating anyone right now, since I just broke up with Justin, and I need to go see my astrologist to find out which sign I should concentrate on trying to date next. But I will do it, to prove a point to you. Then will you believe me?"

"Fine," I said, with a shaky laugh. "Go for it."

The elevator doors opened, and the unsuspecting delivery guy stepped out, holding a plastic bag.

"That'll be eleven fifty," he said to Katerina, as he handed her the bag.

"I'm not paying," Katerina said. "*She's* paying." And she pointed at Lulu.

Lulu got up off the couch and, giving the sash of her fluffy robe a tug to tighten it, approached the delivery guy. I couldn't say I noticed anything at all different about her, except that a beguiling smile had appeared on her elfin face.

But the delivery guy sure seemed to straighten up all of a sudden.

"Well," Lulu said to him. "Hello, there. Eleven fifty, you said? Hold on a second, my wallet is right here. Why, you're all wet. Is it raining out there? Do you want a towel? Here, let me get you a towel. It's getting cold out, isn't it? I wouldn't want you coming down with something. Then who would bring me my banana splits? I sure do love *banana splits*. Here, here's a twenty. You can keep the change. And here's a *big, fluffy* towel. What's your name?"

"Roy," said the delivery guy, in a dazed voice, as he wiped off his face with the towel Lulu had handed him.

"Roy?" Lulu said, taking the towel back. "What a nice name. Is that Hungarian?"

"I don't know," the delivery guy said, still sounding dazed. "What's your name?"

"My name is Lulu," Lulu said. "That's with two *l*'s, and two *u*'s."

"That's a pretty name," Roger said. "Would you want to go out with me sometime?"

My jaw dropped.

"Oh, my goodness," Lulu said, "I'd love to! But only if my husband could come along."

"Your husband?" Roger looked stunned.

"Come on, guy," the elevator attendant said in a bored voice, pulling Roy back onto the elevator. "Let's go."

"Bye, Roy," Lulu said, waving. "Don't catch a cold!"

The elevator doors closed on a still stunned Roy's face. As soon as he was gone, Lulu turned triumphantly toward me and did a little victory dance.

"There!" she cried. "See? I told you!"

I shook my head in wonder. I really couldn't believe what I'd just witnessed.

"That," I said, truly impressed, "was amazing. But how did you do that? You're in a bathrobe! You weren't even wearing anything low cut or revealing."

"I was kind and friendly to him," Lulu said, shaking her head. "And I exuded confidence and charm. That's what I was trying to tell you. Anyone can do it. It doesn't matter how you look or what you're wearing." She crossed the room to the kitchen island, where Katerina had opened the bag containing our banana splits. Lulu swung herself up onto one of the stools until she was sitting in front of one of the plastic containers.

"I don't think I could do it," I said, getting up from the couch and following her. "I don't think I have that kind of confidence."

"Of course you can do it, Nikki," Lulu said, digging into her banana split with one of the plastic spoons the deli had provided. "You used to do it all the time, before the spirit transfer. Sometimes you did it for the wrong reasons, just to be mean, which was why I had to give you the speech about how with great power comes great responsibility, and so on. So you can do it with this Christopher person, too, *easy*. You just have to have confidence. And, like I said, you have to make a *connection*."

"Fine," I said, with a sigh. "I'll try."

Lulu giggled and flicked some ice cream at me. She missed, and Cosabella attacked the glob that landed on the floor.

"Hey!" I said, glaring at Lulu. "What was that for?"

"I can't believe," she said, giggling some more, "you're in love with a high school boy."

"Yeah," I said, aiming my own spoonful of ice cream at her. "Well, you're the freak who believes in spirit trans-fers." The glob of ice cream landed on the wall. Barking, Cosabella raced excitedly to the other side of the kitchen to lick it up.

"Takes someone who's had one to know one," Lulu said, and hurled the cherry from the top of her split at me. It hit the huge plate-glass window behind me and slid slowly down it. Cosabella barked happily at it the whole way.

"Gels," Katerina said. "Stop! I just clean in here! Keep this up, and no more massages."

We cleaned up after ourselves, making sure the kitchen was sparkling when we were done.

TWENTY-FOUR

I FOUND CHRISTOPHER ALONE IN THE computer lab before first period the next morning.

I suppose I could have waited for lunch to bring my new laptop to him, but I knew I wouldn't last that long. When you realize you need to make a connection with someone, you know you have to do it as soon as possible or you'll lose the courage to do it at all.

And this was the only way I could think to do it.

"Um, hi," I said gently, careful not to startle him in the middle of whatever video game he was engrossed in (*Madden NFL* again, I saw a minute later).

He turned in his computer chair and stared. Lulu had dressed me again, though I was getting better at doing it myself. This time I was in skinny jeans, velvet flats, a maroon velvet cropped jacket, and so many necklaces I rattled when I walked. I had only just talked Lulu out of adding a beret. That, I felt, was taking things one step too far. I was a little bit proud of my independent fashion streak.

"Hi," he said without smiling. He had on another short-sleeved Polo shirt, this one gray. His hair was still wet in back from his morning shower.

He looked so good, I wanted to die.

"I brought my computer," I said, pulling the white laptop from my Marc Jacobs tote. "You said yesterday you could set up my e-mail account for me . . . is this a good time?"

Christopher glanced at the wall clock. We had fifteen minutes until Public Speaking.

"I guess so," he said, and held out his hand for the computer.

Hmmm. If he was "in love, but pushing it way, way down," as Lulu had suggested, he was *really* pushing it down. Why couldn't I summon up some of Lulu's awesome aimless chatter and set him at his ease? She was so good at it, while I was as awkward at it as . . . well, a gawky teen tomboy whose brain had been stuck in a supermodel's body.

I handed Christopher my laptop and went to sit in the chair beside his. He looked down at the gleaming — and obviously brand-new — white computer without comment, opened it, and began typing away.

I tried to remember what Lulu had told me. Be confident and . . . what? Make a connection. Right.

Only how? What did Christopher and Nikki Howard have in common? Nothing. Except that they both went to Tribeca Alternative High School.

Oh . . . and *Journeyquest.* Right.

"So what was your high score?" I asked him. "On *Journeyquest?*"

"Forty-eight," he said, without elaboration.

This shocked me. I blurted, without thinking, "You're a liar."

He glanced at me, startled. "What?"

"No way did you make it past level forty-six," I said, completely forgetting there was no way I could know this. "How did you make it past the Dragons of Pith?" The dragons had incinerated our characters every time we'd approached them, no matter which direction we'd come from, barring us from making it past level forty-six. We'd searched the Web for clues as to how to get past them, to no avail.

Christopher was staring at me. For the first time, he seemed really to be seeing me.

"I used the Runes of Al-Cragen," he explained simply.

It was my turn to stare. "The runes? No kidding? Oh, my God, I can't believe I never thought of that. So you just threw them, and —"

"The dragons were powerless in their lair," Christopher said. He was really looking at me now. But not like he was actually seeing me, Em. More like he was wondering what was wrong with me, Nikki. Which made sense, actually. Because what kind of lunatic would look at Nikki Howard and suspect Em Watts was inside of her? "What was your character's name? Your *Journeyquest* character? Maybe I've seen you online."

And I realized I'd made a blunder. I couldn't give him my online character's name, because then he'd know it was me, Em.

But I couldn't just make one up, either, because it would be too easy for him to check.

"Oh," I said, breezily, "I haven't been online in ages. And I doubt you'd ever have seen me, I keep really weird hours. Besides, I don't remember it." I tapped my head. "You know. The amnesia thing."

He gave me a skeptical look and turned back to my computer screen. "Um, yeah," he said. "Sure."

Then, suddenly, he turned and threw me a look that was like someone accidentally pouring a glass of cold water in my face.

"But you remembered you played?" he asked.

I could have kicked myself.

"Y-yeah, amnesia is weird that w-way," I stammered. "Like, I remember some things," I said. "But not others. Like . . ."

And then, just like that, I said it. I don't know why. It was risky. It was probably foolish.

It was exactly the sort of thing, I realized, that Stark Enterprises had been using tracking software to find. This was why it had been installed on Nikki's and Lulu's computers in the first place. This was why Stark Enterprises had been so generous with my family with the free cell phones. To make sure we weren't gabbing to the wrong people about my secret surgery.

But I wasn't typing what I was about to say, or saying it into a Stark-brand cell phone.

"I remember you," I told him.

Suddenly, my heart began to hammer. But I couldn't seem to shut myself up. It was like my mouth was just running away with itself.

But Lulu had said to make a connection. This wasn't the one I'd had in mind. But there it was.

"From that day at the Stark Megastore grand opening," I went on.

Nothing happened. I waited. But no men in black suits burst the door down. No one with guns came busting through the ceiling panels.

We were safe.

Christopher just stared at me, his blue eyes — so different from Gabriel's, more green around the edges and rimmed with light brown lashes instead of dark — wide and incredulous.

I didn't blame him. I didn't know where I was going with this, either.

Shut up, Em, my brain directed my mouth. Or Nikki's mouth. *Or whatever your name is now. Just shut up.* Two million dollars. Two million dollars.

But it was no good. The damage was done.

"You *remember* what happened that day?" Christopher asked finally.

I looked down at my hands. My fingernails — which were fake and still painted black — were perfect. Just like the rest of me. On the outside.

Too bad no one could see that on the inside, I was a big old mess.

"I remember *you*," I said. "I remember how you came with your friend. The one who . . . died."

When I said the word *died*, Christopher looked quickly away from me. His fingers were frozen on the keyboard of my laptop.

But it was too late to turn back. I could only move forward.

"That must have been so awful," I said, my heart twisting for him. "I mean . . . not like you probably want to remember it or anything. I'm sorry to have brought it up. I just . . . I wanted to say something to you about it when no one else was around. You know, about how badly I felt about it."

I had no idea if Frida was right about what was troubling Christopher. About him having been in love with me, I mean. Maybe she was wrong. Maybe he was just still recovering from having seen a girl die right in front of him. Anybody would have been messed up from that.

Maybe Frida was completely wrong about Christopher having had any special feelings beyond friendship for me. I don't know. I couldn't tell by looking at his face, because he was keeping it turned away from me, just staring at my computer screen.

"I'm just so, so sorry that that happened," I went on. "I can't tell you how sorry I am. What happened was terrible. You must . . . you must miss her a lot."

I waited, thinking he wasn't going to reply at all, he didn't say anything for so long.

But a second later, he did. He said, "Yeah."

And then his fingers started moving over the keyboard again.

A minute after that, he said, "Well, here you go. You're all set."

And he closed my laptop and handed it back to me.

Just like that.

I felt my eyes fill with tears. I couldn't help it. I couldn't believe Lulu was wrong. It wasn't that I'd *believed* her stupid theory, exactly. I mean, how dumb would you have to be to believe that all the boys in the world are a little bit in love with you? Sure, maybe it's true for Lulu. But why would Christopher ever have been in love with me?

God, I couldn't believe how asinine I'd been.

I turned around and stuffed the laptop back into my tote, wiping the tears away with my sleeve so he couldn't see that I was crying.

"Thanks," I said. "Well. See you in Public Speaking."

I was halfway out the door when Christopher's quiet voice stopped me in my tracks.

"Nikki," he said.

I froze. I couldn't turn around, because then he'd have seen the tears that had escaped from beneath my eyelids and were trickling down my cheeks.

"Uh-huh?" I said to the wall.

His voice was still quiet.

"She was my best friend," he said.

The tears came gushing down my face, which I still kept hidden from him. Suddenly, I wanted to tell him the truth so, so badly. I wanted to run over to him, throw down my bag, and fling my arms around him, and say, "Christopher, it's me! Em! I'm not dead! I'm in here! I know it's crazy, but it's true!"

But I knew I couldn't. Two million dollars.

Instead, I turned around, not caring if he saw I was crying anymore, and did the one thing I knew I shouldn't — but that I also knew I had to — do. The thing I told myself I was crazy to do. The thing I'd tried to talk myself out of doing all morning, since I'd thought of it, and that I would have left without doing, if he hadn't just said those five little words.

I reached into my tote, pulled something out of it, turned around, walked back over to him, and slapped it down in front of him.

Then I turned and ran before he could ask me why I'd just dropped a sheet of glow-in-the-dark dinosaur stickers on his desk.

TWENTY-FIVE

"WAIT . . ." LULU LEANED DOWN TO undo Cosabella's leash, which had twisted around her legs. "Why are we bringing pizza to these people?"

"Because." I kept my gaze on the numbers above our heads as the elevator rose higher and higher. "I want you to meet them."

"Are they poor or something?"

"No," I said, with a laugh. The elevator stopped, and the door opened. "I thought it would be nice to bring them dinner."

"Oh." Lulu followed me down the long hallway as I balanced the pizza box in one hand and tried to control Cosabella with the other. "I thought it was, like, a charity thing."

"No," I said. I didn't want to mention the truth — that I felt bad for Lulu, because she didn't seem to have any parents . . . who cared about her, anyway. Except for Katerina. But Katerina was an employee.

I felt equally bad for my parents, whom I'd been sort of ignoring. Maybe pizza and a visit wouldn't make up for three days of neglect. But it was a start. That, and the new non-Stark-brand cell phones I'd brought along for each of my parents, as well as Frida.

Besides, I thought Mom should hear some of Lulu's theories. From a women's studies point of view, I thought she'd find them interesting. Or at least worth further investigation.

"I just thought eating in would be nicer than going out for a change," I said.

"Oh," Lulu said. She rooted around in her purse, found her compact, then checked her reflection. "I get it. So, how'd it go with the high school boy?"

I smiled, remembering how Christopher had yet to say a word to me about the stickers.

But he'd been looking. *Oh*, how he'd been looking.

"I think I made a connection," I said. "He's confused, but . . ." I shrugged. "We'll have to see how it goes."

"They're *all* confused," Lulu said, with a gusty sigh. "So why was there a cable guy in our apartment this afternoon?"

"We're getting Wi-Fi installed," I said, stopping in front of 14L. "Not using modem connections anymore should solve our spyware problems. For now, anyway. Why? Did he ask you out?"

"Of course," Lulu said. "But I'm supposed to go out with a Libra next, and he's a Capricorn, so it will never work."

"Are you ready?" I asked her, my finger hovering over the bell.

"I'm ready," Lulu said, putting away her compact. "But are you sure you wouldn't rather go to Nobu? Pizza always does a number on your insides. And we could go to Cave after."

"My insides," I said, "are already messed up. The truth is, they're never going to match my outsides." I rang the bell. "But you know what? I'm starting to think nobody's insides do."

"*I'll get it*," I heard Frida shriek, inside the apartment. A second later, the door to my old home opened, and Frida, in sweats, with face cream all over her T-zone, stared at us.

"Oh, my God," she said, her jaw slack as her gaze darted from me to Lulu and then back again. "Oh, my God, it's . . . it's . . . it's . . ."

"Hi, Frida," I said. "It's me. Can you tell Mom I'm here? I brought pizza . . . and my friend Lulu."

"I — I — I —" Frida was so excited, she let the door bang shut in our faces. I could hear her tearing through the apartment, screaming, "Mo-o-om! Guess who's here?"

Lulu looked at me curiously. Then she said, "Nikki? How do you even know these people?"

"Lulu," I said. "I wouldn't even know where to begin."

BEING NIKKI

SEQUEL TO *AIRHEAD*
BY MEG CABOT

Em Watts is gone.
Nikki Howard is here to stay.

EMERSON WATTS WAS PRETTY SURE there couldn't be anything worse than being a hard-core tomboy whose brain had been transplanted into the body of a teenage supermodel.

But it turned out she was wrong.

Because that supermodel could turn out to have a schedule that gives her barely enough time to breathe, let alone any personal space; an employer who won't stop cyber-spying on her — though Em can't seem to figure out why; and feet so sore from walking around in stilettos, she has to soak them every night while she does her trig homework (and gets romantic advice from her celebutante best friend, Lulu). Not to mention a secret past that Em is only just now uncovering.

How can Em balance all that with school, photo shoots, movie premieres, and weekend jaunts to Paris for runway work — especially when she's got ex-boyfriends crawling out of the woodwork who want more than just a photo op; a British heartthrob who's written a song about her that's topping the charts; a sister who is headed to the high school cheerleading championships; a company she represents that seems to be turning to the dark side. . . .

And, oh, yeah, trying to convince the love of her life, her former best friend, Christopher (whom she can't tell about her true identity), that models aren't really airheads after all . . . especially one model in particular.

But then nobody said it was going to be easy being Nikki.